We at Butterfly Conservation are delighted to be associated with this unusual book. Quite apart from its thought-provoking and intriguing story about growing up, it gives a great deal of accurate information about the wonderful range of British butterflies and their lives. It is suitable for teenagers and adults of all ages.

Butterfly Conservation, through its dedicated staff and volunteers, works hard to protect our endangered species of butterflies and moths, which are under threat on many different fronts. This book is a very welcome step in bringing increased awareness of their fragile beauty to a wider public."

Dr. Martin Warren, Chief Executive, Butterfly
Conservation

THE SUMMER OF THE MOURNING CLOAK

Kathleen Nelson

Kathleen Nelson

Matador
9 Priory Business Park
Kibworth Beauchamp
Leicestershire LE8 0RX, UK
Tel: (+44) 116 279 2299
Fax: (+44) 116 279 2277
Email: books@troubador.co.uk
Web: www.troubador.co.uk/matador

ISBN 978 1783063 024

British Library Cataloguing in Publication Data.
A catalogue record for this book is available from the British Library.

Typeset in Aldine401 BT Roman by Troubador Publishing Ltd
Printed and bound in the UK by TJ International, Padstow, Cornwall

Matador is an imprint of Troubador Publishing Ltd

For Lesley and David

"*The butterfly never meets its mother. It must survive independently and remains a stranger to affection… A child who grows up in a cold and detached home environment is similar to the butterfly, in that kindness is sparing. Once an adult, it will be very difficult for that person to show compassion.*"

HH The Dalai Lama

A Funeral, a Beetle and a Pair of Red Shoes

It is always best to find shelter when a house turns spiteful.

Under the dining room table seemed a safe place, and there was already a companion there waiting for her, a fellow mourner: a shiny black beetle.

He was a large, solid sort of beetle, all in black as she was. He kept her from thinking of the terrifying spectacle of her grandmother lying in her open coffin in the room next door, and distracted her from the wailing of some of the mourners. Her grandmother, who had been everything to her for all of her six and a half years, was there in the next room. At least they told her it was her grandmother, but for Hyslop this was not true. What was laid out in the coffin was a *body*, and a body is not a person. That pale face, cold as one of the marble Madonnas in the hall, was not the familiar smiley face of her grandmother any more. Whether she was in purgatory or in heaven with the Virgin Mary, what was certain was that she was no longer there in her old body. She was not there to make the world all right again. She was not there, but the beetle was.

They were together, and they were staying together. Hyslop found his presence comforting. Beyond the long folds of the tablecloth that shrouded them in a white cocoon was the scary world of the black shoes.

The house was full of old women, all dressed in black. They had been wandering around the house since her grandmother had died three days previously, sitting and walking, endlessly talking, crying, laughing, opening and closing doors, drinking coffee, never silent for a moment. All Hyslop could see of them now was their black shoes: thick ankles, encased in black stockings, ending in those flat matt black shoes.

Some of the old ladies were familiar to her as her grandmother's friends from church, who had called round for cake and sweet white wine, but some of them were strangers. How had her grandmother known so many people, she wondered. They were all speaking at once, voicing their emotions loudly in a way that only old Italian women can. Signora Crolla, a particular friend who always called round on Sunday afternoons, had even begun tearing at her hair and wailing loudly. Signora Crolla was not behaving as she normally did and Hyslop did not like it. She listened as she heard some of the other old ladies clucking and hissing their disapproval.

One or two of them urged Signora Crolla to mourn in a more dignified manner, which led her to wail even more loudly about how she missed poor Violetta. The noise level, as the black shoes drew nearer, made Hyslop put her hands over her ears.

They all talked at once, and no one seemed to be listening to anyone else until one of them approached the table and suggested cutting the pine nut tart. The black shoes were all around the table now. They were closing in, and the beetle moved to her side, twitching its antennae.

In later years Hyslop was to learn of a beetle called The Death Watch Beetle, which would surely have been a suitable name for a fellow mourner. This particular beetle, however, with his large head, bulging green eyes, intelligent expression, and shiny black shell, was a species that she never found again. In later years she also learned that new species of beetle are constantly being discovered all over the world. Her companion may have been one of those rarities, or he may have been a special one-off. He was unique, her personal Funeral Companion Beetle.

"It's not safe for you out there," she whispered to him. "You'll get crushed by those horrible shoes."

The beetle waved his antennae in her direction, and remained still. He was clearly in agreement.

"No one knows we're here," she said. She knew he could understand her.

It was not only the people who seemed scary and different. The house was different too: it was full of spite and malevolence. The house and all the furniture in it would shortly belong to her Uncle Carlo. He was not a kind man, her Uncle Carlo. He had hardly ever visited his aged mother, and when he did, he always ended up shouting at her. He would ignore Hyslop, even when she had tried to speak to him in the early days. It was as if she did not exist for him, though she had no idea what she had done to annoy him. Hyslop had always thought of the house as her home, the only home she had ever known, but now that her beloved grandmother was gone, she realised that "home" is not a place: "home" is a *person*. All the rooms in the house, the furniture and the paintings, the little corners and secret places where she had played, the dusty piano, the air itself, were different now that her grandmother was gone. The house had lost its kindness. Even Hyslop's favourite chair, with its carved wooden legs and its faded tapestry picture on the seat, no longer seemed to talk to her in a friendly way. It no longer said: "Come and sit down, Hyslop!" It had grown cold, and become a stranger. It was as if the house and all its furniture were hissing at her: "We once belonged to you, but now we are waiting for Uncle Carlo. *You* are not welcome here any more."

Occasionally one of the old ladies would mention her name. There would be exclamations of: "Oh, Eesloppa, the poor child!" "How she will miss her grandmother!" "What a tragedy for both of them!" but no one sought her out, and she and the beetle kept a quiet vigil under the table. Together they watched all those pairs of shoes approaching the table and then walking away again, to the sound of glasses clinking and plates clattering. "Oh, it's so sad, but at least dear Violetta will be with her husband now, and her *dear* Sandro. He was always her favourite son." "Yes, it's a shame he's gone, and that other one isn't." This resulted in more wailings of: "Oh, the poor child!" Then there was a chorus of admiration for the pine nut tart: "Violetta taught her well, didn't she?" "Oh yes, Rosa can cook, that's for sure!" "Will she stay on do you think, now that Violetta's gone?" "Oh, I don't think she'll work for Carlo." They were all talking at once, not listening to each other, and Hyslop felt cross at them for being able to enjoy eating and drinking. She felt so sick inside that she had hardly eaten since her grandmother had died. Rosa had made her huge bowls of her favourite pasta with pesto, but she had only picked at it. For Hyslop the world as she knew it had ended with her grandmother's death, but for those others, although they shed tears and lamented loudly, it was different. Yes, they were sad, but drinking coffee and eating pine nut tart was still as important as it ever was.

She put a finger out and touched the beetle very gently on his back. She half expected him to run off, but he did not move. He wiggled his antennae in her direction and Hyslop felt soothed.

"Where is the child?" a male voice cut through the old women's chatter. It was Uncle Carlo. Hyslop shivered.

All the old ladies began talking at once and the din started up again. Each one claimed to have seen her somewhere, either in the kitchen or in the sitting room. Someone said that she had gone upstairs. Several exclaimed again at what a poor child she was, all alone now without her grandmother. Hyslop could see Uncle Carlo's expensive shiny black shoes: he was tapping his left foot up and down impatiently.

"Well, she must be somewhere," she heard him say. "Rosa! Rosa! Where *is* Rosa? Surely she must know where the child is hiding."

"Rosa is in the kitchen." "Yes, she's making more coffee." "I don't think the child is with her."

"Well, she's in charge of her!" snapped Uncle Carlo. "She had better know where she is. The girl's mother has come for her."

This brought shrieks and exclamations from all sides. "Oh Madonna!" cried Signora Crolla above the rest. "La madre!" This was echoed by cries of: "Madre de Dio! La Madre!" It wasn't the mother of God, however, who had come for her. Even more astonishingly, it seemed that Hyslop's own mother had come.

Hyslop gasped. Uncle Carlo had definitely said "the girl's mother." Rosa had told her when her grandmother died, that her mother would come for her, but Hyslop had not dared believe it. She had grown used to not having a mother or a father. Her grandmother had talked often enough of her younger son, Sandro, who was Hyslop's father, but never mentioned her mother. Her mother's name was Vanessa and she was from England: that was all that Hyslop knew of her. She had apparently disappeared when Papa had died, when Hyslop was a baby. "Disappeared" was the word always used. Hyslop had often wondered how someone could just disappear. "Disappeared" was the same as "dead" as far as she was concerned, and she had assumed that her mother was with the angels and the Virgin Mary, the same as her father, and now her grandmother. What an amazing thing to disappear and then to just appear again. How was it possible?

Breathless with excitement, she crawled towards the edge of the table. The beetle made a move at the same time, and scuttled in front of her, as if to head her off.

"It's all right," she whispered to him. "My mother has come."

She peeped out from her hiding place, and saw the most extraordinary pair of shoes she had ever seen. They were bright red with holes for the toes to pop out of, and very high heels. Hyslop had never seen such high heels. The toenails were painted the same colour of red. Surely such shoes and such toenails had never been seen in the house before!

"There she is, la bambina!" cried one of the old ladies. Several others joined in, pointing her out excitedly to Uncle Carlo and the lady with the red shoes. One of them lifted the table cloth up and Hyslop found herself the centre of everyone's attention.

"Come out of there at once!" said Uncle Carlo crossly. "Your mother has come for you."

The word "mother", even said by Uncle Carlo, was so thrilling it made Hyslop shiver deep inside. She looked up at the lady with the red shiny shoes, and opened her mouth wide in amazement.

The lady was wearing a red coat with black buttons, and elegant black leather gloves. Her lips were painted bright red too. All the dowdy old women dressed in black only served to make her stand out all the more. Not even in films or magazines had Hyslop *ever* seen anyone like this, anyone who was so different, so glamorous, so unbelievably beautiful. This amazing creature was her mother!

She stood up and the lady looked down at her. Her eyes did not smile. They were colder than Uncle Carlo's, and Hyslop suddenly felt afraid. She wanted to go back under the table with her beetle. She wanted to run away.

"Hello, Hyslop," said the lady in English.

"It is easy to imagine that an adult butterfly is a purposeless creature that lives out its short life by flitting aimlessly between flowers. Nothing could be further from the truth."
(from The Butterflies of Britain and Ireland by Jeremy Thomas and Richard Lewington)

Five Years Later…

CHAPTER ONE

Hyslop learns that she has a Godmother

It all began and ended with a letter.

The first letter, a flimsy fluttering thing that crossed the continent and heralded the summer in England, the summer that was to change so many lives, consisted of a series of lies…

It began with Hyslop deciding that it was best not to swim when an Uncle is watching. Well, maybe if you had normal Uncles you could, but none of hers had ever been normal. They weren't even proper Uncles, though she had to call them that. She peered through the leaves at the swimming pool shimmering in the heat. A cooling plunge in the water would have been wonderful but today that was out of the question.

Uncle Massimo was sunbathing on a lounger between the pool and the tennis court, and Hyslop hunkered down inside the bush at the far end of the garden, as far away from him as she could. He was smoking one of his horrible cigarettes and he had his very dark glasses on. Hyslop did not like those dark glasses: she could never tell when he was looking at her. The gardener was busy watering hanging baskets with a hose. The trouble was that although it was a huge garden there was nowhere that felt safe. The only good hiding place was here, under the shiny leaved bush at the end of the garden farthest from the house. The bush was uninteresting with no blossoms, just dark green leaves, and the gardeners were not likely to water it or pay it any attention. Hyslop, despite her cupboard experiences, liked being enclosed by the dense branches of the bush, liked being shut off from the world around her with only Nonna for company, and most of all she liked the ants who lived there.

The hum of the insects all around her was reassuring, and the ants' nest at the edge of the bush was as busy as ever. She was sure that ants never woke up hating their lives; they were always rushing around with a sense of purpose. Even when she turned over a stone to expose their eggs, or placed an obstacle in their path, they would deal with the set-back immediately. Hyslop loved watching them.

If their nests were disturbed, the ants would rush to their eggs and carry them deeper underground to safety. Hyslop sometimes longed to be a little ant egg. She would close her eyes and think of how it would feel to be in a dark, secret place, guarded by a delicate eggshell: to be so precious that a whole army of ants would fight to the death to keep her safe.

Sometimes she dropped jam or sugar on their path, which caused huge excitement. They liked melon pieces too. She had to be careful, however, if she wanted to sneak treats for the ants. To her mother all insects were vermin and had to be destroyed. Hyslop did not dare entice ants into the house as they never came singly, but she sometimes brought beetles and millipedes in boxes or jars into her room and hid them under her bed. She also kept a supply of dead wasps, but that was for a different reason.

The cicadas were particularly loud today. In the distance, butterflies danced and hovered, but none were coming in her direction. And there, right in front of her now was a large bumblebee. It was investigating the leaves of the bush and not finding them interesting enough to linger. A teacher at her previous school had told her that the entire Italian tomato crop would fail without bumblebees. It was in a lesson about geography, not about insects. It was just one of those throwaway comments, with no further details. That was typical of teachers and of grown-ups generally. There would be one interesting fact amongst all the boring drivel they talked about, but it was never followed up. Why couldn't she learn more about insects: did bumblebees make honey too? And could they sting? Questions about insects buzzed around her brain, bursting to get out. Her current teacher, at the International School,

Signora Zanetti, had told the class that bumblebees should not be able to fly as they were too heavy for their wings. And that was it. No further explanations or discussions about insects.

Hyslop allowed a dribble of spit to fall in the path of the ants. Several of them stopped in their tracks to investigate, waving their antennae around which seemed to attract others. Quite a little crowd was soon forming round it, and Hyslop wondered how they communicated with each other. Did they dance to each other like honeybees? If only she could get a decent book on insect behaviour, or find someone who knew about entomology. She had recently found out that entomology was the name for her interest in insects when one of her mother's rich American friends had caught her looking at beetles under a stone and said: "Yuck, Hyslop! How disgusting! What are you? A budding entomologist or something?" It led her to look in the English dictionary and to sneak a look at her mother's lap-top. Studying insects it seemed could be a career. There were adults who took insects seriously and who travelled the world in pursuit of their knowledge. How exciting was that! Her secret dream was to study entomology one day at University, and then to spend her life in tropical jungles hunting for rare species.

"Hyslop!" her mother's voice called from the patio.

Hyslop jumped in astonishment. Her mother usually had a long sleep after lunch when the sun was at its hottest. She hadn't expected to hear from her for hours. She got up cautiously and parted the leaves, taking care to stay out of sight.

"Hyslop! Where are you?" There was a sharpness to the call, but it was impatience rather than anger – and Hyslop had learned to recognise all the various nuances of her mother's moods – so it was probably nothing to do with the new collection of earwigs in her room.

Uncle Massimo called out in Italian, laughing, and Hyslop understood that he had seen her all along and was pointing out her hiding place with amusement. She felt something inside her curl up into a ball like a woodlouse. Her secret bush-world was never going to feel safe again if he knew she was there.

"What on earth are you doing skulking about in the bushes!" Her mother approached, waving a sheet of writing paper in her hand. She bent down and peered into the bush. She was wearing an orange sarong and orange rimmed sunglasses, and not even her scowl of displeasure could hide her luminous beauty.

"Stop bugging me, Hyslop. Come into the house at once. There's something I want you to do. It's important."

"She could be worse, Nonna," whispered Hyslop in Italian. She allowed herself the luxury of an imagined ruffle of her hair and a Nonna-hug, then followed the swaying orange sarong and the tap-tapping of expensive sandals into the house. Unusually, there was a sense of purpose about her mother that seemed to involve Hyslop.

There was a pad of flimsy writing paper on the kitchen table and an expensive looking pen.

"We have a letter to write!" announced her mother, handing her the pen. "A letter to your Godmother in England."

Hyslop had not been aware that she had a Godmother in England. Nor had she ever written a letter before.

"Sit down and write what I tell you. *Exactly* what I tell you."

Hyslop picked up a sheet of paper. She noticed that there was a small black ant crawling along the table and wondered if it was from the nest she had just been watching. She must have somehow brought it inside with her. Perhaps it had stowed away on her clothes. She would have to rescue it without attracting her mother's attention, as it would never find its way back to the nest under the bush on its own.

"Who is my Godmother?" she asked, tearing her eyes away from the ant. Her mother did not often reply to direct questions, but it was worth a try.

"Your Godmother is called Sandy. We were at school together. You are to write…" Her mother paused, then scribbled something on a piece of paper for Hyslop to copy. "Here. Write it like this."

Hyslop read: "Dear Xandi," and copied it obediently.

"I've written to her as well, but I'm not going to spell it in that stupid way." Her mother's lips curled up in disdain. "I can't bear names spelt wrongly. Anyway, *you* can spell it like that, Hyslop. It might amuse her. Yes, heaven knows, we want to amuse her."

"Does she know me?" asked Hyslop. The ant had stopped now and was moving its head around in a confused manner.

"Well, she was at your Christening," said her mother. "Probably the last time I saw her, come to think of it."

"How do you know her?"

"We were at school together, Sandy and I. Happy boarding school days!" This was said with a laugh that was not an expression of amusement. It was the sort of laugh her mother often gave, a nasty sort of laugh. "Very well connected was our Sandy! Lots of useful connections in fact. I shouldn't have left it so long, should I? Your Christening must have been ten… eleven… years ago. How old are you?"

Hyslop remembered about Godmothers now. They appeared at Christenings, like in Sleeping Beauty, and gave gifts like being clever or beautiful or having to be pricked on the finger by a spindle. She wondered what Sandy had given her at her Christening.

"Did she give me a present?"

"How should I remember trivia like that? Stop asking questions and write what I tell you."

Hyslop bent her head and prepared to write. She could write in English and French and Italian. All the teachers at the International School were impressed by her skills. Her mother spoke to her in English, and many of their house guests were English or American, but they only had three English books which they carried around with them whenever they moved to a new Uncle: a book of Shakespeare stories, a wonderful book called The Lion, The Witch and the Wardrobe, and a book of fairy tales with a picture of a weeping mermaid on the cover. Hyslop knew all the illustrations and most of the stories by heart, and she always turned to the front page of the Narnia book, where there was a white label announcing: Handwriting Prize, Vanessa Hyslop, Comber Grove Primary

School, 1973 – 74. It gave her a strange feeling to imagine her mother as a small child carefully forming her letters and then going up, with her hair brushed and her shoes shining, to get her prize. Would the child Vanessa have had a cruel tongue and a nasty laugh she wondered, or did those develop later in life?

"Dear Xandi, yes, you've got that," said her mother. "Umm... I am your Goddaughter Hyslop. I have been living in Italy with Mummy for the last... um, let me see... two, no... let's make it five years. Yes five sounds better than two. Sounds more stable. Yes, five years. We live in a little cottage with no heating and no electricity. Can you spell electricity in English? Oh, no matter, probably more appealing if it's spelt wrongly."

Hyslop frowned. The first odd thing was being told to refer to her mother as Mummy when normally she had to call her Vanessa. And then there was the strange lie about having no electricity. The villa they were in not only had electricity inside the house but garage doors that opened and lights outside that came on by themselves after dark. It was not as luxurious as Uncle Paolo's villa, where they had stayed previously, but there certainly weren't any problems with the electricity.

"Write it!" Her mother snapped her fingers and made a clicking sound.. "... no electricity. I go to an Italian village school but I am not very happy there."

Hyslop paused in her writing. The school was the one place where she *was* reasonably happy. In fact it was one of the better schools she had been to, an International School for which Uncle Massimo paid expensive fees. Was it good to lie to a Godmother?

"Keep up!" Her mother snapped her fingers again. "Where was I... yes... I am not very happy there. I would love to come to England and meet you. Mummy often talks about you, and I would love it if we could visit you."

To Hyslop's knowledge, her mother had never talked about Sandy. Surely she would have remembered something as important as a Godmother.

"Got that?" her mother drummed her fingers on the table, very close to the ant which fortunately she had not seen. "Um… It would be good if we could come and stay with you in England. Lots of love, Hyslop. You can put some kisses… you know, large X's, after it. Put three. No, make it four."

Hyslop sensed her mother's impatience and did as she was told. She put four X's, one after the other, beside her name, and thought how odd it looked. Her mother snatched the letter from her and read it through.

"Perfectly neat and no spelling mistakes in your English!" she said, putting it beside a letter of her own and folding them both into an envelope that she had already addressed and stamped. She looked directly at Hyslop and there was no hint of anger or impatience in her gaze. Her beautiful mouth turned up in a smile that seemed to be just for her daughter. It was a *real* smile. Hyslop stopped breathing for a moment. The smile, when it came, was so incredible that you didn't want to miss a second of it. Not even for the brief second of breathing or blinking. Her mother sealed the envelope. "Maybe you take after me, Hyslop. I was always top of my class at school, always ahead of the others."

There was a brief silence, then she said: "It's important to be ahead of the others in life."

Hyslop felt a fluttering of insect wings deep inside her. Praise from her mother was so rare and so precious that she felt slightly dizzy. She lost sight of the ant altogether, though she had intended to rescue it.

"Anyway, take this," her mother said, handing her the letter. The smile vanished now as quickly as it had come. "Take it down to the post-box at the end of the road."

Hyslop took the letter and looked up questioningly. Usually she was told to stay in the shade at this time of the day.

"Just do as I tell you, Hyslop." Her mother's voice was soft as she picked up a glossy magazine and used it to kill the ant which had stopped in front of her. Hyslop gazed at the crushed little body in dismay. Her mother flicked it onto the floor with a long red fingernail, then pointed to the door. "Carla's off duty, so run along and get it in the post before five. Then leave me in peace, for God's sake!"

Nonna walked beside her as she made her way through the garden and out of the side gate into the blinding glare of the street. The air was full of unanswered questions now along with the chirping of the cicadas. Hyslop felt vaguely afraid. Her mother must have some purpose in sending this letter, and often her mother's strange behaviour led to them moving again. Even if she was not happy here, a move was a frightening prospect, especially if it was to a different country. There would be new unpleasant things and new Uncles to get used to if they moved. England itself, her mother's homeland, seemed as remote as the North Pole. As for Godmothers, well, weren't there wicked ones in the fairy stories she had read, Godmothers who made you sleep for a hundred years? There was no guaranteeing that this Sandy person would be of the good variety.

"Oh, Nonna," she whispered.

"It's so hot, tesoro," soothed the invisible Nonna in her ear. "You should have stayed in the shade. Have you put your suncream on? What about a sunhat… "

CHAPTER TWO

Zak disturbs the Butterflies

The trouble about being a daydreamer is that people get mad at you. Some people seemed to like rushing around, flying from one job to another, getting cross, but why couldn't they accept that not everyone liked to live that way? Why couldn't they just leave him alone inside his own head? Zak felt that his whole life consisted of being poked, prodded, shouted at, and generally told he wasn't good at anything.

At the core of him, the very centre, was a stillness that they couldn't touch. Zak reckoned that this was what annoyed people so much about him. He knew his mother had been a still sort of person too. His grandmother often said so:

"Zak Judd, you're as bad as your mother! All she ever did was drift around in a daydream as if tomorrow would do!"

Well, and why wouldn't tomorrow do, was what he wanted to know. The world wasn't about to come to an end just because some chore wasn't completed. Why rush around getting angry all the time? Sometimes Granny said nasty things about his mother to provoke him:

"Bone lazy like your feckless mother, that's what you are, boy!"

He knew she meant to hurt him by saying this, but she didn't succeed. She never seemed to realise that he liked being compared to his mother, even when Granny was saying horrid things about both of them. No one ever mentioned his mother otherwise, so even these insults were a sort of treasure.

He had learned not to ask direct questions about his mother. Both his father and his grandmother fobbed him off. His father's face would change and he would find yet another reason to be out of the house, or to reach for a drink. His grandmother would give one of her sniffs.

"You want to know about your mother, do you? Well, I'm not one for turning people into saints just because they're no longer with us. I tell it like it is: your mother was a lazy, useless woman who couldn't keep a clean house and who didn't know the meaning of hard work!"

Sometimes she would add, pointing a finger: "And you're turning out just like her!"

If only Granny knew how he *longed* to be just like his mother, how he longed for a messy house that had love at its heart. If only she could understand how he longed to have his mother with him, alive and feckless and drifting around in a daydream. Today he tried to slink out of the house unnoticed, but his father accosted him after breakfast and gestured towards the back door.

"Need some help," he said gruffly. "There's extra clearing and strimming to be done." He strode out of the house, indicating that Zak should come with him.

Zak followed some ten or twelve paces behind, as they made their way through the woods to the Hemmingswood estate. Neither of them spoke. To Zak's surprise, instead of stopping at the main garden by the big house where his father normally worked, they moved on past Zak's beloved kitchen garden and the dahlia beds to the empty cottage at the far end of the estate. In an area already full of nettles and thistles and wild flowers, this was a particularly unkempt corner. The path leading to the cottage was completely overgrown.

"They got guests coming," said his father. "We've to tidy this area round here."

Zak stared around him. He watched as his father got out his strimmer and some weeding tools.

"I'll strim round here," he said. "You need to weed the path, Zak."

Zak looked back wistfully at the kitchen garden where he worked for Mrs Braithwaite. He would much rather have tended the salad beds. He could have spent hours happily looking at all the vegetables: recent rain had made the courgettes double in size, and most of the cabbages were being eaten by caterpillars. Every time he came there was new growth to see, always something different.

"Never mind your stupid vegetables," growled his father, as if reading his thoughts. He threw a tool at Zak. "Here. Use this to get them weeds on the path out by the roots. And don't sit staring into space like you usually do."

"The old man won't like it," said Zak. He stood surveying the path, where brightly coloured butterflies were clinging to the weeds.

"Never mind the old man. I take orders from Mr Braithwaite," said his father. "He pays the wages, boy. And you take orders from me. Now get going!"

Zak bent down and began attacking the weeds that were growing between the stone slabs of the path. It was hard to see the paving stones there were so many weeds. Dandelions and couch grass were the worst. Their roots spread far under the slabs and it was impossible to get rid of them without lifting up each paving stone individually. This part of the garden had not been tended for a long time, and it was going to be hard work. Zak hacked at the weeds as best he could, sending up a pair of tiny blue butterflies that had been clinging to a long grass stalk. His father had his back to Zak, with a pair of ear protectors on and was concentrating on strimming the nettle patch at the side of the cottage. A cloud of dust and insects rose up above his head.

"The old man won't like it," said Zak again to no one in particular as he stopped to stare around him. "His butterflies are being disturbed."

CHAPTER THREE

Hyslop and Vanessa leave Italy

"Get all your things together, your clothes and the books. Everything." Vanessa appeared suddenly in Hyslop's bedroom, pulling a jacket over her shoulders. "I've packed everything else. We're leaving for the airport in an hour, so hurry up."

This was how the flight to England was announced to Hyslop. She did not even have time to say goodbye to her friends at school, or to the teacher, Signora Zanetti. It had happened before when they had moved around in France and Italy to stay with the various Uncles. There was no point in complaining about it, however. Her mother's decisions were like the weather; you might not like them but they were a fact of life, and you had to accept them. Protesting of any sort would be punished. There was, however, a new and terrifying aspect to this move: flying. She had never had to cross the sea in an aeroplane before. She had no memory of ever being in a plane and Hyslop felt uneasy. She needed someone to explain to her about flying, to tell her it would be all right. What were the statistics about plane crashes? She tried to conjure up a Nonna hug, but then remembered that she was leaving Italy, the land of Nonna, behind. Would Nonna be available to her in an aeroplane?

They were going to the land of her Godmother, Sandy.

The thought of meeting her Godmother was worrying enough, but first of all she had to survive the flight.

"Are there many accidents in aeroplanes?" she asked her mother from the back seat of Uncle Massimo's red sports car as they headed for the airport. "I mean… you know… plane crashes."

"What?" Vanessa stopped applying lip gloss and met Hyslop's

gaze in the car mirror with a scowl of irritation. "Accidents? What do you mean accidents? Oh my God, it's your first flight isn't it, Hyslop? Well, well! I hadn't thought of that!"

Her mother's tone was both amused and scornful. She explained the situation in Italian as if it were a joke to Uncle Massimo, but he just growled in reply. He was hunched over the steering wheel and he was not in a good mood.

"I was just wondering," said Hyslop, "about accidents in aeroplanes. I don't suppose they happen very often."

"Well, of course there are accidents," said Vanessa, reverting to English again. "Accidents happen all the time. Life is an accident, my dear. One enormous unpredictable great big accident. You and I are accidents… " she paused, then gave a joyless laugh: "especially *you*, Hyslop."

Hyslop was silent. She should have known better than to have shown fear to her mother. She dug her thumbnails into the flesh of her fingers and said nothing more.

The car stopped at a taxi rank with a squeal of brakes, and Uncle Massimo began talking rapidly in Italian to her mother. He seemed angry, not at all happy that they were leaving him and going to England. He thumped his fist on the roof his car, and cursed loudly. Hyslop was pleased that her mother had lied to him and said they were going to a place in the north of England called Newcastle, when in fact she knew that they were going to stay with the Sandy person somewhere about thirty miles from London. Her mother had told him they would only be gone for two or three weeks but Hyslop suspected that the move was more permanent. She had come to recognise the signs of her mother's restlessness, the endless need to move on. The only good part about moving was that the Uncles always got left behind. They got left behind, but Hyslop never did. Massimo, his face dark with displeasure, went round to the boot to get the luggage out. He cursed at the weight of the cases and tossed Hyslop's case at her, almost knocking her over. Then he and Vanessa began kissing and Hyslop walked away from them. She wanted to get as far away from Massimo as possible in case he wanted to kiss her goodbye too. She looked down at her feet for any sign of a dead wasp to protect her, but there were none. She did not think she would need any, however, as Massimo was so busy saying goodbye to her mother he seemed to have forgotten her.

"Once it is all sorted out over there, you come straight back," he was saying, twisting a lock of her mother's hair in his hand. "Telephone me every day. I won't be happy until you are back here with me. Phone me as soon as you land. Remember I love you."

Hyslop felt a little surge of triumph. "You may love Vanessa," she thought, "but she doesn't love you. She's leaving you behind. She's taking me, only me, with her."

Finally Uncle Massimo called out "Ciao, bambina!" to her and drove off, with a great deal of noise, in his expensive shiny car.

Hyslop muttered a rude word after him in Italian. It was a word she was not allowed to use (though adults often used it), but her mother did not hear as she was heading for the glass revolving doors ahead of them.

The airport was enormous and full of people rushing around, all with a sense of purpose and all in a hurry. It was a bit like an ants' nest, but not so orderly, and with no apparent teamwork. Her mother handed their luggage over to a lady in a green jacket and it disappeared on a moving conveyor belt. Hyslop felt rather bereft once it had disappeared from sight. Then her mother bought a magazine and drank an espresso. She plonked a glass of orange juice in front of Hyslop.

"Drink that," she said. "It's very dehydrating in the plane."

This was the only information that Hyslop had to go on. She wasn't sure what dehydrating meant, but knew it was something to do with being dry. Her mother talked a great deal about feeling dehydrated after she had been drinking wine in the sun. Why would the plane be like that wondered Hyslop, as she drank the orange juice. Was it because they would be flying close to the sun, like Icarus in the legend, and it would get very hot? Was it because there wasn't enough air for everyone on the plane? There were so many questions buzzing around in her head, but she kept quiet as usual.

When they were shown onto the plane her mother made her sit on an aisle seat away from the window, which was a pity as Hyslop would have liked to have seen the clouds. A girl at school had once shown her a photograph on her phone that she had taken of clouds from a plane window, and they had looked amazing.

"If you're going to be sick by the way, aim over there, not near me," said Vanessa, settling back in her seat with her shiny magazine.

Hyslop did feel sick and nervous. There was a lot to think about. Ladies in green jackets were wandering up and down the aisle smiling at everyone. Little television screens appeared and boomed out instructions in both Italian and English about what to do if there was an emergency. It was serious stuff. Lifebelts were mentioned. Hyslop could not see where the lifebelt was, and did not want to poke around searching for it as no one else was. They were not that near an emergency exit either. She glanced round anxiously at her fellow passengers. No one was paying the slightest bit of attention to the instructions. Lifebelts were all very well anyway, but what if they crashed on land?

Hyslop tried to conjure up Nonna, but it was difficult to be soothed as she imagined Nonna would be pretty scared in a plane too. She knew that Nonna would have been saying her Ave Maria and fingering her rosary. She said the familiar words to herself in her head: "Ave Maria, piena di grazia… "

The plane was moving faster and faster along the runway. It was taking off. The wings did not flap, but there was a huge sense of power from the plane's engines. It was incredible! People still flicked through newspapers and magazines in a bored fashion or chatted with their neighbours. The safety talk was finished now and the ladies in the green jackets had gone to sit down and fasten their own seatbelts.

"Il Signore e con te," murmured Hyslop to herself. She had not been to church since Nonna's death, as her mother said all religion was a load of rubbish. Actually she used a ruder word than rubbish, but Hyslop tried not to think of that. She often muttered the words of the Ave Maria in secret to remind her of Nonna: "Tu sei benedetta fra le donne... "

Her ears felt strange, and she shook her head to clear them. In her head she continued in Italian, though the last line was more alarming than comforting: "Prega per noi peccatori, adesso e nell'ora della nostra morte... " Hyslop had muttered it so often to herself as a sort of magical mantra, not considering the meaning of the words, that it was only now when she was afraid of the plane crashing that she translated the ending to herself in her head: "Pray for us sinners now and at the hour of death." She shouldn't be drawing attention to the hour of death in her prayers, she decided. It could be dangerous. Maybe she should try the Lord's Prayer instead. Was there much about death in that? She screwed up her face as she tried to remember it all.

"Try and have a little nap, Hyslop," said her mother suddenly, in a tone that was kind and concerned, patting her on the arm. Hyslop look up in astonishment. Her mother was smiling over her at a man in the seat across the aisle. "It's my daughter's first flight," she said. "She's a little bit nervous, aren't you, darling?"

"Back home to England?" the man asked, nodding briefly at Hyslop, then turning to Vanessa in open admiration. Hyslop could tell at once that this man was of no interest to her mother, but still she had to ensnare him. She had to keep making sure that no one was immune to the power of her smile.

"Yes," sighed Vanessa. "Back home after a long time away."

"Oh, that sounds interesting!" said the man. He was leaning forward now. The poor fool was well and truly caught.

For much of the journey her mother and this man talked. Vanessa had shown him her smile, and she made him go to great efforts to amuse her, in order to make her flick the smile back at him again. His silly stories soon ended up with the stupid things that men always said, about how she didn't look old enough to be

Hyslop's mother, how beautiful she was, and could he perhaps take her out to dinner in London. Hyslop could tell that her mother had no intention of meeting the man again, but she allowed him to buy her a drink and to compliment her. Vanessa, it seemed, had to make everyone acknowledge her power. No one was allowed to escape. It made Hyslop yawn in boredom as she listened to it all. This proved to be fortunate, as she found that loud yawning helped the funny sensation in her ears so she carried on doing it. The conversation over her head was so monotonous that eventually, despite her anxiety, she fell asleep.

CHAPTER FOUR

Arrival in England, a Godmother and a Bumblebee

Godmother Sandy met them at the airport near London. She was smaller than Hyslop had expected, with a bare scrubbed looking face. It took Hyslop a moment to realise what was unusual about this, before she decided that she had never met a friend of her mother's who did not wear high heels and whose face was not orange with make-up. Her jeans were rather grubby looking, and there seemed to be some sort of dusty white powder in her hair. Instead of a designer handbag she was carrying what looked like a supermarket carrier bag.

"Sandy, darling!" Air kisses were exchanged. "Long time no see!"

"Oh my goodness, Vanessa!" exclaimed Sandy. "Look at you! As gorgeous as ever! Do you have a portrait in the attic or something!"

Hyslop was not quite sure why a portrait in the attic would make her mother laugh and shake her head. It had to be a compliment about her beauty though. It always was.

"Hardly, Sandy, I'm such an old bag now! Surprised you knew me!"

"You look younger than ever, you lucky thing! *And* slimmer – it's not fair on the rest of us. And Hyslop!" said Sandy turning to Hyslop and beaming at her. "My dear girl! I last saw you when you were a baby. At your Christening. And you must be eleven now!"

Hyslop wondered if Sandy had given her a gift at her Christening but didn't like to ask. Her mother had warned her about asking questions. It felt good but strange to be addressed as "My dear girl!"

"In case you were wondering why I said your Mum must have a portrait in the attic," Sandy said, still addressing Hyslop, "it was just a way of saying she looked so young. It's from a story you probably haven't read, a book by Oscar Wilde, where the portrait in the attic ages but the person remains young and beautiful!"

"Oh," said Hyslop.

She was astonished at hearing her mother referred to as "Mum" and also at being provided with an explanation. Most of what Vanessa's friends said was weird or stupid but generally no one took the trouble to explain anything to her. Adults laughed at things that were not funny and became angry about things that Hyslop loved (like insects). She could have told Sandy that Vanessa stayed young because she was always on a diet, spent a fortune at the hairdresser, and used expensive cleansers, toners and moisturisers. To Hyslop's knowledge there was no portrait in the attic. It was always best to say nothing, however. Her mother had told her not to "give away any information". Luckily Hyslop had learned the art of slipping invisibly into the background when adults were about, so she did not find it difficult to avoid talking. She stared down at her feet, and waited for her mother to claim her share of attention.

"Darling, do fill me in on the set up where you live!" Vanessa gave Sandy the heavier of her two cases to carry. "Now, did you say you live in a barn conversion?"

"Yes, I live in a barn with a pottery attached where I have my own workshop."

"How *wonderful*! And we are to be in a little cottage nearby, is that right?"

"Yes, Keeper's Cottage."

"How perfectly *sweet*! It sounds delightful. And what about neighbours?"

"Oh yes, you'll meet the neighbours. There's the main house, Hemmingswood House, where Uncle Northy – he's my Godfather – grew up. It's been in his family for generations – a real old country house, full of dark wooden panelling and antiques, lots of atmosphere. A huge old pile! Penny and Hugo live in it now. They are dear friends. Then there's the Dower House, where Uncle Northy lives – he's a bit of an eccentric by the way and he… "

"Tell me about Penny and Hugo in the big house," said Vanessa. "Do you see much of them?"

"Oh, all the time," said Sandy. "We're very close. Quite a little community. There's Penny and Hugo and Uncle Northy and then there's Ilga and Malcolm. You'll like them all, I'm sure, and they're dying to meet you!"

"Darling, whatever have you been telling them about me?"

Sandy turned round suddenly and looked at Hyslop struggling along behind them.

"Hey, let me take that brown bag, Hyslop," she said, her face creasing into a smile. "It looks pretty heavy to me."

"Oh, Hyslop likes to be independent," said Vanessa. "She doesn't need help."

Hyslop walked a few paces behind them as they chattered away. She felt cautiously optimistic about Sandy. She had a smile that came from deep inside her and sparkled through her eyes. She was also a sort of relation in a way: a Godmother. In a world that seemed to be made up of other people's families, of brothers and sisters and grandparents and aunties and cousins, Hyslop had a serious shortage of relatives. There was only her mother, nasty Uncle Carlo and the even nastier string of fake Uncles they had been living with over the years in France and Italy. Of course there were Papa and Nonna in heaven, but they were not much practical help to her.

"Come on, Hyslop," said Sandy, stopping to turn round again. "You really *are* struggling with that."

"I'm fine thank you, Sandy." She had been taught to answer politely and not draw attention to herself.

"No, no, hand it over," said Sandy. "I insist! It'll help me balance this thing of your mother's that weighs half a ton!"

Hyslop looked ahead at her mother to see what she should do, but Vanessa was busy with her mobile telephone. Hyslop handed the bag over to Sandy. It was rather heavy as she had been given the books and the dictionaries to carry.

"Goodness me, you're stronger than you look, littl'un!" laughed Sandy. "This is a ton weight too. Come on, the car's not too far away."

As they emerged out into the fresh air a bumblebee appeared. It flew in a clumsy circle around them as if to welcome them. Hyslop was delighted to see her first English insect.

You could never trust first impressions, but if there were fat furry bumblebees and Godmothers who carried your bags, then maybe England would be bearable. Just as long as there were no Uncles.

CHAPTER FIVE

Hyslop explores an English Garden

In the night Hyslop dreamed she was back in France, in the Normandy chateau of vile Oncle Xavier. He was definitely the worst Uncle. It was the dream where she was trying to escape from the horrible journey upstairs, past glassy-eyed boars' heads, past endless pictures of dead animals, up, up, up to the wooden door into the haunted attic room. Oncle Xavier's mocking laughter echoed hideously in her head as dream-Hyslop struggled to get away from him.

She found herself muttering Nonna's Ave Maria as she woke up, her heart pounding, and wondered where she was. The sun was sneaking in to her room through a gap in the curtains. The English sun was different from the Italian sun. That was her first impression: it was more polite, less brashly insistent. "You might just want to get up and come outside," it seemed to say. "But in your own time of course." The Italian sun was an attention seeking shouter, who would burst in rudely unless forced out with wooden shutters.

It was a gentle relief to find that it was morning, that she had survived the plane journey, and that she was in England, the Land without Uncles. She had the tiny upstairs part of the cottage all to herself. Her mother had the big bedroom downstairs with French doors that led onto a patio, and Hyslop's room was up in the eaves, all snug and private, up some worn wooden stairs.

The cottage was smaller than anywhere they normally stayed. It seemed cramped after the huge French and Italian houses they had grown used to, but Hyslop liked it better. It seemed to beckon her in and embrace her in a secret hug. Her new bedroom was not much bigger than the single bed and tiny chest of drawers it contained, but there was a little fireplace there with chipped green tiles round it and a broken grate. It looked as if it hadn't been lit for a hundred years. To Hyslop's delight there were cobwebs there and two woodlice. There did not seem to be any likelihood of maids bursting in to clean and polish.

She opened her curtains. Her window looked out onto a stone patio, and beyond that to a meadow of tall grasses. Giant nettles at the edge of the meadow bent their heads towards the patio area, nodding in the breeze. Some of them had been hacked at roughly, as had the creeping briars and brambles, but they looked as if they wanted to come and invade the little paved patio as soon as they were given a chance. It all felt like a neglected corner of somewhere more important, and as she opened her window and listened to the birdsong, Hyslop felt a restless urge to be outside. She wondered what the rest of the garden was like, and decided that it was time to explore.

Her mother had been drinking wine with Sandy until late, and Hyslop knew better than to disturb her sleep. She dressed quickly and crept downstairs. There was no sound from her mother's room so she went outside. As well as morning birdsong, she could hear the buzzing of bees, though not the familiar sound of the cicadas. She rather missed the Tuscan cicadas. She would need to attune to different bird and insect noises here.

As she stepped out beyond the tiny garden gate, more grasses and nettles surrounded her. She did not know the names of the flowers she saw but they looked like the kind of plants which would grow randomly in a field, rather than be cultivated in a garden. There were lots of plants with pinky-purple flowers which smelt like oregano in Italy. Bees were buzzing all around them, and butterflies hung from purple thistle heads. It did not look as if gardeners ever came near. Hyslop liked the feel of the grassy wilderness.

Soon she came upon a large kitchen garden. It was not all

straight and orderly like vegetable gardens she had seen before. The vegetables had not been planted in rigidly straight lines, and weeds grew in profusion amongst them, green and lush. There was a cabbage patch too, whose cabbages seemed to have been stripped to shreds. Hardly an edible patch of green remained, and Hyslop smiled to see little caterpillars of varying sizes munching their way through what was left of them. There were different sorts of lettuces: red and green, straight leaved and frilly, shiny green courgettes with large yellow flowers, peas and potatoes, and two scarlet wigwams of runner beans. The tomatoes were in greenhouses, and she put her head in and sniffed the intense tomato smell. There were aubergines and peppers inside too, in terracotta pots, looking healthy enough but not large and bursting with ripeness like they would be in the Italian sunshine. Two wasps were buzzing against the glass unable to understand why they couldn't get out. How long would it take insects to understand glass, she wondered. Might it take a thousand generations? Or a million years? It must seem like a hard piece of air: it just wouldn't make sense. Hyslop set about rescuing them. She found a piece of cardboard and shooed them out into the fresh air and freedom. "Fly away, little wasps," she murmured.

The morning air was warm but not fiercely so. Perhaps her mother would not need her long beauty sleep after lunch here, although Hyslop could not decide whether that was a good or a bad thing. She followed the overgrown paths past the vegetable garden until she came to beds of tall brightly coloured flowers, some as high as her head. They were deep shades of purple, vibrant red, yellow, pink and orange. They were almost too exotic looking to be English, and Hyslop was pleased to see bees and bumblebees buzzing around. England might not be as hot as Italy, but there seemed to be no shortage of insect life.

After the beds of tall flowers, through an archway in an enormous hedge, she suddenly came upon neatly mown lawns and saw the main house itself. Her heart sank. Her mother's friends, or rather the friends of Godmother Sandy, lived here, the people who were letting them live in the cottage. It looked very grand: not the sort of house that beckoned you in with a smile, but the kind of house that had stood for hundreds of years, confident of itself and its grandeur, the kind of house that told you to keep out unless invited. Such a house meant rich people and this made Hyslop sigh. She did not care for rich people. Most of her mother's friends had silly amounts of money: rich people with their rich toys. For as long as she could remember, they had flitted from one group of wealthy people to another, and Hyslop was tired of them all with their big houses and fast cars and boats, with servants who ran after them and poured them far too much wine. This part of the garden, so formal and tidy, must have staff, and she did not particularly want to meet the gardener. She decided it might be best to head back for the safety of the wild garden. She did not want to meet anyone at all, although it would be good to meet a dog or two. She had thought she had heard dogs barking earlier, and had a fantasy that the dogs would be let out. They would be big fierce dogs, wolf-like and terrifying, and they would all run at her snarling and foaming at the mouth, but she would not be afraid.

She would stand her ground, looking at them calmly and they would whine and sit down in a circle around her. There would be a Doberman amongst them, Hyslop decided, with its lip curled up viciously. "I'm not afraid of you," she would say, pointing a rebuking finger at it. Perhaps a German Shepherd would also be baring its teeth at her, but one look from Hyslop would calm it too. Snarling would turn to low growling, and foaming at the mouth to gentle drooling. Most children would run in terror but Hyslop had no fear of animals. It was people she usually wanted to run from. After a while she would put her hand out to the lead dog (there was always a pack leader), the fiercest of them all, and he would approach her slowly, head lowered submissively and tail wagging. Then the others would bark excitedly and follow his lead, all wagging tails and licking her hands. Perhaps the owner of the house would come running up and cry in astonishment, "Good heavens, I've never seen the dogs do that. How *did* you tame them?"

"YOU THERE, LITTLE GIRL!" boomed a real voice, bursting into her reverie.

Hyslop whirled round and saw an old man moving towards her at an alarming speed, pointing a walking stick at her.

CHAPTER SIX

Hyslop meets a Peculiar Old Man, a Brimstone and some Peacocks

"Can I help you?" The old man made the question sound more like a threat as he pointed his walking stick at her. "This is private property."

"I live in the cottage beyond the vegetable garden," said Hyslop. She decided to remain as calm as she could, despite her heart thumping. She would treat him like a snarling Doberman and show no fear. Unlike with dogs, she knew she could outrun him if she had to, and she tensed her body, ready for flight.

"You *live* there, do you?" he said in rather an unpleasant tone. "In Keeper's Cottage!"

"My mother is renting it from the owner of this house," said Hyslop. Was renting the correct word when no money changed hands? What exactly was the connection between the owner of the house and her Godmother, Sandy? Perhaps this old man *was* the owner of the house, though he did not seem like the sort of rich person her mother usually targeted. Not like an Uncle at all. It was best to say nothing more. Perhaps she had already said too much.

"*Renting*, are we!" he said, eyes bulging at her in an angry-old-man-staring kind of way. "And where do you pay your *rent* I wonder. Do you know who owns this house? Hmmm?"

In fact Hyslop did *not* know who the owner of the house was so she said nothing, but held her head up in a calm "I'm not frightened of you" sort of way. It was an attitude she had learned over the years: you had to show that you were not being insolent, but that at the same time you were not afraid. Showing fear to any predator was dangerous.

The old man stared at her for a while, then muttered something to himself. It sounded like a rude swear-word, so Hyslop pretended not to have heard it. She was more sure of Italian swear words, but the English word sounded similar to a term she knew in Italian. At least he did not seem to be directing it at her; it was as if he had forgotten she was there. He leaned on his walking stick and looked beyond her. Suddenly his eyes took on a look of fondness as if he had just seen his favourite child, though there was no one in sight. He slapped his head with his hand and muttered to himself a few times. Hyslop decided that he was a very strange person, and wondered if all old people in England were as peculiar as this. As she watched him, his face creased into a lop-sided smile that showed his yellow old man's teeth.

"D'you know what that is?" he said. He seemed to be addressing her directly now, and Hyslop turned around to follow the direction of his gaze. He was staring at a butterfly.

"It's a butterfly," she said. How young did he think she was, for goodness sake?

"A butterfly. Yes, just a butterfly. That's all it is to you, isn't it? That's all you can say about it. How pathetic!"

"Well, I don't know what else to say about it," said Hyslop. "What do you want me to say? It's a yellow butterfly," she added to appease him further. It was indeed a very yellow butterfly, and Hyslop mused on this: a butterfly that was the colour of butter.

"It's a BRIMSTONE!" he said, glaring at her. "Don't they teach you about butterflies in school these days?"

"No, unfortunately we don't learn about insects in school," said Hyslop. She pondered for a moment. In the various French and Italian schools she had attended no one had taught her anything about butterflies. In France they were all papillons and in Italy they were farfalle. Maybe English children had learned about butterflies in school and she had missed out. That would be typical: something she would have been interested in learning about, and the moment might be gone forever. She would go back to English and arithmetic and geography in some strange class and never learn about butterflies.

"Hah! I know who you are," said the old man, pointing his walking stick at her. He didn't seem to need it for walking as far as Hyslop could see, but used it for pointing and poking at things. She kept a careful watch on where he was pointing in case he turned violent with it. He was a very posh-sounding old man, but no one seemed to have told him it was rude to point at people and shout, let alone mutter swear words. "You're guests of Sandy, aren't you?" he said, narrowing his eyes at her. "Haven't been in touch for years, and now that you've run out of cash in Italy you sell her a sob story and come over here for some free board and lodging. Oh yes, I've heard all about it."

"Yes, I am Sandy's Goddaughter," said Hyslop with as much dignity as she could, "but I think it's rude to talk about running out of *cash*," she paused to show that she found it a vulgar word, "to a child. Quite bad manners in fact." This seemed to be an effective strategy, as it made him frown and pause.

"I suppose it is," he said after a while, nodding slowly as if she had said something which, upon consideration, he agreed with. He glared at her again: "But if you're so keen on manners, *child*," he spat the word out at her, "don't you know that it is rude to trespass in someone else's garden."

"I am not trespassing, I am exploring," said Hyslop.

"Exploring in someone else's property *is* trespassing," he said. "I should have thought that would be perfectly clear to even the youngest and stupidest *child*. Or how would you define the word?"

"Well, I didn't *know* I was trespassing," said Hyslop. For some reason she was not afraid of this rude old man, and the realisation astonished her. She thought of him as a noisy dog, growling and snarling but not dangerous: all bark and no bite. "Anyway," she added, "I thought people in England were meant to be polite to guests, and I am a guest of my Godmother Sandy. I assumed that no one would mind if I took a walk around the garden. If this is your garden and you object to my presence, then I am very sorry."

There was a silence as he seemed to think about this. Then he began slapping his head again and Hyslop wondered if he were slightly mad. He was muttering swear words to himself as if he had forgotten that she was there, and suddenly in a strange accent, quite unlike his normal posh voice he bellowed a strange word at her: "Dunderheids!" He said it several times.

Hyslop did not know what the word meant or why he had shouted it. She decided to ignore it. "Oh well, I had better go back now," she said, pretending to consult a watch, as his slapping movements became more extreme. She thought it best to keep facing him and walk backwards rather than turn her back on him. Her talk of politeness to guests seemed to have deflected his aggression, but it was best to keep him in view. There was something unpredictable, almost wild about him.

"Sandy's Goddaughter, are you? Hey, don't leave just yet! Come with me!" he ordered, waving his stick in her direction, setting off towards the other end of the garden. Hyslop followed him, even though he was – in the most literal sense of the word – a stranger, and Nonna and her school-teachers in Italy had always told her not to talk to strangers. She was curious, however, and reassured herself again that she could outrun him if she had to. Besides, he seemed to know Sandy. They passed many flowers and shrubs, all neatly pruned and tidy. A gardener had obviously been around this part of the garden. The old man peered closely at some of the flowers, and finally stopped beneath a tall purple-flowered bush and looked up. He raised his stick to point upwards.

"D'you see?" he said, his voice much quieter and gentler now. "Do you see? The butterfly bush!"

Hyslop looked up and opened her mouth wide in wonder. She had never seen anything like it in her life. The long purple flowers of the bush in front of her were covered in butterflies. At first they seemed like exotic blossoms shimmering in the breeze, then two of them flew up and changed places. Some were predominantly red, some were multicoloured, two were black and orange, and one was white.

"They're… they're amazing!" she cried, her eyes shining. It was one of the most wonderful things she had ever seen. A butterfly bush! Why had no one told her about such things!

"There are eight butterflies!" she cried, counting swiftly. "Oh, here's another. Oh my goodness, nine!"

She glanced at the old man. His face looked quite different, softer, almost kind.

"Do you know their names?" he said.

Hyslop frowned. Surely he didn't have names for all the butterflies. Then she realised he did not mean names like Lucia or Carlo; he meant did she know what sort of butterflies they were.

"Oh," she said. There were no more yellow Brimstones as far as she could see. There was, however, a white one with black spots on its wings, and she was sure she had heard gardeners cursing about their caterpillars eating cabbages when they had lived with Uncle Paolo. Everyone got cross with the poor caterpillars and Hyslop had tried to stop the gardeners from killing them. "That one is a Cabbage White."

"Only if you're American," said the old man. "Are you American, little girl?"

This was a random question.

"No, I'm not," she said.

"Didn't think you were," he said. He slapped his head, then returned to pointing at the butterflies. "Strictly, there's no such thing as a Cabbage White here. In America they call them that, but here in England we call our white butterflies different names. That one's a Large White."

"I thought the caterpillars ate cabbages," said Hyslop. She wanted to show that she did in fact know a thing or two about insects herself. She could have told him that the cabbages she had just seen in the vegetable garden beside the cottage were pretty much eaten up by caterpillars.

"That's true," he said. "Bit of a nuisance at times." He shrugged. "But then again, we've all got to eat. I don't allow them to kill the caterpillars. It really annoys my son-in-law." He pointed at a particularly beautiful butterfly. "Don't you know that one?"

It was the most exquisite creature that Hyslop had ever seen. It had eyes on its wings like a male peacock and its colours were iridescent in the sunlight. She shook her head sadly.

"No, I don't know its name," she said.

"Dunderheids!" He said his strange word again, in an accent that sounded unlike his normal posh voice. Was he imitating someone? Hyslop wondered if he was talking about her, or the butterflies, or about some unspecified people in his own mind. It was as if he didn't know he was saying the strange word, as if it had just tumbled out of his mouth. She hoped it wasn't the name for the beautiful butterfly. That would be most unfortunate.

"It's a Peacock!" He spoke in his normal voice again. "See the Peacock eyes on its wings? Look, there's another over there. Mind you, when I was a boy you used to see dozens round here."

He turned to face her, his eyes flashing: "I mean it, literally *dozens*. My grandfather's garden was alive with them. The place was *dancing* with butterflies." He almost sounded angry at her, then his shoulders sagged and he looked sad. He shook his head. "You just don't see that now."

He was staring off into the distance as if at the long-gone world of his childhood, a world that had been full of those wonderful Peacocks. Hyslop looked back up at them. Seeing two of them was exciting enough, and she tried to imagine the beauty of dozens of them dancing around the purple bush. Where had they all gone, she wondered and the sheer sadness of it brought a stinging sensation to the back of her eyes.

CHAPTER SEVEN

Failed Pots and Blueberry Muffins

As Hyslop ran back to the cottage for breakfast, Peacocks and Brimstones were still fluttering around the butterfly bush in her head. She had to go and look at them again more closely. She wanted to study the colour and the shape of those "eyes" on their wings. The strange old man had become less grumpy when she had showed an interest in the butterflies. He had stopped calling her a trespasser, and told her that he had a grove full of buddleia, or butterfly bushes. He had stopped scowling and muttering swear words when she asked him if she could come back and see the butterflies again. Hyslop knew that she would not be afraid to go back into his garden.

To her astonishment, however, when she opened the door into the cottage, her mother was up and about, dressed in "going out" clothes and high heels.

"Where have you been, Hyslop?" The tone was irritable rather than angry. "I've been waiting for you. I hope you haven't been collecting insects for God's sake. I have to go to London, so you're going to Sandy's."

Hyslop felt a surge of panic.

"I'll be all right here on my own," she said.

"Well, you probably would be," said Vanessa, "but as I said, you are going to Sandy's." She patted her hair to check it was perfect. "It's not the done thing to leave children here on their own and there are no staff to dump you on. Believe me, I'd be quite happy to leave you with your creepy crawlies, or hiding under bushes, or whatever it is that you do, but Sandy insisted you go there. She is doing some sort of tedious ceramic activity with a couple of the neighbours. They all get together and make funny little pots and things. I said you'd love to join in, so smile and pretend to be enthusiastic."

"I don't want to go," said Hyslop looking down at the floor.

"What you want or don't want is quite irrelevant," said Vanessa. "We all have to do things we don't want to do. You're going, and you're going to take that surly expression off your face. It's amazing what you can achieve in life if you smile at people. I've told you that before. Learn to use your smile."

"I don't know these people," said Hyslop.

"Well, then, get to know them," Vanessa's voice was cold. She opened the door, indicating that Hyslop should follow her. "And I want you to be pleasant and look interested in this pottery thing that they're busy with. Pretend, act the part, smile and simper. And remember, you're to call me "Mummy" here. Not "Vanessa" like you did in Italy. Do *not* talk about our life in Italy by the way. Just smile and join in."

The thought of "Sandy and a couple of the neighbours" and having to "smile and join in" filled Hyslop with horror. Why had she come back to the cottage, she wondered. How could she have guessed that her mother would be up and about with plans for her? She had hoped to come in, find some bread to toast and perhaps some jam, before rushing out to see the butterflies again.

For a moment she considered running away, but she knew that there was nowhere to run, and her mother would punish her if she did. As she looked up at the sky, she saw an orange butterfly soaring up towards the trees and wished, with an aching longing, that she could fly up and join it.

Vanessa walked briskly ahead, and Hyslop followed in a zig zag fashion behind her.

"Don't dawdle!" Her mother turned round to scowl. "I have to get to the station and catch a train."

"I don't feel well," said Hyslop. It was worth a try, though in truth it was not something that had ever worked before with her mother. "Can't I go back?"

"I'm *so* not interested," snapped Vanessa. She knocked at the door of Sandy's pottery, and put on her radiant smile.

"Sandy!" she called. "Hi, can I come in!" She pushed the door open and went inside. "Wow, what a busy scene, and my goodness, what a *wonderful* place you've got here!" Her voice was full of laughter and fun. The others were going to be charmed of course. People always were. "And look at all these *amazing* things you've made! I wish I didn't have to go to boring old London – this is incredible. I could spend all morning here watching you all."

Hyslop stood still, poised on the doorstep, not wanting to go in. She really did feel sick.

"Nessie!" Sandy called from inside the room. It was odd to hear her mother called by this short form of her name. It must have been her nickname at school. "Penny, Ilga, this is Vanessa, the old schoolfriend I've been telling you about!"

Hyslop lingered outside as she heard her mother being introduced to two people, called Penny and Ilga. She waited to hear if there was a man's voice. If there was a man in there she would take off. However, as she listened intently it seemed there were just these two women and Sandy: three adults to cope with.

"Where's Hyslop?" she recognised Sandy's voice and her mother turned round in a kindly way, using the in-front-of-other-people voice: "Come in, darling! Come and see this lovely pottery!"

Hyslop walked in and the first thing she was aware of was Sandy's beaming face.

She found herself in a huge, bright room with shelves and shelves of plates and jugs and mugs and vases, all in colours of blue and terracotta and olive green. There was a large table in the centre of the room and two women Hyslop had never seen before were seated there, looking up at her mother with interest.

"Sandy, you are a sweetie lending me your car and looking after Hyslop for me," said Vanessa, laying her hand on Sandy's arm. "I can't tell you how grateful I am. And Hyslop's terribly excited to be meeting you all and seeing the pottery. What a treat for her! Oh dear,

I wish I could stay too but I'd better run, I've got tedious business appointments in London."

She did not say goodbye to her daughter, but included Sandy and the other two women in her gushing farewells and was off, leaving just the smell of her expensive perfume behind.

Hyslop stood by the door, inhaling the last of her mother's scent, not daring to meet anyone's eye.

"Right, Hyslop," said Godmother Sandy. "The first thing I need to do is get you an apron or something to protect your clothes."

She bustled about in the corner and fetched a torn old green shirt.

"Pop this on," she said, "it's a bit messy in here, especially if you're going to be doing a bit of throwing."

Hyslop had no idea what "a bit of throwing" meant. It sounded rather alarming, but she obediently put the large shirt on over her T-shirt.

"This is Penny," said Sandy, and Hyslop looked sideways at a slightly older looking lady, whose eyes were tired-looking but smiley, "and this is Ilga." Ilga's eyes were not so smiley. She wore thick make-up, huge shiny earrings and she looked more like her mother's usual sort of friend. Hyslop scowled.

"Welcome to our pottery class," said the lady called Penny. "Though 'class' isn't really the right word for it I'm afraid. We're truly awful at pottery."

"Speak for yourself!" said the Ilga woman.

"I am speaking for both of us," laughed Penny. "Sandy is of course a wonderful teacher, Hyslop. It's not her fault that we're so untalented. In fact, if I'm to be really honest," she leaned towards Hyslop and said in a loud whisper, "don't tell Sandy, but we only come here for the tea and the chat."

"That's enough, Pen," said Sandy. "You're on the wheel today. I've prepared some clay for you, so get on with it. You can show Hyslop your throwing skills."

Hyslop had no idea what "on the wheel" meant and she watched as Penny got up to sit at a blue plastic contraption in the corner of the room. She placed a lump of clay on a round silver disc. Penny sat down on the seat and put her feet on a pedal. It was all very strange, and Hyslop dreaded being asked to get involved in the process. She moved into the corner of the room, as far out of their way as she could. She hoped no one would notice her. She wished they would forget about her altogether and let her slip outside, back into the wild garden.

"The pedal controls the speed," explained Sandy, smiling over at her.

Hyslop wriggled further into the corner, trying to make herself invisible. Usually it was easy to do this with adults but Sandy kept looking at her and talking to her directly. She kept *noticing* Hyslop.

"I'm going to paint my effort from last week," announced Ilga, who was sitting at the table. Her voice was loud and booming. "Sandy, how very attractive your friend Vanessa is. Quite unbelievably stunning! I can see why she was queen bee when you were all at school. I want to hear *everything* about her. Hyslop – is that your name, child? – she doesn't look old enough to be your mother!"

Hyslop ignored her and stood watching Penny and Sandy.

"You have to centre the clay before you can work on it," said Sandy, addressing Hyslop again, as Penny, her foot on the pedal, made the clay go round and round in a circle. She hunched over it, intense concentration etched on her face, with her hands each side of the wet lump.

"Faster, Pen," said Sandy. "Don't let me down now. You know you can do it."

"I know I can't," wailed Penny.

"Come on, faster still," urged Sandy. "Faster, and stay in control. You've both centred dozens of times. You know how to do it."

"Do we?" Ilga brandished a tiny paintbrush. "Well, it's not my strong point either I must say."

"Ilga, you managed to centre that last pot perfectly well," said Sandy.

"Sheer luck, I assure you," said Ilga.

"Mmmm," said Penny, the clay wobbling under her hands. "Me too. It's the clay that's in charge, not me, I'm afraid."

"Don't be silly, you have to stay in control," said Sandy.

The wet clay was wobbling around now quite violently, and it did not seem to Hyslop as if Penny had any control over it at all.

"Darlinks," said Ilga. Hyslop decided that Ilga was German or Hungarian and was putting on a silly exaggerated form of her own accent. She was showing off, and it made Hyslop scowl. "Darlinks, I assure you I only ever centre by luck. I think that is what is meant in English by pot luck!"

Penny giggled at this, with disastrous results for the clay beneath her hands. It now wobbled all over the place, and Penny stopped the machine by taking her foot off the pedal. Hyslop was not sure what was meant to have happened, but it didn't seem to be right.

"Oh dear, I've made a blob," said Penny, surveying the wet mess of clay.

"I think it might be best if I show Hyslop myself how to centre," said Sandy, shaking her head and then smiling over at Hyslop. "That, my dear Goddaughter, is a lesson in how *not* to throw!"

Hyslop shrank back against the wall. She wished they would just leave her alone and let her be invisible. With adults around, it was the safest strategy. Sandy, however, persisted in paying attention to her in a way that Hyslop found rather disconcerting. It was also strange, though not unpleasant, to be addressed as a "dear Goddaughter."

"Well, let me put the kettle on," said Penny, washing her hands at a little sink. "I can do that at least. I'm rather good at it in fact!"

"Have you had breakfast?" Sandy asked Hyslop. "You can't have much stuff in your larder, though we did leave bread and milk and teabags I think."

"And some homemade damson jam," added Penny. "Made by my own fair hands."

Hyslop did not know what to say. Her stomach was rumbling with hunger but she did not want to admit that she'd eaten nothing. Her mother became very angry when she told strangers things like that. She looked down awkwardly and mumbled that she was fine.

"I have some muffins," said Sandy. "Blueberry muffins!"

"Not for me, darlink!" cried Ilga. "Let the child eat those. We shall have your funny old Earl Grey tea and Rich Tea biscuits. It's our tradition."

Hyslop felt wistful as she thought of Penny's home-made damson jam. She would have to investigate the kitchen cupboards back in the cottage.

"Hyslop!" said Sandy, addressing her suddenly, making her jump. "I don't expect you will like our Earl Grey tea, but how about a glass of milk or orange juice and a blueberry muffin? They're just mini muffins, so do tuck in!"

"May I have orange juice, please?" said Hyslop, her eyes not leaving the muffins.

Sandy busied herself helping Penny make the tea, and while they chatted and ate rather boring looking biscuits, she handed Hyslop a glass of orange and a plate with four muffins on it.

Trying not to look too greedy, Hyslop ate two of them in rapid succession and sat staring at the remaining two.

"Sandy!" Ilga held her dry biscuit aloft. "Are we allowed to dunk?"

Hyslop had no idea what was meant by this, but the others laughed.

"God, yes, we have to dunk Rich Tea," said Penny, dipping her biscuit into her mug.

"So very English," said Ilga, thrusting her own biscuit into her steaming mug of tea.

"Yes, though not the sort of thing we were allowed to do at school," Penny smiled over at Sandy and Sandy smiled fondly back at her. Hyslop decided that Penny and Sandy must have been at the same school as her mother, and that they were proper friends. How unusual for adults, she mused. They were friends in a way that was different from the way her mother related to her friends. There were jokes and teasing, but it was all meant kindly. The teasing was not meant to hurt the other person. It made her feel sad, though she did not know why.

"Oh, I don't know," Sandy nibbled her soggy biscuit. "I seem to recall dipping our bed-time biscuits into our hot chocolate in Matron's study."

"Well, Sands," laughed Penny. "You are nine years younger. Standards must have slipped in those nine years!"

"Yes, back to your schooldays," said Ilga. "Now, I demand to know my share of all this. Are you telling me that Vanessa was in your year at school, Sandy?"

"Yes, Ilga," said Sandy. "Now, don't you dare say it! I know. I know. She looks *so* much younger."

"Well, darlink, I wasn't going to say so," said Ilga.

"Yes, you were, Ilga, in your normal tactless way," laughed Penny. "Go on, Sandy can take it. And I don't mind. I'm the ancient one round here anyway."

"Well, she does look young," said Ilga. "You said she was beautiful, Sandy, but I had no idea she would be quite so extraordinary. I would like to get to know her."

"Oh, she's just your sort, Ilga – I think she speaks at least four languages," Sandy now seemed to remember Hyslop again and turned to include her with a smile. "Hyslop, I know you speak French and Italian too. Anyway, Vanessa and Hyslop are welcome to stay at Keeper's Cottage for as long as they need, thanks to Penny's generosity, so I'm sure you will have plenty of time to get to know them, Ilga."

Hyslop frowned. She had no desire to get to know Ilga. She waited until they had begun chatting again and furtively took another muffin.

"I'm not surprised you all had boarding school crushes on her," said Ilga.

"Well, not exactly," said Sandy. "No, I didn't have a crush. It was just that Vanessa was sort of the coolest girl in our year. You know, there's always one, isn't there? She was good at games, the prettiest girl in the year by far, and popular with everyone. She was a scholarship girl as I recall, had come from a state school in south London, so she was bright in class too. Everyone wanted to be with her. In fact, I think everyone actually wanted to *be* her. If she snapped her fingers, we all went running."

"Really, even you, Sands?" Penny put her head on one side and smiled at Sandy.

"Yes, even me I'm afraid. No one could stand up to Vanessa's charm-bombing, then or now. It was totally full-on!"

Hyslop listened intently, taking in all that Sandy was saying, whilst reaching for the last muffin on the plate. It seemed that her mother had exerted her magic on everyone even when she was at school.

"And if boys were around, the rest of us might as well have been invisible," sighed Sandy. "You can imagine it, can't you? Talk about bees round a honey-pot! No point in being jealous, though. Nessie was a force of nature. Wonder what your Malcolm will make of her, Ilga."

"I assure you, she won't charm Malcolm," laughed Ilga. "I'd rather like it if she did. I wish he *would* learn to flirt and let himself be charmed. He wouldn't notice if a glamour model walked into his workshop and began stripping off."

"He'd probably say in his broad Scots accent: 'If you've nothing better to do, could you plane that piece of wood!'" said Penny in an accent that reminded Hyslop of the old man shouting his strange word at her. They all began giggling at the image.

"'Aye, and cover yerself up, lassie, or ye'll get a splinter!'" Sandy's accent was even more extreme. Hyslop wondered who this Malcolm was, and if he really spoke in such an extraordinary manner.

"I think, Sandy, your Scottish accent is slightly better than Penny's but you are both rubbish!" said Ilga. "In any case, I shall be amazed if even such an attractive woman as Vanessa can interest Malcolm."

Hyslop decided that this Scottish Malcolm must be Ilga's husband.

"Well, anyway," continued Ilga, "she will liven up our dull little lives. No doubt she'll give us something to gossip about over our failed pots."

"I hope she charms Hugo at least," said Sandy. "I do feel a bit guilty, Pen, about friends of mine being in the cottage. I know Hugo sort of considered it his mother's domain."

"Well, she'll never be out of the nursing home now, poor old thing," said Penny. "And Hugo can jolly well butt out of it anyway. I said it would be fine and it is. It's lovely to have the cottage being used again."

"I don't want him being grumpy about it, that's all," said Sandy.

"Yes, well, Hugo's always grumpy about something," the laughter had left Penny's eyes. "And as for being charmed, well, I don't know. If Vanessa doesn't have a double first from Oxford or a high-flying city job, I can't see him being interested."

Hyslop was quite sure that her mother had neither of those things, but it had never prevented her from attracting men before. It sounded as if there were two men, Malcolm and Hugo, and she did not much like the sound of either of them. She hoped neither of them would prove to be Uncle material. As she savoured the last crumbs of her muffin, she decided that she would keep out of their way.

CHAPTER EIGHT

A New Pupil comes to School

However slowly he walked, however often he stopped to stare at a spider's web between two tall stalks of grass, or pick a slab of moss off a stone, the journey to school ended, as it did every morning, at the school gates.

Occasionally Zak's father would let him stay home for the day. It all depended if he had a hangover or not, or if there was a job to do that required Zak's help.

"Yes, stay off school. It never did me any good," his father would sometimes say nodding at him. His grandmother's main concern was for herself: "As long as they don't come knocking on my door asking where the boy is!" she would shout, "I'm not taking the blame!" At other times, if Zak asked to stay off school, he would get a smack from his father and be told: "You need to get some learning into that thick skull of yours, boy. Get yourself to school. Never did me any harm."

This morning he hadn't even tried to ask for a day off. He shuffled slowly through the school gates, ignoring the shouts of children greeting each other all around him. Somewhere to his right he heard his name called: "Judd! Hey, Judd, *love* your trainers!" This was from Tristan Pringle, a boy in his class, who was Zak's main tormentor. It encouraged some of the younger children to chant his surname mockingly: "Ju-udd! Ju-udd!" Zak did not quicken his pace. He slowed down slightly, in fact, pretending not to hear. Running away was pointless as there was nowhere to run to, and in any case it would show a weakness which would be pounced upon. Nor did he meet anyone's eye: that could be dangerous too as it might be seen as a challenge. He walked slowly on, kicking at a stone, calculating that they would soon lose interest in him.

As he made his way towards his classroom Zak looked down at his trainers. They were filthy, and falling apart, but that in itself was not the shameful aspect of them. In fact some boys managed to make scruffy trainers look cool. What marked them out for ridicule was that his grandmother had bought them from the local market, and there was a hint of pink around the toes which probably meant they were intended for a girl. No one else bought trainers in the market. No one else chose trainers for cheapness alone. There was no designer logo on them, nothing to brand them as acceptable, let alone cool. For his own part Zak did not really care, but he preferred not to draw attention to himself, and decided that second-hand trainers from a charity shop might be better in future.

The noisy hubbub in the classroom informed him at once that Miss Carradine had not arrived. The girls' high pitched chatter and excited shrieks of laughter dominated the room. As he listened to them speculating about the arrival of a new boy, Zak glanced around with faint curiosity. He could not see any new faces.

"Oh my God, the poor new boy will have to sit next to you, Zak!" laughed Emily Glover. "That's the only spare seat."

"What has he done to deserve *that* treat!" This was Emily's best friend, Olivia. The other girls giggled, and a few of them said: "Oh, my God!" several times in succession.

Zak was used to paying no attention to the mocking laughter of the girls in the class. He went to the back of the classroom and put his filthy schoolbag on his desk. He gazed up at the huge poster of Queen Victoria. They were learning about her, doing a project. Some of the children had work pinned up on the wall, pictures and drawings and essays, but Zak had not contributed. He did know that the old queen dressed in black because she was mourning a husband whose name Zak couldn't remember. She had mourned him for forty years, which seemed a long time. He couldn't recall his father wearing black or doing much mourning for his mother. Unless you counted drinking too much as mourning. His father certainly did plenty of that. Why didn't the old queen wear a crown, he wondered. There wasn't much point in being royal if you couldn't wear a crown. She didn't look very good-natured either, probably one of those adults who was always shouting and grumbling at you, a bit like his granny.

The classroom seemed to be unusually full of flies, and one of them settled on his hand. He flicked it off, and tried to remember a film he had once seen where the hero had been able to catch flies with his hand. Zak had practised it himself for some days afterwards, but it was something he had never been able to do. The fly was always too fast. He only looked up when he realised that the noisy chatter had subsided to a "teacher's-in-the-room" sudden hush.

Miss Carradine walked towards her desk and smiled at the class. She was not alone. A small, slim girl with dark hair tied back in a pony tail, followed her into the room, looking round at everyone with the most extraordinary eyes that Zak had ever seen. The children looked on with puzzled interest.

"Morning everyone!" called Miss Carradine in her sing song voice. "This is Hyslop, Hyslop d'Agostino who has joined us from a school in Italy. She is going to be starting in our class and I hope that you will all make her very welc… "

"You said Hyslop was a boy, Miss!" cried Tristan Pringle, and there was a male chorus of "Yeah!" and "You said a boy, Miss!" from his cronies.

"All right, Tristan!" said Miss Carradine sharply. "Yes, I admit I was wrong. I only saw Hyslop's name on a sheet of paper with no other information, and it is a slightly… um… unusual name for a girl. I confess I misinformed you all that a new boy would be starting. However, Hyslop will be all the more welcome as the girls are outnumbered by the boys, so it's a good thing for all of us."

Zak pondered on the phrase : "A good thing." Normally he didn't agree when adults said something was "a good thing" or "good for you." In his experience it never turned out to be much good. Was a new girl really such a good thing? Some of the girls in the class had cruel mocking tongues.

"Can we all sit down, please!" said Miss Carradine. "Hyslop, dear, now where will you sit?"

"Don't make her sit next to Zak Judd!" called out one of the girls, and there was the familiar chorus of giggling and groans.

"Chloe, don't be so silly!" snapped Miss Carradine. "Come on now, everyone, settle down, could you!"

"Yuk, Miss, there are flies everywhere!" The children all seemed to be talking at once. "I hate flies!" "We need to zap them with something." "Why are there so many?" "Has something died in here in the night and left its rotting carcass!" "A carcass with maggots!" "That's gross!" "Oooh, maybe there's a dead body!"

"For goodness sake," said Miss Carradine. "What sort of impression are we giving poor Hyslop?" The teacher smiled down at Hyslop, but there was no smile in reply, just a solemn stare from those large eyes. "Sit down, all of you, and ignore the flies. They won't harm you. Zak, move your bag off the top of the desk and make room for Hyslop please."

"Flies can give you diseases, Miss." The chorus started up again. "Yes, like malaria." "That's mosquitoes, stupid!" "Well, how do you know these aren't mosquitoes?" "You only get mosquitoes in Africa!" "Not just Africa. My auntie went to India and they had them there too." "You can die from malaria." "Yeah, well, we're not in India or Africa, are we?" "No, but you can get malaria if you… "

"Yes, yes," said Miss Carradine in a weary tone. "Well, I can assure you that none of you are going to get malaria. Nor is there a dead body anywhere nearby. I shall get the janitor to fetch some flyspray. In the meantime, could we sit down and be quiet. Thank you!"

For Zak it was all meaningless background noise. He found himself transfixed by the new girl, Hyslop d'Agostino. It certainly was a strange name, and she looked somehow different from the other girls in the class too. She stood, straight and self-contained, as if she was apart from everyone else in her own head.

It came to him slowly, as he watched her approach the back of the classroom where there was a spare seat beside his. She was the girl who was staying at the Hemmingswood estate where his father and grandmother worked. He had heard that there was a mother and a daughter who had come all the way from Italy, and their surname ended in Tino. This was the girl who was staying in Keeper's Cottage. Zak wondered if she spoke English. It would be difficult for her if she only spoke Italian. He watched her place her pencil case on the desk, but she did not sit down.

"We don't need flyspray," she said suddenly, in perfect English. The other children fell silent, as they would if a teacher had spoken, and the girl Hyslop walked over to the window. She opened the window as wide as it would go and then stood there, waiting. To Zak's astonishment, all of the flies flew at once towards the window, probably attracted by the breeze, and then flew out in a great swarm. It was really rather extraordinary.

There was an astonished silence, then Miss Carradine spoke. "Well! That was clever of you, Hyslop. Yes, well, jolly good. No need for flyspray as you say. That was well done. Now… um… where was I?"

No one said anything, and Zak stared, open-mouthed, at the new girl as she took her seat beside him.

"Yes, I know what I was going to say," said Miss Carradine. "Yes, I think before we start with lessons, we should all introduce ourselves to Hyslop."

The teacher smiled at the new girl with a bright false smile. Zak could see that the fly incident had made her a little uneasy.

"You won't remember everyone, Hyslop, but it will be a start," she said in her teacherish voice. "And then maybe you can stand up and tell us a bit about yourself and your school in Italy." There was no smile in response from Hyslop, no expression at all. The teacher cleared her throat several times and turned to her favourite: "Emily, could you begin, please!"

Emily, whose desk was closest to the teacher's, stood up and acknowledged her audience with a series of nods. One of the boys across the aisle from Zak imitated her smile and her supercilious stance, and in truth his impression was fairly accurate. Zak was relieved that someone else was being mocked for once.

"My name is Emily," said Emily. "Emily Louise Glover. I am eleven and a half, and I have one brother, Liam, who is six, and who is a complete pain!" She paused for emphasis and a few of her friends tittered obligingly. "I do ballet lessons and I'm on Grade Three piano. I actually passed my Grade Two with merit. I play netball for the school. My BFF is Olivia." She beamed at the girl next to her, who beamed back. "We've been best friends since we were three. We used to be in Brownies together. We have secrets and stuff that we don't tell anyone else about." Once again, she and Olivia exchanged knowing smirks. Zak thought they were welcome to their silly secrets. He had no interest in knowing what they giggled about in private. "I have a cat called Mishka. Um… I like different sorts of music." She paused and went on to name various groups and singers she liked, an interminable list of boy bands that Zak hadn't heard of. The resume ended up with, "and I want to be a ballet dancer when I grow up."

As usual, the girls were more forthcoming than the boys. They were all keen to advertise the names of their best friends. Zak wondered if the Italian girl would know that BFF stood for Best Friend Forever in silly girl-talk. The boys concentrated mainly on their football teams, amid boos and groans from their fellows. Zak allowed it all to merge into meaningless noise, and continued studying the girl Hyslop. Her face betrayed no emotion, and he wondered if she was listening or taking any of it in. Was she deep inside a place in her own head, or was she aware of what the children were saying? It was hard to tell.

He was suddenly aware of giggling and staring at him, and Miss Carradine saying his name in a cross voice.

"Are we daydreaming again, Zak?" she said. "Zak? Are you with us?"

He turned his gaze reluctantly to the teacher.

"Well?" she continued staring at him. He realised that something was being expected of him.

"Yes," he said.

"I said it's your turn now, Zak," said Miss Carradine. "All the others have introduced themselves to Hyslop."

Still Zak said nothing.

"So, if you could do the same!" Miss Carradine's tone became sharp.

"I'm Zak," said Zak. He stopped staring at Hyslop and settled his gaze on the open window instead. He was unsure what else to say. After a while he added: "Zak Judd."

There was a long silence. Zak knew something was expected of him, but was not sure what it was. Surely he had already introduced himself.

"Stand up, properly, Zak," said Miss Carradine. "Stop fidgeting, and talk a bit about yourself. Would you like to tell Hyslop about your hobbies?"

"Not really," said Zak. The class roared with laughter, and Zak wondered what he had said that was so funny. He had answered truthfully, but he had found that telling the truth was not always the best policy. He felt his face grow red, as he wondered what the new girl would be thinking of him.

"Sshhh, everyone!" Miss Carradine sounded crosser than ever now. "Come on now, Zak, just tell Hyslop about *something* that you like doing." She cleared her throat and raised her eyes to the ceiling. "Anything at all."

"I like vegetables," said Zak. He sat down awkwardly and decided to say no more as everyone was laughing at him again.

"You *are* a vegetable, Judd!"

"Tristan!" shouted Miss Carradine. "That's enough! Quite enough! Right, thank you Zak." She turned to the girl Hyslop. "I think Zak is trying to tell us that he likes gardening and he likes growing vegetables."

The laughter subsided and Miss Carradine cleared her throat again.

"Now, Hyslop, perhaps you can tell us a little bit about yourself."

The new girl did not look at anyone. Zak recognised that she was somehow different from the others. Like he was.

The silence as the class awaited her answer was unlike the normal classroom silence. There was no mocking giggling or whispering, and everyone was watching the girl Hyslop with respectful interest. No one could look away.

After what seemed a very long time she stood up. She directed her gaze at the window she had opened earlier.

"My name is Hyslop," she said. "Hyslop d'Agostino, and I like insects."

CHAPTER NINE

Zak finds a Purpose in Life

No one knew the Hemmingswood estate like Zak Judd.

He had been taken there by his father ever since he could remember, to get him out of the way of his grandmother. Whilst his father mowed and edged and weeded and pruned, Zak had gone exploring. He was good at knowing his way around, but not good at remembering things people told him to do. If his father asked him to fetch a particular edging tool from the shed he would get side-tracked on the way by a new plant or a vegetable. The world was full of things to stop and stare at: Mrs Braithwaite's brightly coloured dahlias and chrysanthemums, the runner beans which seemed to double in size overnight, and the cunning courgettes which hid behind their larger brethren, then suddenly emerged as giants. His father's impatient bellow would send him scuttling on to the shed, and there would be a bewildering array of tools and weed-killers and composts, and it would not be clear what he had been sent to do. Often his father found it quicker to come stomping in to fetch the tool himself. He did not screech or scold like Granny did, but his head-shaking disappointment was harder to bear. If he'd had a drink he would give Zak a smack around the head. Zak did not mean to sit staring into space, or to forget errands. It just happened.

Today was the first day of the school holidays. He was free from the sniggers of his class-mates and the constant nagging of Miss Carradine. No one knew or cared where he was and he wandered through the woods, past the nettles and brambles where the old man's butterflies were fluttering around. His father was forbidden by the old man from tending to some of the wilder areas, though Mr Braithwaite did not like all the nettles and thistles everywhere. The old man seemed to like plants only if they were good for caterpillars to eat, or for bees and butterflies to feed on, while Mr Braithwaite liked the place to look neat and tidy. Zak's father was often given conflicting orders about what to do. The old man might have been the boss at one time, but now it seemed that Mr Braithwaite was the one with all the money.

"You got to be polite to the old boy," his father instructed him, "but you do what the Braithwaites tell you. Specially Mr Hugo. It's him that pays the wages."

Zak had intended to sit surveying the vegetables he tended for Mrs Braithwaite. She was a kind lady who never seemed to mind if his lettuce rows were not straight. Much of his tending of the vegetable garden consisted of sitting and watching the plants grow. He could pass hours just drifting around the rows of spinach and beans and leeks. Occasionally he would pull a weed out. If he saw his father or Mr Braithwaite coming, he would leap into action and start filling his weed bucket more quickly. People got cross if you were just sitting there. They didn't understand that plants sometimes wanted a bit of quiet companionship. You were expected always to be doing stuff. Lettuces didn't mind a few bits of groundsel or chickweed growing beside them in a friendly sort of way.

Today he had found something far more interesting to survey, however. The old man and that new girl from school, the girl with the boy's name who was staying at Keeper's Cottage, were coming towards him from the direction of the big house. Zak dodged behind a tall scarlet wigwam of runner beans and watched them. The old man was pointing out butterflies to her and she seemed to be interested, more interested than anyone else ever was. Well, she had said in school that she liked insects, and butterflies were insects. That would please the old boy. No one ever showed an interest in his butterflies and moths. He wasn't slapping his head and shouting at the girl like he did with Zak. He looked almost kindly. He gave her something, which looked like a large book, and pointed in the direction of the woods.

The girl seemed pleased with the book, though Zak couldn't see what it was. She held it like a treasure and couldn't take her eyes off it. After a while she said goodbye to the old man and set off on her own. She went slowly, looking all around her as she went. Zak kept her in view and followed, being careful to stay far behind and out of sight. She was too busy looking at the plants and trees to notice him. He knew all the best places to hide and how to make himself invisible.

They reached the edge of the woods and Zak watched her as she approached a bramble patch and stood staring intently. She seemed to have found something there that held her attention.

She had a core of stillness about her that Zak recognised. She was in no hurry to get somewhere or do something; she was just standing there staring. It reminded him of how he could sit and stare at the vegetable garden for long periods of time, just looking and looking. It was a gift that few people seemed to have. Everyone was so busy rushing that they didn't see the plants and the insects. After a while she opened her book and began flicking through the pages of it. It seemed as if she was comparing a picture in it with what she was looking at. Maybe it was a book of butterfly pictures. Zak didn't know the names of any of the butterflies but he was familiar with those brown ones with creamy spots that she was watching. They always flew above the bramble patch, though he didn't find them particularly interesting. There were brighter coloured ones in the nettle patch and in the main garden, and lots of different black and white chequered ones in the fields. He wondered if she knew about those.

Slowly she put her hand out and pointed an index finger. What could she be pointing at? Zak peered round the tree and tried to see what she was doing. After some time a brown butterfly swooped and hovered around her finger and landed on it briefly before dancing off again. He had never seen the old man doing that.

"Zak Judd."

The two syllables of his name floated towards him on the breeze.

Zak felt startled. He wondered where the voice had come from. The girl Hyslop had not turned around. Zak felt the back of his neck tingling. It was as if he had been addressed by a supernatural being. He pressed himself flat against the trunk of the beech tree, his heart beating in his chest so that he could feel it.

A long time passed and he began to think he must have imagined the voice.

"I know you're there, Zak Judd," said the voice again. It was, unmistakeably now, the voice of the girl Hyslop.

Zak peered round the tree and found that she had turned to face him. She stared at him with her dark, dark eyes and he felt scared, more frightened than he was of his grandmother in a temper, though Hyslop was smaller than him and not particularly violent looking. He wanted to run away yet at the same time, longed to stay where he was, just looking at her. Spooky, that's what she was, spooky rather than scary.

"Why are you watching me?" she asked at last.

Zak did not know what to say. It was true that he had been watching her, but he did not know how to answer her question.

"You sit watching me at school too, don't you?"

Zak mumbled something inarticulate.

"You're the boy who likes vegetables." If any of the other girls in the class had said this, it would have been said with either a giggle or a sneer but the girl Hyslop did not seem to be passing judgment on him. Then again, she was in no position to sneer at him, he decided, when she stood watching insects herself.

She stared at him for a moment longer then turned away. Zak felt a pang of loss when those intense dark eyes were no longer directed at him. He knew he had to follow her.

She walked slowly through the woods and did not look back at him. He knew that she knew he was following, however, so he did not try to slink behind trees or walk quietly over twigs this time.

Hyslop came to a stop near a nettle patch, where there were a couple of orange butterflies with raggedy wings.

He stopped some way behind her, and for the first time in his life felt an urge to make conversation. What an odd feeling it was. He wanted, more than anything, to make her look at him again.

"I know where there are more butterflies," he said at last. "If that's what you're looking for."

She did not say anything, and continued looking at the butterflies in front of her.

"I know where the big colourful ones are," he said, made brave by her silence. "I know where the old man goes to look at them."

This last statement made her turn round and look at him again. He felt the same trembling inside him, and he wanted, more than anything, for her to keep looking at him.

"Which big colourful ones do you mean?" she asked.

"I… I don't know their names," said Zak. "But I know where there are lots of them."

She had opened her book again, and was consulting it about the orange butterflies in front of her.

"These are definitely Commas," she said. Zak thought that was a funny name for a butterfly. It was a teacher's sort of word, not a butterfly sort of word. "Come and show me the pictures of the ones you are talking about."

She held the book out to him and he stepped forward towards her awkwardly. She was looking at him again with those eyes. He held out his hand, realising as he did so how dirty his nails were, and took the book.

He hoped it wouldn't be full of big words and small writing as his reading skills were not up to much and although he had grown used to being laughed at by the girls in his class he did not want this Hyslop girl to laugh at him. To his relief the book was full of pictures of butterflies. As he flicked through it, he realised that he had seen many of them before in the woods and in the garden. After a while he found the ones he wanted.

"I've seen them," he pointed at a butterfly in the book, and the girl Hyslop came over to stand beside him. He turned over a page: "And I've seen lots of them too, them with the eyes on their wings. I can show you where they are."

"Red Admirals and Peacocks," she said.

"And… and there's lots of them about too," he said, turning to the next page.

"Painted Ladies," said Hyslop. "Yes, I've seen quite a few of those this morning. It's a good year for them. Take me to the place where Sir Northcote goes then. Show me."

Zak bounded ahead, eager as a gun dog, to show her the way. They stayed on the main path for a bit, then he took her through some rough briars, and held low branches out of the way for her. They came to the patches of marjoram and nettles and other plants that Zak didn't know the names of. He felt his heart beating inside him again, and he hoped that some of the brightly coloured butterflies would be here.

"Wait!" cried the Hyslop girl behind him.

He turned round and found her staring at a butterfly on a tall nettle that was sitting with its wings closed.

"That's a Red Admiral," she said. He recognised the butterfly and its name. It sounded a better name than a Comma, that was for sure.

For a long time they stood together and looked. Hyslop looked at the butterfly and Zak looked at Hyslop. He'd never really wanted to look at a person before. Usually he avoided looking at people. She was somehow very lookable-at.

The butterfly opened its wings and flew up in the air. It was red and black, and Hyslop was obviously delighted with it.

"Where are the others?" she said.

Once again Zak took the lead and they came to the edge of the wood, beside a barbed wire fence where nettles and clumps of wild plants grew in profusion. This was the place the old man spent most of his time peering at butterflies, sometimes through his funny binoculars.

"This is a good place!" said Hyslop, her eyes shining with excitement.

The air was full of butterflies, and as far as Zak could see there were many different sorts. He knew he would never remember their names, but the girl seemed happy. Her pleasure in the butterflies made him feel funny: he had heard of the phrase "butterflies in my tummy" but had never understood it before. How strange that real butterflies could make him feel their fluttering wings deep within him. Of course he knew that it wasn't the butterflies which were making him feel like this : it was the girl Hyslop. It was good and scary and spooky all at the same time.

"Painted Ladies and Peacocks!" she cried.

She turned round to look at him again and this time she smiled. She smiled right *at* him.

Zak shuddered.

Once, when he had spent a morning weeding the lettuces without being too distracted and had got most of the chickweed out, and had even gathered fourteen small slugs which he had picked off the leaves of the lettuces, Mrs Braithwaite had come along and smiled down at him, and said: "Well done, Zak! What *would* we do without you!" It had been a great moment in his life. His father had been nearby, and had witnessed the scene. It was a memory that consoled Zak through many an unhappy evening. He could conjure it up and see Mrs Braithwaite's smile and his father's quiet pride, and it consoled him for so much that was bad in his life.

Good as it was, it was nothing compared to this moment.

It was nothing compared to the girl Hyslop's smile.

He felt his heart beating violently, as if it were full of a thousand fluttering butterflies, and he knew that Mrs Braithwaite and her vegetables were no longer the most important things in his life. When the girl Hyslop smiled right at him with those dark eyes he knew he had found what he needed to do in his life: he needed to find butterflies for her and make her smile.

"The Painted Lady is one of the world's most successful butterflies…"
(from The Butterflies of Britain and Ireland, by Jeremy
Thomas and Richard Lewington)

CHAPTER TEN

A Drinks Party

Hyslop had spent another wonderful day identifying butterflies. The book the old man had given her, with pictures of all the British butterflies, was now her most treasured possession. The old man's name was Sir Northcote Hemmings and he was Penny's father and Sandy's Godfather, which made him – in an indirect sort of way – a relation of hers, since she was Sandy's Goddaughter. Did that make him a God-grand-father? Was there such a thing?

Now, as she opened the cottage door her happy feelings shrivelled. She had been so free outdoors, but now she remembered that she was supposed to accompany her mother to a drinks party at the big house.

Vanessa's bedroom door was open and Hyslop could see her sitting at a little dressing table putting on her make-up. Make-up always took a long time. Her mother was studying her face in the mirror with no expression in her eyes, examining first one side, then the other. She was like an artist painting a beautiful mask, adding a daub here and there, smoothing, blending, colouring, with an air of detachment. Her features only became animated in the company of others. It was as if, on her own, her face was not in use; it was waiting for someone to switch it on. Hyslop sometimes felt she was the only one who saw her mother's real face. Vanessa did not flatter and flirt, or throw her head back in laughter with her daughter. She only seemed to really "see" Hyslop when something irritated her or if she wanted something done.

Her mother's eyes met hers in the mirror.

"Why are you standing around gawping?" she asked, lifting her head up to blend her face make-up into her neck. "I told you to be back an hour ago. Are you ready to go out? Your hair looks revolting."

"Yes," said Hyslop. She smoothed down her hair to make it look tidier.

"Take that T-shirt off and put a different colour on," said Vanessa.

"Why?" asked Hyslop.

"Don't answer me back," said Vanessa. "I said to take it off and put a different one on. Hurry up. I don't want you wearing the same colour as me, so any colour but that particular shade of blue will do."

Hyslop turned and went upstairs to her little room. She tore off her T-shirt and threw it on the bed. Roughly, she opened the drawer where she kept her clean tops, and took out the first one she came to. It was a dull beige colour. Surely that wouldn't be offensive to her mother. Hyslop preferred her blue one, but there was no point in arguing. She muttered a swear word defiantly in Italian, and allowed herself a hug from Nonna. It didn't feel quite the same as in Italy. It was hard to conjure Nonna up in England: she belonged in Italy somehow. To Hyslop's dismay, she was finding it harder and harder to remember Nonna's face at all. She would be able to recall the brown eyes, those dark Italian eyes, but then the shape of the nose would go, or she would finally be able to recreate her grandmother's smile in her head, then it would shimmer and vanish like a summer heat haze. The memories kept shifting and changing, and sometimes she would see the cold dead face in the coffin, and she would push that image away. She knew it would have been easier if she had a photograph of Nonna. Her mother did not approve of photographs of the past. In fact, she did not seem to approve of the past at all. If she referred to past events, dates would be changed randomly, and the events themselves were not solid but fluid and subject to constant alteration. And so Hyslop had no pictures of either Papa or Nonna, or even her English grandparents. So many dead people in her life, precious dead people, and she was not allowed to mention them. Hyslop kicked the wall in anger.

A honeybee had got into her room and was buzzing furiously against the window. Hyslop opened the window wider and ushered it out into the fresh air. She hoped it wasn't too exhausted from beating against the glass window, and that it would find its nest before it got dark. Bees weren't like wasps: if they had to sting, they died afterwards.

"Right, I'm ready to go!" called her mother from the foot of the stairs. "Hurry up, Hyslop."

Vanessa barely glanced at Hyslop as she emerged. Obviously the colour was not displeasing to her or she would have said something.

They were invited to the big house to have drinks, and to meet Hugo and Malcolm. Hyslop loathed such occasions. It always seemed so pointless meeting to have a drink when everyone surely had plenty to drink at home. She had no desire to meet either Hugo or Malcolm or to witness their inevitable fawning over her mother. There would no doubt be the endless chatter of rich people talking about their possessions and their holidays and the silly forced laughter that got louder the more wine they drank. Hyslop guessed that there would be rich people in such a large house. Her mother needed to be with rich people, and so far it didn't seem as if Sandy was rich. It had to be Penny and Hugo. They had to be her mother's target. She dreaded her mother finding another Uncle to latch onto. That's when things always changed for the worse.

She had met Penny in the pottery, and she had seemed friendly enough, even if she was both posh and rich. She wasn't so keen on the Ilga woman. Hyslop wondered if old Sir Northcote would be there. She brightened a little at the thought. Maybe she could tell him about the butterflies she had identified from his book.

Vanessa was wearing very high heels so their progress was slow. The lights of the big house twinkled, and just as they were approaching the front door along a crunchy gravel drive Sandy arrived breathlessly behind them.

"Blimey, Vanessa!" she exclaimed. "We don't do dressing up for drinks round these parts. Oh dear, you will put us all to shame."

"Sandy!" Kisses were exchanged. "You look wonderful yourself. Do forgive me, darling, if I've got the dress code wrong. It's so long since I've lived in England."

"Oh, you'll bring a touch of glamour to the evening," smiled Sandy, her laughing eyes including Hyslop. "I'm still in my jeans. And I've probably still got clay-dust all over me. Has young Hyslop been telling you about our pottery session?"

"What... oh... um, yes, it sounded great fun!" said Vanessa, and at that moment Penny opened the door.

There were more pointless exclamations about what people were or were not wearing, more air kisses and they were all ushered inside.

Hyslop gazed around her. This house was big and old and solid. It seemed more substantial than the luxurious Tuscan villa which had been their last home. There was a great deal of dark wood everywhere, and pictures in gold frames with dark landscapes. There was only one other couple there.

"These are our dear neighbours, Ilga and Malcolm," said Penny. "I know you've met Ilga. And this is Malcolm, who made that wonderful ebony table to your right. He's a bit of a genius with wood. Unfortunately, Hugo is working late. He did say he would try and be back early, but he's not always very reliable in that department."

"Oh, I'm sure he has some frightfully important job in the city!" said Vanessa. "Now, Ilga, we met briefly in Sandy's pottery. I have heard that you are from the Black Forest area. One of my favourite parts of Germany!"

"Do you know the area?" beamed Ilga. She was clearly destined to become one of her mother's hangers-on.

Vanessa replied in German and she and Ilga laughed loudly at something she said. No one else could understand them, and Sandy and Penny chatted to each other in low voices over their drinks.

Hyslop felt a surge of panic as she saw a tall reddish haired man approaching her.

"I'm Malcolm," he said. "I don't think we've met."

He was holding out his hand and after a brief hesitation, Hyslop darted her hand into his, then pulled it away quickly. She stepped back and looked away, to show him that she did not want to talk to him.

"It's Hyslop, isn't it? I hear you've been doing some pottery with Sandy." He offered her some salted peanuts from a bowl he was holding. "What were you making?"

Hyslop looked at Malcolm suspiciously. Why would he take such an interest in her?

"I'm making a coil pot," she said in a tone which was as surly as she dared to be in company. She wanted him to go away.

"Useful things, coil pots," said Malcolm. "I could do with one to put my pencils in."

Hyslop scowled, but could not resist taking another peanut when offered the bowl again. She was hungry as usual.

"Have you glazed it yet?" he asked. He wasn't taking the hint that she did not want to talk, and her scowl deepened. If he thought he could become a potential Uncle by chatting to her like this, he was wrong.

"It's looking rather promising, Hyslop's little coil pot," said Sandy, coming over to join them. "Mind you, I have warned her never to get too excited about things in pottery until they're safely fired. I guess things can go wrong with wood at times too, Malc."

"Oh yes," said Malcolm. "Things can go wrong with wood." He looked at Hyslop and spoke to her in a normal sort of voice, as if she were an adult: "What sort of stuff do you like to do in your spare time, Hyslop?" She stared down at her feet. Usually at these drinks parties the deal was that she wandered around on her own while Vanessa and her friends drank more and more wine and shrieked with laughter at nothing. Sometimes she stayed home alone, which she preferred. Why was Malcolm bothering to talk to her unless it was to ingratiate himself with Vanessa later? That *had* to be the explanation. Men had used her before as a means of approaching her mother. How long would it be before he was flying to Vanessa's side to pay silly compliments? She turned her back on him and did not reply.

"Hyslop, dear, what can I get you to drink?" said Penny, suddenly appearing. "We have all the usual soft drinks in cans or there is orange juice or lemonade. What would you like?"

"May I have lemonade please," said Hyslop. Penny seemed a friendly person, even if she did have a very posh accent. The lemonade came in a crystal tumbler with a bendy straw.

"Sandy, I cannot imagine you two at school in the same class together!" called Ilga from the other side of the room, switching back to English again. "I shall need to ask Vanessa to divulge some tales from the classroom. She can tell me her secrets in German!"

Hyslop sat in a corner of the room and watched them all. Malcolm and Vanessa were shaking hands now and to her astonishment he did not gush and fawn over her, but seemed to be calmly asking her about which part of Italy they had been living in and how was she finding the English weather. He then drifted back to talk to Sandy. Ilga, on the other hand, seemed to be the one enslaved by her mother. Hyslop knew the symptoms and wondered if Ilga were very rich. Was it possible that *she* was the target? A woman? That would be a new development.

"If you have no plans, I insist you all come round to ours on Saturday night for dinner," Ilga beamed round the room at everyone.

"How very kind," said Vanessa.

"More kind than you know," said Sandy. "Ilga is a fabulous cook. Though perhaps unkind would be a better word – it will be death by calories."

"Quite!" agreed Penny. "Ilga doesn't do small portions."

"Vanessa looks as if a few large portions wouldn't do her any harm!" said Ilga. "Are you on any sort of diet, Vanessa? How *do* you stay so slim?"

"Heavens, no!" laughed Vanessa. "I eat anything and everything I'm given. Can't be doing with diets. Far too boring!"

Hyslop frowned at the lie. Her mother picked at fruit and salads, and never cooked proper meals. She spent her life on a diet, and often Hyslop had to go hungry too.

"And of course Hyslop must come," said Malcolm. "We have two cats, Hyslop, that you can look after if you get bored with us lot at dinner. We can get pretty boring I'm afraid."

Hyslop hesitated. Usually she preferred being left at home, but the thought of large portions and two cats was very tempting. If Sandy was there she would feel safe enough. She wondered what her mother wanted her to do.

"Can I come?" she asked.

"Well, of course, darling," said Vanessa. It was the warm loving-mother tone that she only ever used when other people were present. "You must come if you want to!"

"That's settled then," Ilga clapped her hands. "Sevenish at our place. Hyslop – I can't get used to this strange name – is there anything you don't like to eat, child?"

"Oh, Hyslop will already have eaten," said Vanessa.

That was unlikely and Hyslop thought longingly of the good cooking and the large portions.

"Well, when I was her age I could eat two meals quite easily," said Malcolm, "so you can decide if you want to eat or not when you come, Hyslop."

Hyslop did not look at her mother.

"Thank you very much," she mumbled politely.

Already she liked Sandy and Penny, and Malcolm, though she was suspicious of him, did not seem like obvious Uncle material. Ilga was becoming one of her mother's fans, with all the familiar signs of enslavement, but she did not seem to present an immediate danger to Hyslop. It was a shame that Penny's father, old Sir

Northcote, wasn't around, though she couldn't imagine him at the drinks party with his funny head slappings and mutterings. Perhaps he was in his own home, looking at his butterfly books. The only one they hadn't met was Hugo, Penny's husband, and how bad could he be?

CHAPTER ELEVEN

Too Late for Orange-Tips

Hyslop was out in the garden again before her mother was up.

She had encountered the old man several mornings in a row now. Despite being the strangest old man, indeed the strangest person, she had met, he was also turning out to be the most interesting. He wandered around with a dirty old hat on his head, and a cardigan with leather patches at the elbows which was often not buttoned up properly, and – even on the hottest day – a tartan scarf around his neck. He did not behave like other grown up people. He spoke in a posh voice, but muttered swear words to himself, and sometimes shouted out his funny word: "Dunderheids!", in what she now recognised was a Scottish accent. He contorted his face into peculiar expressions and sometimes slapped his head, which looked painful at times. Hyslop decided that he was like a child in an old man's body. She, on the other hand, sometimes felt like an old person in a child's body.

What was most exciting about him, however, was that he was the first adult she had ever met who was interested in insects. He wasn't just vaguely interested in them, or mildly curious. He was *obsessed*. He seemed to spend all his time hunting for them, and he knew the answers to all her questions. Butterflies were his passion and Hyslop was happy to concentrate on those too. After all, of all the insects in the world, butterflies are the most beautiful.

With Sir Northcote she quickly learned that she did not have to think before she spoke. *He* certainly didn't. She also didn't have to ration her questions. If she asked him twenty questions in a row about a particular butterfly he never tired of answering. She was sure, in fact, that the more questions she asked, the happier he was.

"How many butterfly species are there are in Britain?" "Have you seen all of them?" "How long do they live?" "How do caterpillars actually turn into butterflies?" "What do they do in the winter?" "How can they fly to different countries over the sea?" "Do birds ever eat them?" "How can you tell the difference between males and females?"

At first she paused between questions to be polite, but after a while she let the questions come rushing out of her mouth as they occurred to her. This was a novel sensation. Usually it was safest to be silent in front of adults, and to think carefully before speaking. As for asking questions, it was something she had not done since she had lived with Nonna, when she had chattered away non-stop in Italian. Nonna had never tired of listening to Hyslop, and even if she did not have answers to all the questions, she had called Hyslop a clever bambina to be asking them. Then everything changed : her mother came, and it was no longer considered clever to ask anything at all. It was best to be quiet, and to keep all thoughts and questions locked inside her own head.

She realised how tiring it had been, having to be careful what she said, always having to watch out for impatience and bad moods, always living in fear of what would happen next. Here in the old man's wild and beautiful garden she could speak her thoughts out loud. It was restful.

She once apologised for asking so many questions, and he turned on her, his eyes flashing : "Quite frankly, any child who does *not* want to know the answers to all these questions is a very tedious child indeed. Certainly not the sort of person I'd want to be around."

"What's your favourite butterfly of all?" she asked him.

"Now, that *is* a difficult question," he said. At last she had asked something that made him pause. "Hmm. Very difficult. I have many favourites. My grandfather and I particularly liked the Orange-tip. The male Orange-tip is a splendid fellow. Yes, I rather think he is my favourite British butterfly. He is white with bright orange tips to his wings. In parts of Europe they call the species The Sunrise Butterfly."

"Can I see one round here?"

"No, I'm afraid you cannot."

"Why not?"

"Well, it's too late in the year. Read about them in your book. Our Orange-tips appear in April and they don't hang around for long." He paused then spat out the word: "Dunderheids!" several times, with a particularly violent slap of his head.

Hyslop waited until the shouting session was finished then resumed her questioning. She knew he was not referring to the Orange-tip butterflies with his funny word. He behaved as if nothing had happened, and so did she.

"Do they come here in this garden?" she asked.

"Oh yes," he said. "But you'll need to wait until next year now. The Orange-tips are a great joy when they appear I can tell you. The garden here is particularly lovely in the spring, and those Orange-tipped chaps seem like heralds of the summer ahead. You'll see what I mean next April."

Hyslop felt a happy shiver at his assumption that she might still be around next year, but this was followed by a dropping down into sadness as she reflected on how unlikely this would be.

"I probably won't be here next year," she said. "I don't know where we'll be. We may have to go back to Italy. Or somewhere else."

There was a long silence, broken only by snorting noises caused by the old man puffing his cheeks in and out in a peculiar fashion.

"Well," he said after a while, "you can see plenty of butterflies in Italy. Oh yes, Italy has more sunshine and more species than we do here in England."

Hyslop knew that this thought should have comforted her, but somehow it did not. For the first time, ever since she could remember, she wanted to stay in one place. She knew she wanted to be around to see those Orange-tips the following April. She knew she wanted Sir Northcote to be there to point them out to her.

"It was the twenty sixth of March when my grandfather died," said the old man. He slapped his head once, and looked around wildly almost as if he expected to see his grandfather. Then his voice grew softer again. "We wheeled him outside in a wheelchair. He was too weak to walk by that time. He could hardly stand up. We all knew he was dying but no one would admit it. He knew it too – he said he wanted to be taken out into the garden one last time. It was a warm spring, one of the warmest I can recall." He nodded his head, and his eyes narrowed as he peered over the unseeable hill in his mind where the past lay hidden. "Warm and sunny, and I hoped, gosh, how I hoped, that we would see an Orange-tip for him. It was earlier than they normally appeared, but it was so warm that we thought we might be lucky. For a long time there was nothing, and then he saw one, yes, it was him who spotted it, the first of that year – a fine bright specimen it was – and he said to me: "All is well with the world. I can go in peace now, my boy." He died later that night."

"What age were you when he died?" This was the first personal question she had asked him. She wondered if she were trespassing again.

"Oh, I was nearly twenty, quite old really," he said. "It's a long time ago now, but I still miss him. He was like a father to me more than a grandfather, and we did everything together. My parents died out in India, and I was brought here with my nanny when I was six. Dear old Nanny McDonald. She was a funny old Scottish lady – she liked butterflies too. Anyway, I've lived here ever since!"

"Oh," said Hyslop. She then added, without thinking: "That's the opposite of me. I lived with my grandmother in Italy until I was six, then my mother came for me and I lived with her after that."

The old man nodded and seemed to be consulting thoughts in his own head. He then slapped his head a few times. Perhaps he did it to make the thoughts clearer.

"Dunderheids!" he said again, in that strange Scottish accent. Was it a word that he had learned from his funny old Scottish nanny? Hyslop decided that "Dunderheids" must be a sort of clearing-of-the-mind word. Maybe it helped him to think more clearly. And maybe you had to do it in an accent that was not your normal way of speaking. It was an interesting technique, not one that she had witnessed in anyone else of her acquaintance.

"My grandfather was an eminent lepidopterist," he said after a while. "Do you know what that is?"

"I know what an entomologist is," said Hyslop. "I'm not altogether sure what a lepidopterist is."

"You're on the right track," he said. "An entomologist studies insects, and a lepidopterist specialises in butterflies and moths."

"What is the difference between butterflies and moths?" asked Hyslop. "Is it just that moths come out at night?"

"Well, there are plenty of moths which hang around in the daytime," he said. There was a pause and then a particularly long bout of swearing began with a few violent head slaps. He seemed to be trying – and failing – to say "Dunderheids" instead of a swear word.

At this point they were interrupted by the loud barking of dogs, and the rather stern tone of Sandy.

"Uncle Northy!" She put her hand on her Godfather's shoulder. "What are you trying to say?" Hyslop realised that she was concerned about the old man swearing in front of her.

"And Hyslop!" Sandy beamed down at her. "I didn't know that you and Uncle Northy were such good friends!"

Hyslop was troubled by the use of the word "Uncle" – it always made her shudder – but she was soon caught up in a boisterous greeting from Sandy's two large dogs, Sasha and Skye. They were beautiful creatures, Bernese Mountain Dogs, and Hyslop leaned down to fuss each one in turn.

"Sandy, my dear," said the old man, his face crumpling into a wrinkly smile. "How are you this morning?"

He gave Sandy an affectionate kiss, and Hyslop felt a stab of pain. She was used to the sensation: she had often witnessed friends being kissed by their mothers and fathers, and had felt angry and sad at the same time. It always made her aware of what was missing in her own life. She tried not to scowl.

As if in some way catching a hint of this secret pain, Sandy put a hand on Hyslop's arm.

"Don't tell me!" she laughed. "Don't tell me you are into butterflies, Hyslop!"

"Into butterflies!" spluttered the old man, his voice rising to a shout. "INTO butterflies! Why, this child has learned more about butterflies these last few days than you and Penny have learned in a lifetime!" Spittle flew from his lips: "*Into* butterflies indeed!"

"Well, I'm pleased to hear it," said Sandy. "I'm well aware that Penny and I were a great disappointment on that front. You've found an ally at last, Uncle Northy. I couldn't be more delighted for both of you!"

The strange thing was that Sandy seemed to mean what she said. As she and the old man looked at Hyslop, she could feel some of the warmth that they had between them, radiating out towards her. They were sharing with her.

She was included.

CHAPTER TWELVE

The Bad Dream with a Happy Ending

That night Hyslop dreamed about the haunted cupboard again.

Something was different, though. The dream did not follow its usual pattern.

There was Oncle Xavier, the worst of all the Uncles, and there was his horrible French chateau. It was the familiar scene of her worst nightmares.

He was leading her up the stairs as usual to The Cupboard.

Hyslop had experiences of Italian cupboards too, but this cupboard – so large it was almost a room in itself – was the worst of them all. It contained the ghost of an eyeless little girl, a girl with bleeding stumps for fingers…

Oncle Xavier was laughing, as he always did, when he took her upstairs. His laughter, echoing and exaggerated, sounded as hideous as ever. The glassy eyes of the dead boars and stags on the walls looked on impassively. They had never been able to help her despite her pleas over the years. Up those endless dark wooden stairs past the gold framed pictures of Oncle Xavier's ugly big-nosed ancestors. They all seemed to be laughing at her too.

"Oh, Eezlop!" She hated the way he said her name. "I like it when you struggle. You are like a leetle fish on the end of my line… "

For once Hyslop stopped struggling. She knew only too well what happened next.

"Have I ever told you the story about the naughty girl who lived here two hundred years ago?" She made no reply, as she knew he was going to tell her anyway. He always did. "A very naughty, stupid little girl, who annoyed everyone!" He stopped laughing and pulled her hair viciously. He always did that on the second landing, right in front of a picture of dead deer piled on top of each other. Hyslop loathed that picture and tried not to look at the poor broken bodies of the deer.

"Oh, yes, she was a nuisance to everyone, this stupid little girl." He was marching her up the next flight of stairs, to the top of the house. "So they decided to take her up to the attic, up here, Eezlop, where we are going now!" She waited for the burst of laughter at this point. "Up to the dark cupboard where nobody ever goes. And they shut her in!"

She did not struggle, and for once she did not cry aloud in terror as she saw the hated wooden door of the cupboard before her. Oncle Xavier shook her, as if in disbelief.

"They shut her in," he said again. "They *locked* her in!"

His horrible face was right next to hers now, and he stopped laughing, as if he were puzzled at her lack of response.

"You know what happened then, Eezlop?" She knew only too well, but waited for him to tell her. He did not seem to be enjoying the story as much as he usually did. "Well, this little girl was such a nuisance that they all found they were much happier without her. *Specially* her poor mother!" This was said with particular triumph but still she did not react. "They forgot all about her. That's what happened!" He hissed this right in her face. "It was six months before someone had to go into the cupboard, and guess what they found?"

This was Oncle Xavier's favourite part and she was spoiling it for him by neither screaming nor struggling. She stared right back at him and found that for once she was unafraid. She felt proud of her dream character.

"They found her skeleton, her staring eyesockets. She had tried to scratch the door down. It was all covered in scratch marks and blood, and her hands were scratched to bleeding stumps. And now, you stupid little girl, you are going in beside her." Dream-Hyslop did not react in the slightest. Oncle Xavier was growing desperate to make her afraid. He shook her and shouted right in her face: "She had been eaten by insects!"

It was when he said this that Hyslop changed the order of things completely and she burst out laughing.

Oncle Xavier raised his hand to strike her. "This time I am going to shut you in *forever*!" He shouted and cursed as she dodged his blow, and he reached for the cupboard door.

"It's only a dream and it doesn't scare me any more." Dream-Hyslop pushed him away, realising that she could make herself super-strong if she wanted to. It was *her* dream.

She was in control.

"I could lock *you* in the cupboard if I wanted to," she said grabbing him by the hair so that he yelped in pain. He tried to kick her but failed, and she pulled his hair even harder.

"I can do what I like with you," she said, "It's *my* dream! But the cupboard is much too good for you! I have a better idea. A much better idea ! Listen! Who do you think is at the door?"

As she said this, there was a thunderous knocking at the hall door far below, a knocking so loud it echoed right up the stairs and into every corner of the chateau. The portraits of the hideous ancestors trembled in their frames.

"Open this door!" called a voice from outside. Oncle Xavier went pale with fear.

She wondered whether to give Papa a gun in his hand, a machine gun to destroy all her enemies, but decided that a sword was better. She smiled at the trembling Uncle.

"I have come for my daughter!" What a deep, thrilling voice her dream-father had! The door was knocked down completely, and he rode into the great hall of the chateau on a dappled grey horse. Yes, dappled grey was even better than black. "I have been searching for her all over Europe and now I have found her!" At this point Hyslop decided that her mother would be screaming.

Papa dismounted and grabbed her mother by the hair, dragging her upstairs with him. Oncle Xavier struggled to escape from Hyslop's grasp, but she held him tightly.

"Papa is going to chop your head off!"

As she said this, real Hyslop woke up, sooner than she would have liked. It was the first time she had ever felt sad that the dream was over. She was disappointed not to have witnessed Oncle Xavier's execution.

She was even more disappointed not to have seen her Papa's face.

The ending was good, however. She had taken control of her dream, and it was good to wake up in England. England was a land without Uncles or ghostly girls or horrible cupboards. England was a land of butterflies.

CHAPTER THIRTEEN

Zak Makes a Mistake

Zak knew as soon as he clambered down the steps from the high stone wall onto the road, without checking, that he had made a mistake.

Normally he was vigilant. Normally he saw people long before they saw him. He had to watch out for nasty kids at his school, for teachers, for his grandmother or his father in a bad mood (which was most of the time), or for Mr or Mrs Braithwaite, or for the old man, who was liable to shout and swear at him. Now, however, he had concentrated all his watchfulness into looking out for the girl Hyslop. Nothing was quite the same as it had been before.

Today he was sure he had glimpsed her entering the wildflower meadows, but somehow she had disappeared again. The grasses and flowers were waist high and dancing with bees and butterflies. He wandered around but could not see her anywhere. Perhaps she was lying down somewhere, with her precious book in front of her, watching a butterfly that interested her. His eyes had scanned the meadow in every direction, but there was no sign of movement, no sign of anything that would betray her whereabouts. The meadow was still and the summer air was heavy. Irritating little midges swarmed around him in clouds, and he found he had to continually scratch his face and arms, and swat them away. He kept an eye out for horse flies too, as they had a particularly nasty bite, and the itch lasted for a long time. It was best to keep moving in the meadow.

The thought then occurred to him that she may have gone for a walk along the road. Even she, who loved insects so much, might have got a little tired of swatting flies away. She may have headed into the village to buy an ice lolly at the shop. He knew that if he had any money he would make a bee-line for some delicious cold ice cream.

He found himself at the edge of the Hemmingswood land, at the point in the high wall where there were stone steps up and down each side. Without thinking or checking, he climbed up the steps and jumped down onto the other side. It was only once he had landed down on the grass verge beside the road that he was aware of voices.

"Way-hay! It's Judd!"

Tristan Pringle and his gang of cronies were only yards away, gathered round something by the other side of the road.

"Judders!"

Zak turned at once to climb back up the stone steps, but the boys were too fast for him. He was only half way up when he felt himself grabbed from below.

"What's your hurry, Judd?"

Zak said nothing, and made himself go limp so that they would loosen their hold on him. He was waiting for his moment to make a run for it.

"You're not saying much, are you?" One of the boys poked him in the ribs. "Speak when you're spoken to!"

"What shall we do with him, Triss?"

As he felt a slight loosening of the grip around his arms, Zak wriggled and tried to escape. It was no use. They caught him at once. There was an air of excitement about them all. They were a gang, a pack of animals, surrounding their prey.

"Trying to run away, Judders, are you? That's not very polite, is it?"

"Judd doesn't know anything about manners, do you, Judd?"

"Hey, he might be interested in our little find, guys!"

Zak was aware of a foul stench coming from something nearby, and he struggled as hard as he could to escape, sensing something horrible was about to happen to him.

"Something wrong with our company is there?" This was Tristan Pringle now, who thrust his face right into Zak's. "God, your breath stinks, Judd."

Zak longed to tell Tristan Pringle that his own breath was pretty smelly too, but he said nothing.

As the boys gathered round to hold him fast, Zak became aware of the rotting carcass of a dead badger on the other side of the road. He wriggled as best he could to get away, as he recalled how once before they had caught him and rubbed his face into cow dung in the fields. He had had to wash himself in the stream before he went home. The memory of the humiliation – and of the smell – remained vividly in his mind, and he felt a surge of panic. He finally succeeded in freeing one of his hands, and he lashed out at one of the boys nearest him, catching him on the side of his head.

There was a string of curses and he was held fast again. The boy who had been hit took aim and punched Zak full in his face.

"That's it, Grant. Give him another, the little swine!"

There were more curses, more punches and several hard kicks which Zak tried to dodge as best he could. It was not easy when five boys, all bigger than him, were holding his arms.

"OK, that's enough," Tristan Pringle asserted his authority and smiled at Zak. It was not a kindly smile.

"Come on, guys, let's not be too rough on Judd. Let's give him a little treat, a special treat he won't forget."

The others ceased their violence and looked to Tristan, as if awaiting orders.

"His breath stinks. I don't think he ever brushes your teeth, do you, Juddy boy?"

Zak said nothing, but felt sick with foreboding. His knees were buckling under him.

"You seem to have a hygiene problem, Judd, as well as a problem with manners. I reckon you like things that stink! I think we should let you get a taste of the dead badger there!"

There were enthusiastic whoops from the other boys, and Zak

felt himself being dragged towards the stinking carcass. He was close enough now to see that it was moving with maggots and flies, and half eaten away. The stench was enough to make him want to vomit, and he struggled as he had never struggled before.

It was no use. He felt his head being forced down towards it and there was nothing he could do to stop it. He closed his eyes tightly and whimpered in fear.

"It's all right, Mrs Braithwaite, I've found him!" A high clear voice pierced his consciousness, and his captors jumped to the side and released him.

Everyone looked up to the top of the high wall, at the head and shoulders of the girl Hyslop. She must have been standing on the stone steps on the other side.

"Zak!" She said crossly. "What *are* you doing playing in the road when you know Mrs Braithwaite here has been looking for you this last half hour? You are behind with your weeding and you're in *big* trouble!"

Never had Zak rejoiced so much to be in big trouble. He staggered away from the boys and the dead badger, his legs trembling.

"Are any of you boys here to help with the weeding? If not, please leave Zak alone!" Hyslop looked at them all in turn, her dark eyes flashing. The boys shuffled around, looking uneasy. "There are quite a few lads here, Mrs Braithwaite. I am sure they would all love to help with the gardening."

"No way!" said Tristan Pringle at last. "I'm off. Come on, guys!"

They all walked off in the direction of the village. One of them stopped to pick up a stone and throw it at the dead badger, and there were a couple of half-hearted curses. Zak crawled towards the stone steps and climbed up to the top of the wall, and down the other side, before he collapsed onto the long grass. His whole body was shaking so badly he couldn't speak. He still felt as if he might be sick.

"You're going to have a black eye tomorrow," said Hyslop, surveying his face. "And probably a few bruises on your legs."

Zak was unable to say anything.

"Otherwise you should be fine."

She picked up her butterfly book, and dusted it down. After another close scrutiny of his face she set off across the meadow.

"By the way," she turned round once. "I made that up about Mrs Braithwaite wanting you for weeding. As you can see, she isn't here at all. But if I were you I'd keep out of the way of those village boys. They're not exactly friendly, are they?"

Zak sat in the long grass, not even bothering to swat at the flies. He was still trembling, and his head was buzzing with so many different thoughts and emotions that he felt he might explode.

CHAPTER FOURTEEN

Butterflies are not Dunderheids!

Hyslop found the old man leaning over his walking stick staring down at something in the flower border. She walked up behind him, and found that, as she had suspected, it was a butterfly he was looking at.

"A Painted Lady," she said.

"Mmmm," he said, not turning round. "It's a good year for them."

"Amazing how fresh they are," said Hyslop," considering their long flight over the sea from North Africa."

Sir Northcote whirled round to face her, his eyes narrowed. He could look quite wild and angry at times, but Hyslop was not afraid of him. She found him the least scary adult she had ever met.

"Been reading the book I gave you?" he said, taking a hand off his stick to slap himself on the head.

"Oh yes," said Hyslop. "I know the Latin name too : Cynthia cardui."

The old man gave a peculiar snort.

"Well, actually, it's Vanessa Cynthia cardui,"

His head beating became more intense.

"Come this way," he commanded and set off towards the end of the garden. He stopped abruptly after a few steps and pointed with his stick at a butterfly spreading out its wings on the path in front of them. "There. What's that one then, Missy?"

"It's a Small Tortoiseshell," said Hyslop. "Aglais urticae."

"Mmmm," he said, leaning over his stick to survey the insect in front of him. "Been learning their Latin names, have we?" He seemed pleased, though, and Hyslop thought he was trying to hide a smile. "When I was young we had Large Tortoiseshells round here too, not just Small." His half smile turned to a scowl and his voice rose. "You don't see them now. Been gone for years. They've gone extinct in Britain. Extinct! D'you know what that means, hmm?"

He pointed an admonishing finger at her, and seemed to be trying not to say his usual word. She said nothing. He surely couldn't be blaming her for the sad demise of the Large Tortoiseshell. All of a sudden, he shouted at the top of his voice: "They'll ALL be extinct shortly, but NO ONE cares!"

"I care," said Hyslop calmly.

"Yes," he said, pointing at her with his stick. "It's all very well learning the Latin names, and reading the book. Oh, yes." Again, he seemed to be about to say his word but stopped himself. Sometimes he seemed able to do that. "But there's work to be done, Miss Smarty Boots. Work to be done to save what's left."

Hyslop took a step back as his walking stick was now waving perilously near her face.

"What work?" she asked.

"Habitat!" he shouted, putting his stick back down and leaning over it again. "It's *all* about habitat."

Hyslop waited while he made some more peculiar snorting and clicking noises.

"If they keep destroying habitat there'll be no butterflies left," he said, his voice softening slightly, then rising to a crescendo again: "We don't need sentimental tree-huggers! We need practical work. Funding. Butterfly conservation! We need people to care about butterflies, d'you hear!"

It would have been difficult *not* to hear as he was shouting so loudly.

"This garden is a good habitat," she said, partly hoping to pacify his anger and partly because she wanted to know more. "I mean the estate in general, with all the nettles and wild flowers and stuff. It's not like other people's gardens, is it?"

"Well, it's the work of years of research, and it's a project that is ongoing." He nodded. "It didn't happen overnight, you know. My grandfather and I created an environment that would contain plants for the caterpillars, and a variety of wildflowers where adults can nectar. Different butterflies have different preferences, as you will know if you have been reading your book."

The stick came up again and Hyslop eyed it warily.

"But it's not enough," he said. "Never enough. The butterflies need corridors of habitat. We need to look at what they like to call nowadays the big picture. The whole of the UK." He gave a snort. "It's a hard enough struggle here in the *small* picture. I have opposition in my own garden, you know!"

He muttered swear words under his breath and Hyslop turned her attention to the Small Tortoiseshell. She knelt down to examine it more closely.

"Yes," he continued, flecks of spittle flying in her direction. "Oh, yes. It's not easy conserving habitat here with my wretched son-in-law around! He wants to turn this whole estate into silly manicured lawns and a pheasant shoot for his overpaid city lawyer friends. Can you imagine?"

Hyslop frowned as she forced herself to imagine.

"Well, as long as there's breath in my body, I'm not having it," he said. He became agitated again. "I'm *not* having it."

"Can't you stop him?" asked Hyslop, standing up. "Surely it's your land, not his."

"My great-grandfather bought this estate," he said. "Back in Victoria's reign."

Hyslop recalled seeing a picture of Queen Victoria on the classroom wall at the local school. Rather a stern looking old lady, dressed in mourning black.

"Trouble is," he gave a wheezing sort of noise that sounded like a strange laugh. "Trouble is, there's no money in butterflies. Never has been. Son-in-law's money has bailed us out." It was definitely sounding like a laugh now, a rather bitter laugh. "I'd have had to sell long ago, if he hadn't stepped in with his big city money. He owns it all, lock, stock and barrel. What he wants now is to shove me in a nursing home and invite all his fancy lawyer friends here to shoot birds."

Hyslop looked at him in alarm. She did not like the sound of this Hugo person. He sounded violent and dangerous.

"He can't do that against your will," she said.

"Well, if they think I've lost my marbles, they can," he said, slapping his head. "And, apart from Penny and Sandy, they *do* all think I've lost my marbles"

He gave another wheezy laugh: "I think even Penny and Sandy have their doubts sometimes!"

Hyslop decided that losing your marbles was another way of saying going mad. She could not help thinking that the old man did not help his case by his odd mannerisms and outbursts of swearing and shouting. The continual slapping of his head couldn't help either. Most people would think he *was* slightly mad.

"Do people want a world without butterflies?" he cried, and the stick came up again. "Do they? Hmmmm?" He said a swear word loudly. "Butterflies going extinct, hmmm? Butterflies which are… " He seemed to be making a huge effort not to say another swear word and his funny word came tumbling out in all its Scottishness: "Dunderheids!"

"I am willing to learn and to help," said Hyslop. "Please don't shout at me. Why do you call butterflies Dunderheids? What does it mean ?"

Sir Northcote shook his head. He put his stick down.

"I'm not swearing at you, child," he said. "It may sound as if I am, but I'm not." He shook his head sadly. "And obviously butterflies are not dunde… " His voice tailed off, and it was as if he could not say the word in his normal posh voice. "It's just a word my Scottish nanny used to say. She called everyone a dunder… well, that word. In fact she called everyone that word except me. She was always kind to me." He gave a smile and seemed to be looking into the past again. "She taught me to say that word so that I didn't swear and curse in front of people. If a swear word wants to come out I say that word instead. Dear old Nanny understood and wanted to help me. It doesn't always work, but it's pretty effective most of the time, specially if I imitate her accent. It may seem odd, but you'll just have to get used to my ways."

"And you'll have to get used to mine," said Hyslop without thinking.

There was a silence when she said this, and then the old man began to laugh. It was a funny wheezing laugh, but Hyslop found that she was pleased she had provoked it. He laughed for quite a long time, wheezing turning to chuckling, and then to snorting and head slapping.

"Come and see my butterfly collection, child," he said. "It's quite famous, you know. Come tomorrow early. I'm always up and about by seven. Don't expect food or anything but come and see me. You know where I live."

With that he headed off in a different direction, pointing his stick and muttering as he went.

CHAPTER FIFTEEN

Zak Ponders on the Nature of Beauty

Zak had positioned himself amongst the bracken and brambles behind Keeper's Cottage patio. He had flattened the nettles so that he wouldn't get stung, and he had to dodge the bramble thorns as best he could. Some insect had just bitten him on the arm and his knees were itchy and sore with crouching, but the view more than compensated for such discomfort.

There, sitting at the table on the patio reading a book, there in all her beauty was the girl Hyslop. She seemed to be looking at her book, then writing in another book, possibly a notebook, and he guessed it would be about butterflies. Occasionally she chewed the end of her pencil, or ran her fingers through her hair. Her hair, her amazing hair, danced in the sunlight with all its colours. When she began writing, there was no stopping and pondering, just swift, hurried writing as if she could write as fast as she could think, the way a teacher might. Not that you'd want to watch a teacher. No teacher had hair or eyes like Hyslop. Zak watched her hungrily. There was no danger of her spotting him and he could just look and look and look.

After a while she raised her head and peered around her in a puzzled way. Zak had noticed before that if you watched people secretly, some sixth sense told them they were being spied on. They would look around, as Hyslop was doing, but when they saw nothing would return to what they had been doing before. He had chosen his spot well, and knew that he was invisible. The girl looked around her in every direction, and he waited patiently for her to return to her books. Finally she stopped and turned her head in the direction of his hiding spot. She frowned and stared over at the patch of bracken and blackberry where he was hiding. He was confident that she could not possibly see him, but at the same time her gaze gave him a shivery feeling, and he felt all the hairs on his neck and arms, hairs that he never knew he had, stand up like a dog's hackles. The girl narrowed her eyes, then rose from the table. It looked as if she was about to approach his hiding place, but before she could do so she suddenly whirled round in the opposite direction.

"Hyslop!" A sharp voice called from inside the cottage.

Zak watched as a woman in a shimmery dress came out onto the patio. This had to be the girl Hyslop's mother, though she did not look particularly motherly. She did not look like anybody's mother he had ever seen. She seemed shiny and radiant like a film star, one of those people from the magazines Mrs Braithwaite sent over to his grandmother once she had read them. She had to be quite old too if Hyslop was her daughter but she didn't look old. She didn't look any age. She didn't even look real. She was like an adult doll.

"Are you coming to this dinner party or not?" he heard her say in a snappy voice that didn't sound kind at all. "I mean, personally I don't care either way, Hyslop, but you are expected, so could you hurry up. I'm ready."

Hyslop gathered up her book and notebook.

"Oh, God, a book on insects," said her mother. "I might have guessed. You are *not* bringing *that* to the dinner party!"

Well, she might be beautiful, this mother of Hyslop, but she was not a kind person. Her voice had a nasty tone that reminded him of his grandmother on a bad day.

"That's what you're wearing, is it?" she asked next. This seemed a curious question to Zak. "You look quite hideous, Hyslop." Zak felt angry on Hyslop's behalf when he heard this. He saw the mother's face more clearly as he parted some leaves, and her expression was a cruel one. She actually looked more scary than his grandmother. It was strange to see such a horrible expression on a beautiful face. Beautiful people should be smiley and happy. After all, his grandmother was poor and old, had never been pretty, and had lots of washing and cleaning to do, so she probably had a right to be grumpy and sharp-tongued. Why did this lady, who was so radiant and beautiful, have to be nasty to her daughter, he wondered. Hyslop was only reading a book. And she certainly did *not* look hideous. Zak decided that he didn't like Hyslop's mother at all. He would definitely take care to keep out of her way.

Hyslop mumbled something that he couldn't catch, and then followed her mother into the cottage. If they were going to a dinner party he wondered if it was at the big house or at the German woman's house. That lot often trekked round to each other's houses to eat each other's food. Mrs Braithwaite at the big house was a kindly lady with sad eyes, but Zak tried to avoid Mr Braithwaite. He often shouted at Zak, not in a mad way like the old man, but always angry and impatient. Then again, although he wasn't keen on the German woman, the Scottish furniture maker always had a friendly smile. You couldn't trust any of them, but some were definitely worse than others.

CHAPTER SIXTEEN

A Dinner Party and a Potential Uncle

The one good thing about her mother being dressed up in tight skirt and high heeled shoes was that she could not walk very quickly. Hyslop was spared the usual scowlings and hissings to hurry up and stop dawdling.

"Hey, you two!" a voice from behind them called out, and Sandy joined them on the path to Ilga's and Malcolm's house. Her mother and Sandy air kissed and then Sandy gave Hyslop a hug. She had not been prepared for this. It was a proper, all-enveloping hug, and Hyslop felt her whole body stiffen and freeze. She had not been hugged like this since Nonna died, and she did not know how to respond.

"Now then, Sandy," Vanessa said, linking her arm in Sandy's, pulling her away from Hyslop. "You have to fill me in again on this set up."

"Well, Nessie, I know you are used to wining and dining at some wonderful places, but I think you'll enjoy Ilga's cooking," said Sandy. "And their house is pretty amazing too. Not grand, not all out to impress in a look-at-me sort of way, but Ilga's an interior designer and Malc's a furniture maker, so everything is unique, lots of hand-made stuff, and somehow just "right" if you see what I mean."

"Not all arty farty and pretentious then?" Vanessa's voice was full of laughter, but Hyslop could detect a hint of scorn.

"Oh, no," said Sandy. "No. Ilga doesn't like houses to look too perfect with everything matching. She likes to create a welcoming atmosphere, with a bit of clutter and mismatched stuff here and there. She takes a pride in making their house homely and warm.

She always says too much money and too much good taste can ruin a place. There's a German word she uses. I've forgotten it."

"And Hugo," said Vanessa. "The famous big city lawyer. He'll be here this time, won't he? He didn't make it last time, and I'm curious to meet him."

"Oh yes, he won't miss out on an Ilga supper," said Sandy. "He and Malcolm actually get on rather well too, despite their different outlooks on life. Malc is very artistic, a real craftsman, but… "

"Hugo's the guy with all the money round here, though, isn't he?" Vanessa interrupted as they reached the door of Ilga's and Malcolm's house. "The one with the international reputation in European law?"

Her mother seemed suspiciously interested in Hugo, and Hyslop began to have a sense of foreboding.

"Darlinks!" Ilga flung the door open the minute they knocked. She gave Sandy and Ilga effusive kisses on both cheeks but Hyslop managed to stand clear. She needn't have worried about being noticed. Ilga was soon gushing about her mother's dress and appearance, rushing around with little plates of nibbles, and Malcolm poured drinks for them all. There was no sign of either Penny or Hugo.

"Well, Ilga," she heard her mother saying, as she looked around the room. "I *am* surprised by your house."

"Really! Why is that?" asked Ilga.

"I imagined that an interior designer would have a very interior designer-y sort of house if you know what I mean," said Vanessa. "This is not all matching and perfect, it's almost homely. Everything is original and wonderful, but it's warm and welcoming too. You have created a wonderful… ambience… or Stimmung. Is that the word?"

Ilga beamed with pleasure: "Well, that is *exactly* what I have tried to achieve," she said. "A welcoming atmosphere! Stimmung! So few people understand the concept. Come with me and see my kitchen. All hand-made by Malcolm to my design!" Saying this, she slipped her arm through Vanessa's and led her out of the room.

Hyslop looked over at Sandy. Her Godmother caught her gaze and smiled at her in a conspiratorial way. Hyslop felt a connection between them at that moment.

"Have some peanuts, Hyslop," Malcolm suddenly appeared at her side, almost making her jump. "And a lemonade. I'm having a whisky, but I thought I'd better not offer you one of those."

Hyslop took a large handful of peanuts. She had hardly eaten all day and was ravenously hungry. She had a sip of lemonade and decided that his comment about the whisky was a joke. He didn't seem like one of those adults who would try and force her to drink alcohol. On the other hand, it was best to be on guard. Sometimes at her mother's parties, the Uncles had slipped vodka into her orange juice. They had thought it funny when she was dizzy and sick.

"Can we come in!" called a voice from the door and Penny appeared with a man who must be Hugo behind her.

"Hey, Malc!" said the man who must be Hugo, slapping Malcolm on the back. "On the whisky without me I see!"

"Poured you one already," said Malcolm. "We're on Ardbeg tonight."

"Fantastic!" cried Hugo. He was a loud man, much louder than Malcolm. Hyslop took a step back, as Hugo seemed to take up a lot of space. He took a noisy drink. "Just what the doctor ordered. Or even if he didn't, just what *I'd* have ordered."

They clinked glasses together, then Hugo began looking around him. He took Hyslop in with a dismissive glance, then gave Sandy a quick kiss on each cheek.

"Well, Sandy, where's this glamorous old school-chum of yours I've been hearing about?" he said. "Chickened out of meeting us all, has she!"

"Sssshh, Hugo," said Penny. "I think she's in the kitchen with Ilga. Hello, Hyslop, how are you?"

"I'm well, thank you," said Hyslop politely. She moved back into the corner of the room to keep out of everyone's way.

Ilga and Vanessa appeared at that moment, and Hyslop watched Hugo closely. She was an expert by now, and she could see by his reaction that her mother's beauty had literally taken his breath away. She felt a sickening sense of déjà vu.

"Vanessa, how lovely to see you again," said Penny. "This is my husband, Hugo."

"Hugo, piacere!" said Vanessa, greeting him in Italian for some reason, and turning on the full headlights of her smile. She said in English : "I've been told you speak rather good Italian!"

"Um... hardly," said Hugo with an awkward little laugh. He seemed less boisterous and confident now. "Don't know who told you that. I can do holiday Italian, get by in a hotel sort of thing, but... um... that's about it I'm afraid." His laugh was definitely nervous . He reminded Hyslop of an embarrassed schoolboy.

"Oh, but I hear you are an expert in European law, Hugo, always travelling round the world, and Sandy was singing your praises as a linguist." Vanessa's smile now encompassed Sandy too. Sandy's slightly puzzled smile in return showed that she probably had no recollection of saying any such thing. "Well, we were sorry to have missed you the other night, when Penny kindly had us over to your house for drinks."

"Yes, I... um... I was sorry too," said Hugo. "Tried to leave work early but I think I just missed you all."

"Missed them by a good four hours as I recall," said Penny in a loud aside to Malcolm, as she took a glass of white wine from him. "Thanks, Malcolm."

"Well, if I'd known what I was missing I'd have made more of an effort!" Hugo was simpering like a silly schoolgirl now. Hyslop recognised the scene all too well. Her mother was targeting him, and he was taking a direct hit. He stood no chance. Despite her instant dislike of the man, Hyslop could almost feel sorry for him.

"We are so grateful to you, Hugo," said Vanessa, her eyes shining with sincerity as she gazed up at him. "You and Penny have been so kind letting us stay in the cottage. Bit of a safe port in a storm for us, but I know it's a special place for you. Wasn't it where your mother lived at one time? You must let us know when we have outstayed our welcome."

"Oh, no question of that!" said Hugo. "Stay! Stay as long as you like. I told Penny it wouldn't be a problem."

From Penny's wry smile, Hyslop guessed that Hugo was not telling the whole truth here. Adults rarely did, she found.

"Well, we shall try and stay out of your way as much as possible," said Vanessa. "We don't want to be a nuisance."

"I assure you, Vanessa," said Hugo, not taking his eyes off her for a moment. "You could never be a nuisance."

Hyslop moved into the corner of the room. It was a familiar scene and she had heard enough. She had no interest in listening to her mother flirting and Hugo saying stupid things to her.

"I feel I have found a kindred spirit here at last amongst you all!" Ilga said, bursting in to claim some attention for herself. "Vanessa has a European soul. I do adore you Brits, but you can be so insular, you know!"

Hyslop wasn't sure what insular meant, but Malcolm clarified this for her.

"Could be because we live on an island," he said.

It seemed to Hyslop that both Hugo and Ilga were under her mother's spell. They were being drawn into the Vanessa web, though one was a woman and one was married, which was not the normal situation. Who or what was the target here? There had to be a purpose, but it was unclear to Hyslop what her mother was up to. Was she just toying with these people? Although Vanessa seemed playful and full of fun, her actions always had a motive, a calculated purpose. Malcolm seemed immune to Vanessa's charms which was unusual, and Penny was polite and aloof, so it was hard to tell what she was thinking. Sandy was the one who had worked Vanessa out in a way the others hadn't. It must be because they had been at school together. She, like Hyslop, had seen the charm-bombing before.

"I have a suggestion to make, Hyslop." Once again Malcolm was at her side, offering her a bowl of peanuts. Hyslop took a handful warily.

"We boring adults are going to sit down to dinner shortly," he said. "Now, of course you are welcome to join us, and there is a place set for you."

Hyslop glanced over at her mother to see what it was she was meant to do, but Vanessa was throwing her head back, laughing at something that Hugo had said and was not looking in her daughter's direction.

"On the other hand, there is rather a snug wee room, just across the hallway, with a television," he said. "where you could have some supper on a tray and make the acquaintance of Miss McKenzie and Miss Hilda McKenzie."

The snug wee room sounded tempting, but the thought of two more adults was daunting. Who on earth were they, and why were they not joining the dinner party?

"There's even a laptop in there that you can use," continued Malcolm. "I hear you like butterflies, so you can look them all up on the internet."

Hyslop weighed up the joys of a computer to herself with the fear of having to make conversation with two grown-ups who were also going to be there.

"Miss McKenzie and Miss Hilda are our cats," explained Malcolm, his mouth still straight and unsmiling, but his eyes full of sparkling humour. "They can be a bit demanding, but it'll just be you and them in there. Away from all of us."

This time Hyslop did not even glance in her mother's direction for approval. She followed Malcolm.

CHAPTER SEVENTEEN

A Face at the Window and the Anatomy of a Bee

Hyslop decided that this was the ideal dinner party: she was having the food but not having to sit with grown-ups drinking and getting loud and stupid.

Malcolm had brought her some tiny pancakes with a delicious creamy topping and smoked salmon, a chicken curry dish with lots of peppers and rice, and then a sort of zingy lemon ice cream with home-made shortbread biscuits. It was not a sensation she was used to, but she felt so full she could hardly move. She flicked through channels and watched television distractedly, then turned her attention to the cats who had been trying to get on her lap throughout her meal.

Miss McKenzie and Miss Hilda McKenzie were two beautiful tabby cats. They were called after two of Malcolm's aged aunts from his Scottish childhood. Malcolm said they were Missy and Hilds for short, but Hyslop rather liked the long versions of their names. A cat's contented purring was the most relaxing noise in the world she decided, and these two were purring so loudly it was as if they had little engines inside them. Miss McKenzie stretched out her claws to show them off, extending and retracting them repeatedly. Miss Hilda pushed her way past her sister onto Hyslop's lap and settled down without a break in her purr. They both had large green eyes and a general air of knowing how wonderful they were in every way. Hyslop knew her mother would never consent to a dog as a pet as they were apparently too dirty and too demanding, but she wondered if she could perhaps sneak a cat into her room. A cat could purr loudly through the night and keep all the bad dreams away.

She switched the computer on and began looking up butterflies on the internet. What a joyous activity. She felt like purring herself as she looked up image after image of butterflies from all around the world. There were so many species that a lifetime would not be enough to see them all. The cats tried to get between her and the screen, jealous of her paying so much attention to the flickering pictures.

The noise and laughter from the dinner party across the hall was a familiar sound to Hyslop. Adults took such a long time to eat a meal. Surely they were all full by now if they had eaten as much as Hyslop had eaten. They just sat round the table for hours and talked about boring things. Usually they drank far too much alcohol and got even sillier as the night went on. Voices rose and fell, and the loudest sound was always Hugo's deep guffawing laugh. Hyslop decided that he was a show-off. She could also hear Ilga's loud, rather strident voice. It sounded as if she and Hugo were vying with each other to make Vanessa laugh. Everyone always wanted to amuse her mother in order to be rewarded with her wonderful smile and her tinkling laugh. There were no smiles and laughs when mother and daughter were on their own, but in public the smile was used to great effect, enslaving and ensnaring everyone around. There was not much to be heard from Penny, Malcolm or Sandy, just a low background murmur. Hyslop sat and thought about Sandy. She did not say unkind things and she was always warm and welcoming. They had had three sessions in the pottery together now, and Sandy had told her to pop in any time and glaze her little coil pot. Malcolm was also being kind to her, but although there didn't seem to be any sinister motive for his behaviour, you could never be sure with men: just when you thought they were safe, they turned into Uncles. Then there was Sir Northcote who had promised to show her his butterfly collection. He was definitely not going to become an admirer of her mother. She felt a buzzing of excitement at the thought of drawers and drawers full of Victorian butterflies. Sir Northcote, she decided, was a sort of God-Grandfather and the thought made her smile to herself. In theory her mother should not object to her visiting the old man, but it was impossible to tell in advance what would make Vanessa angry and what would please her. Hyslop had learned never to show too much enthusiasm for anything or anyone in her mother's presence, as no sooner did she become attached to people than she would be taken away from them.

Hyslop narrowed her search on the internet to British butterflies. There was so much information about each one. It was incredible. None of the photographs matched the beauty of the illustrations in her wonderful book, but she was able to find up-to-the-minute information about sightings of particular butterflies. She wondered if Sir Northcote ever used the internet, and idly she typed in his name. To her astonishment there was a website all about the Hemmings collection of butterflies. It was described as an "important national treasure." As Hyslop read about the unique collection of butterfly aberrations that were the special feature of the Hemmings Collection, Miss Hilda placed herself between Hyslop and the screen in a very determined manner.

"You want more attention, do you!" Hyslop stroked the cat's arched back and tickled her behind her ears. The purring grew louder.

Suddenly a scream rang out and Hyslop jumped.

It was unmistakeably her mother who had screamed. Hyslop stood up at once and ran for the door. Miss Hilda gave an indignant meow, as she was pushed aside. Hyslop was fearful. This was not a normal dinner party sort of noise. Something had happened. She rushed across the corridor and peeped in at the dinner party through the slightly open door.

"I tell you, it was a face!" Vanessa was saying, her voice full of genuine alarm rather than fake-dinner-party-emotion. "An old man's face pressed to the window pane, watching us! He was staring right at me!"

"There's no one there now," said Ilga, getting up and going over to the window.

"Oh dear, I'm afraid it was probably my father," said Penny.

"I think I told you about Penny's father, Sir Northcote." This was Sandy now. "My Godfather. He is an old sweetie, but sometimes he gives us all a bit of a shock by appearing at windows. He's what you might call an eccentric."

"Well, he did give me a fright I must say," Vanessa's voice returned to dinner-party-amusement. She was once more in control. "Sorry if I startled you all. What's he doing out and about anyway? Isn't it past his bed-time?"

"Oh, he's often out much later than this," said Hugo. "Silly old codger goes mothing. Sets moth-traps and goes around checking them at odd hours of night and morning."

"Mothing!" exclaimed Vanessa. "What on earth does he want moths for?"

"A very good question, Vanessa!" laughed Hugo. "I often ask myself that."

"Not creatures I'd want around, thank you. I can do without holes in my clothes!"

"Daddy's a bit of a naturalist, a lepidopterist in fact," said Penny. "Butterflies are his speciality. His grandfather, my great-grandfather, was a renowned Victorian collector and Daddy has a whole room full of drawers of butterflies and moths from all over the world. It's rather famous in fact."

"Hasn't Hyslop mentioned him?" asked Sandy. "She bumped into him in the garden and he's got her interested in butterflies. He gave her a book I think."

"How sweet," said Vanessa. "Yes, Hyslop was showing me that book earlier. It looked really interesting."

Hyslop repressed a snort.

"I believe he's going to show her his collection of butterflies," said Penny. "It's a great honour, I can tell you."

"Oh, please," Hugo put his hands up. "No more talk about

butterflies. I had to feign an interest in the wretched things when I first came to the house as Penny's boyfriend. I even sat through drawer after drawer of those dusty old Victorian specimens. And as for moths, don't get me started!"

"Well, it's good that the old boy still feels passionate about it all," said Malcolm. "More wine, anyone?"

"Passionate? What rubbish!" said Hugo loudly. "The old duffer's going senile. Like my poor Mamma. I suppose it comes to us all in the end."

"Daddy's not senile," said Penny. "Just a bit eccentric I suppose. His mind's still razor sharp and you know it, Hugo."

"Eccentric! Just a bit eccentric you suppose!" Hugo mocked Penny in a tone that made Hyslop want to go in and slap him. "A bit more than eccentric I think. If you haven't met him, Vanessa, you ought to be prepared."

"Oh, why's that?"

"He insists on keeping the estate here full of nettles and thistles and ghastly weeds. I give the gardener instructions to tidy up, and the old boy makes a scene and gives the man different orders behind my back. He won't allow us to keep the place decent. Madness I tell you. Then he wanders around looking for butterflies by day and moths by night, muttering nonsense to himself, smacking himself on the head and shouting curses in a silly Scottish accent at anyone and everyone he happens to meet. Now that's more than eccentric by my reckoning!"

"Nothing silly about a Scottish accent." This was said quietly by Malcolm to no one in particular.

"Well, he certainly does sound odd," said Vanessa. "Thanks for the warning."

"Oh come on, Hugo. You are being harsh. Now, please don't worry about Uncle Northy spending time with Hyslop, Nessie," said Sandy. "He is quite harmless. He doesn't actually swear at people. He just mutters to himself and shouts randomly. It's sort of an involuntary reflex. It's true he sometimes shouts out in a Scottish accent as a sort of tribute to his beloved old Scottish nanny. She helped bring him up. But he really is an expert on butterflies – quite eminent in his field – and will be delighted if he has found someone to share his interest. I'm afraid Penny and I were a bit of a disappointment there, weren't we, Pen?"

Hyslop was grateful for Sandy's defence of the old man. Her cheeks were flushed with anger at Hugo's insulting words.

"Is Hyslop all right next door, Malcolm?" asked Penny suddenly. Hyslop tensed at this mention of her name, her body poised for flight, but she relaxed when she heard Ilga's voice calling from the kitchen to say that coffee was ready.

"Now, Vanessa, would you like me to make decaffeinated? This lot will drink strong coffee until the sheep come home!" Ilga had such a loud voice. "But I was just checking that you were OK with real coffee. It won't keep you awake, will it?"

"Oh, real coffee for me, please, Ilga!" laughed Vanessa. "Count me in until those sheep come home too!"

"Ilga is well aware that the expression is 'till the cows come home'," said Sandy. "She enjoys the odd Malapropism to keep us on our toes. Don't be fooled into thinking she's made a mistake in her English."

"Oh, I'd already noted that Ilga speaks English better than most English people," said Vanessa, smiling at Ilga.

Ilga made a clucking noise of pleasure, and Hyslop could see she was thrilled at this compliment. "I am trying to improve the English language!" she said. "I sometimes like to change expressions round. It's my German logic."

"A classic is the bee's bottom," said Malcolm.

"The bee's bottom?" asked Vanessa. "What, instead of the bee's knees do you mean!"

"Well," said Ilga, "a bee does not have particularly interesting knees – rather boring, spindly little things, whereas it has a wonderful black and yellow bottom! So if something is particularly exciting I would call it the bee's bottom. I feel I sometimes have to improve English idiom."

"I for one approve!" cried Vanessa. "From now on I shall never refer to a bee's knees again. Only to its wonderful bottom!" She raised her glass with a giggle: "Bees' bottoms up!"

How stupid they were, thought Hyslop. Didn't they know that a bee carried its pollen in its knees, which was its greatest treasure. As usual, adults were ignorant about insects.

"And as for knee high to a grasshopper," continued Ilga. "Well, that's just silly. I prefer to say knee high to something more logical, like knee high to a buffalo."

That did make more sense, thought Hyslop, so maybe Ilga wasn't entirely stupid.

"German logic indeed," said Malcolm, passing a large glass decanter to Hugo. "Port, Hugues?"

"Don't mind if I do," said Hugo, though he was getting louder and louder and it seemed that he had already had more than enough alcohol to drink. Although he had not spoken to her directly, Hyslop decided that she did not like Hugo at all. He had been rude about Sir Northcote and the butterflies, and he was showing a dangerous amount of interest in her mother. She sighed. He was a rich man after all, but how could he be a new potential Uncle when he was married to Penny? These people were close friends of Sandy's and all so kind. They had created a happy, harmonious environment, and it was unbearable to think of her mother disturbing it all.

"These delicious looking Italian chocolates are from Vanessa," said Ilga. "Now, I have rather naughtily just sampled one in the kitchen, and I can assure you, darlinks, they literally are the bee's bottom!"

Hyslop watched Hugo reach over and take a chocolate. His face was flushed and he looked radiantly happy. It was the kind of happiness men displayed when her mother was giving them her special attention. Oh, how stupid they were.

"Well, I know which part of a bee's anatomy they remind me of," he announced, launching into a series of crude words which he seemed to find amusing. "I must have another!"

Vanessa threw her head back and laughed.

Hyslop felt indignant again on Sir Northcote's behalf. Why did Hugo feel that he could criticise the old man for swearing and shouting, especially when he knew Sir Northcote couldn't help it, when he himself thought it was entertaining to shout rude words so loudly? She knew that if she said the words Hugo had used her mother would probably have smacked her, yet there she was laughing merrily at Hugo as if he had just said something unbelievably funny and witty.

"No coffee for me, Ilga, I'm just going to check that Hyslop's OK."

Sandy was getting up, pushing her chair back, so Hyslop fled back into the little sitting room. She threw herself down on the sofa and pulled Miss Hilda onto her lap. The cat gave an aggrieved yowl, then began to purr again.

"Hi Hyslop," said Sandy, putting her head round the door. "Are you OK in here?"

"I'm fine thank you, Sandy," said Hyslop.

"Are you watching television?"

"Um, no, I was on the internet," said Hyslop. "And I'm enjoying being with the cats."

"I confess I'm not normally a cat-person," said Sandy, coming in and perching on an arm of the little sofa. "Dogs are my thing. But I do make an exception for these two. They are the dearest creatures!"

She began to stroke Miss McKenzie gently on the top of her head.

"I love it when they purr," she said.

There was a long silence, then Sandy said: "Do you mind if I sit in here with you for a bit? The others are having coffee and liqueurs, and the men will be lighting up cigars shortly. I think I've had enough of it all."

"I don't mind," said Hyslop, and to her surprise she found that she didn't.

CHAPTER EIGHTEEN

You Don't Lie about Butterflies

The girl Hyslop was sitting, with a book on her lap, staring at a dandelion. It looked like a dandelion anyway. From where Zak was sitting, it was hard to tell. She had been sitting there quietly for at least ten minutes, just looking and looking. Well, it felt like a ten-minutes-ish sort of period of time. Ten was a good round number, and it didn't seem to offend people. Zak wasn't actually sure what ten minutes felt like. He had never owned a watch and was not good at telling the time, though he tried to disguise the fact. Time spent staring at things was in any case hard to measure. Sometimes, when he had been surveying Mrs Braithwaite's plants and watching the bees buzzing around them, an hour would go by, and he would only know that because his father would be cross and shout at him for not doing anything for a whole hour. A whole hour was a dangerous amount of time to be caught staring it seemed. His father never shouted about a whole ten minutes, so that must be a safer amount of time.

Zak wondered if she was studying a butterfly. Would a butterfly stay still for that long? He edged round the large ferns he was hiding behind to try and see what she was looking at. He had good eyesight, but it was hard to make out if there was something there or not. She wouldn't be sitting looking at a dandelion for this long. There must be an insect of some sort, and he decided it was most probably a butterfly.

The sun was shining on her hair, and it brought out all sorts of different colours he had never seen in anyone's hair. He had thought she had dark hair, so dark he might even have called it black, but now he realised that her hair was more complicated: he could see dark brown, light brown, copper, various shades of red that he couldn't name, some of it almost golden. Maybe each hair on her head was a different colour, so that it only looked dark when you saw it from a distance, or when the light wasn't bright. Was everyone's hair that complicated? He had never really looked at anyone else's hair properly.

He longed, yet feared, to make those spooky eyes look round at him again. Maybe he should pluck up courage and tell her that those Peacock butterflies she liked so much were back round the nettle patch at the edge of the wood.

"It's a female Common Blue," said Hyslop suddenly.

Zak started. Was she talking to him, or to herself?

"At least I think it is," she continued. "It's hard to tell. Come and see what you think."

Zak stood up. There seemed to be no point in hiding from this girl. His grandmother sometimes told him she had eyes in the back of her head and that if he did something wrong she would see it. He had never believed his grandmother, but the girl Hyslop really did seem to be able to see things that were at the back of her head.

Once he got closer he could see that there was a butterfly with its wings closed on the dandelion. It didn't look very blue to him.

"It's hard to tell it apart from the Brown Argus," she said. "You have to look at the spots really closely."

As she turned round to show him the picture in the butterfly book, the butterfly she had been looking at suddenly opened its wings and flew off. There still didn't seem to be much blue about it.

"The Common Blue males are blue, but the females are brown," she said, as if reading his thoughts. "It's good when they let you stare at them for ages."

Zak nodded. That was one of the reasons he liked the vegetables. They didn't mind being stared at. He realised, however, that since the arrival of the girl Hyslop he had hardly visited the kitchen garden. He had forgotten to take his grandmother one of the large courgettes she had asked for, and he had done no weeding at all.

"It's called sexual dimorphism," she said, "when the males and females of the same species are different from each other."

Zak had no idea what she was talking about. It sounded like the kind of stuff a teacher would say, but, unlike with any teacher he had ever encountered, he could have listened to her speaking for whole hours and hours. Her voice wasn't like other people's voices: she didn't speak like the kids in his class at school, but she wasn't posh like Mrs Braithwaite or the old man either. She spoke like a teacher, using big words, but she was never boring. Listening to her was almost as good as watching her. He wondered if she knew how much he liked watching her.

"You like watching things, don't you, Zak?" she asked. It really seemed as if she could read his mind.

"Some things," he said, meeting her spooky gaze.

"You like watching me, don't you?" she said in a matter of fact tone. It was a question, but not the sort of question that needed an answer. That was the kind of question he liked. He did not reply.

She turned back to her book and began flicking through it. She seemed totally engrossed in the pictures of butterflies. Zak felt a strange unfamiliar desire to make conversation. Somehow he had to get her to pay attention to him again.

"Them Peacocks are out again," he said after a while.

She did not look up. He waited for a while.

"Quite a lot of them about," he added.

"Yes, I've seen them," she said. "And the Speckled Woods on the brambles."

Zak wasn't sure about the Speckled Woods. Maybe they were those chocolate brown butterflies with yellowy spots that were always flying above the brambles in the woods.

She continued reading her book for a long time, ignoring him. He felt self-conscious staring at her now, and he shifted his weight from one foot to the other and cleared his throat a few times. He wanted to get her attention, but the Peacocks weren't going to do it today.

"I… eh… I know where there's other butterflies," he said.

Hyslop looked up.

"Which other butterflies?" she asked.

"I don't know their names," said Zak. "I can never remember names."

"Show me," she thrust the book at him, and Zak's mind began moving with unaccustomed haste. Thinking fast was new to him, but he did so now.

As he turned over the pages of the butterfly book, he knew he would have to alight on something exciting to make her get up and follow him. There seemed to be lots of orange ones, and quite a few white ones. He glanced up at the girl Hyslop. She was staring at him with the dark unblinking gaze of her full attention, and he didn't want her to stop. He turned awkwardly back to the book, and flicked through page after page. His hands were trembling slightly. He found the pictures of the Peacocks and the others, whose names he had forgotten, that they had seen the previous day. No, it would have to be something more dramatic. He had to impress her.

There was a picture of a large butterfly with one wing purple and the other one brown. Surely that wasn't right. The artist must have drawn it wrongly. He was tempted to say that he had seen it, but then thought it might be a trick picture. He turned the page over again and came to the largest and most dramatic looking butterfly he had seen so far. It was yellow and black and blue with raggedy sort of wings, sharp pointed at the bottom. He guessed that she would get up and follow him if he said he had seen one of these.

"Seen one of them today," he said.

Hyslop put her head on one side.

"That one there?" she said, pointing to it. "Where was it?"

"Other side of the woods," said Zak. "I can show you where it was."

"Are you sure, Zak?" she asked.

He nodded, not trusting himself to say any more.

The huge dark eyes stared right into him. He certainly had her attention now, but somehow her gaze was making him feel uneasy. Something was wrong.

"That's a Swallowtail," said Hyslop. "It's only found in parts of Norfolk now." She paused, and then said softly: "Parts of Norfolk, and nowhere else in the country."

Zak felt his heart thumping. He didn't know what to say. Words could get you into trouble, so he said nothing more. He did not know where Norfolk was but it wasn't anywhere nearby; he was sure of that.

"You lied, Zak," said Hyslop. "Didn't you?"

He had no idea how long the silence was between them. It felt like a few seconds, and it felt like a hundred years.

"You know, it's OK to lie to adults," she said at last. Her tone was light, and she didn't seem cross, but it was still scary somehow. "We all have to lie sometimes. But you don't lie about butterflies. Not to me. Not *ever*."

Zak sneaked a look up at her. The sun was shining on each individual hair on her head, and he knew he had never seen anything or anyone so beautiful in his whole life.

"Butterflies are important to me," she said. "Do you understand that, Zak?"

She seemed to be wanting an answer this time, so he nodded his head slowly.

"If you lie to me about butterflies, I will not spend time with you," she said, her voice suddenly cold. "I will not allow you to come here following me around. And believe me, I *will* know when you are following me."

Zak felt miserable. It was like the sun had gone in behind a cloud, though in fact there were no clouds in the sky. Even his father shouting at him couldn't make him feel this bad. He stared down at his feet, utterly wretched.

"I won't lie again," he whispered, "not to you, and not about butterflies."

Hyslop said nothing for a long while, and seemed to be pondering something.

"I might be going on a trip soon," she said after a while. Zak looked up, puzzled. School was over for the year, and the girl Hyslop had missed out on all the school trips.

"A butterfly trip," she added. "To look for the Purple Emperor. To Bernwood Forest."

"With the old man?" he asked.

He knew that Sir Northcote went on butterfly trips to various places nearby, sometimes to Bernwood Forest, and his father drove the car for him. Zak had never wanted to go before, but now he wanted to go so much it felt painful. He longed to go with the girl Hyslop and help her find this Purple Emperor butterfly.

"Northy is taking me," she said, slamming her book shut.

"Oh," he said, his eyes shining with eagerness. "I… would… I mean, I would… like… "

"I just thought I'd let you know," she said, and she walked off, her book tucked under her arm. "Now leave me in peace."

Zak did not dare follow.

CHAPTER NINETEEN

A Serpent in Paradise

It was all very well knowing the seventy two butterfly species in the book that could possibly be found in Great Britain and Ireland, but there were also over two thousand species of moths. How could lepidopterists contain so much knowledge in their heads! One would simply have to specialise. Hyslop, curled up in bed reading her beloved butterfly book, was reminded of nocturnal insects by the appearance of two brown and fawn moths fluttering around her bedside lamp. Several more were flinging themselves against the window pane. It was strange, she mused, that creatures which chose to live in the dark should be so attracted by light. If they liked light so much why didn't they choose to fly in the daytime? That was a question for Sir Northcote when she next saw him.

The two at her bedside light were now joined by a third. They had managed to come in through the open window. Hyslop put her book down and watched them for a while. She realised she would have to capture them and release them outside. There was nothing for them here in her room.

"You silly creatures," she said, putting them outside the window. "Stay away from windows."

She put her light out so as not to lure any other moths in and looked out into the night. She knew that Sir Northcote sometimes wandered around in the dark, and she peered out to see if she could detect any sign of him.

Despite her experiences in dark cupboards, Hyslop was not afraid of the night. She did not mind darkness, as she liked being invisible herself. Nor was she scared of things that most people would be afraid of in the dark, like winged insects brushing against her cheeks, bats squeaking, or owls hooting. Such natural phenomena were comforting to her. The other scary things of the night, which her schoolfriends in both France and Italy had talked of in terrified tones, were ghosts. Hyslop, for the first time in her life, felt she had banished her fear of the ghostly girl in Oncle Xavier's cupboard. She smiled as she thought of the new ending to her recurring dream. Either there was no such thing as a ghost, she decided, in which case there was nothing to fear; or, if spirits really did exist, Hyslop was confident that the two people who had loved her most in the world, her Papa and her Nonna, were ghosts themselves and would protect her from anything bad in the spirit world. In truth, she was more afraid of her mother than of anyone or anything else. How different she was from most children, who turned to their mothers for comfort from night terrors. Hyslop could not imagine *ever* disturbing her mother to tell her about a bad dream or a scary noise.

It was a very black darkness outside and Hyslop wondered if all the butterflies were safely roosting, and if there were any night predators which might take them unawares. Her head was still full of the book she had been reading. She wanted to impress Sir Northcote with her knowledge when he showed her his butterfly collection. Of course, in one way it wasn't very pleasant to think of butterflies being killed and pinned, collected and labelled like stamps, but in Victorian times it was the only way to record them. There was no need nowadays when sophisticated cameras could record every detail, every brightly coloured scale of their wings. In any case, Sir Northcote seemed far more interested in conserving habitat for butterflies, and in saving them from extinction. Killing them was the last thing he would want to do now.

For some time Hyslop had been vaguely aware of a background noise, and had assumed that her mother was watching television downstairs. Now she heard laughter, both her mother's and a man's. Her whole body tensed and she had a moment of horror as she imagined that Uncle Massimo had somehow returned. She stood motionless at the window as she heard the patio doors below her being flung open and the outside lights went on to illuminate the wooden table and chairs.

She stood to the side, though she knew they would not be able to see her in the darkness. Her mother was carrying two glasses and the man behind her was carrying a bottle.

"This is terribly decadent." Her mother's voice rang out, full of fun and laughter. "Champagne and it's nearly midnight. Whatever are we celebrating?"

"We're celebrating you, Vanessa," said the man. It was Hugo. Relief that it was not Uncle Massimo coursed through Hyslop's blood, though it was quickly replaced by puzzled suspicion. What was Hugo doing here at this time?

"Well, it's not my birthday or anything," said Vanessa, putting the glasses on the table. "Though these days I don't admit to birthdays that often I must say!"

"You don't have to worry about birthdays." Hugo seemed to be struggling to open the bottle, probably because he was staring at Vanessa rather than at the task in hand. "My darling girl."

Hyslop scowled to hear Hugo refer to her mother as "my darling girl." She watched as several large brown moths began circling around the patio lights.

There was a loud pop as the bottle was opened and he filled the glasses with foaming, golden liquid. Hyslop had tried champagne once or twice when adults had forced her to drink it. She did not know why they all made such a fuss about it; she much preferred lemonade.

"To us!" Hugo clinked his glass against Vanessa's and she gave him the full radiance of her smile. Poor man, thought Hyslop, poor silly man, he stands no chance against that.

"To us, Hugo?" said Vanessa. "That's a funny old toast. I didn't know there was an 'us'. Our acquaintance is rather recent."

They drank their champagne and there was more silly banter. Hyslop heard snippets of conversation.

"Don't toy with me, Vanessa," Hugo's voice sounded desperate, pleading. What an idiot he was. "The minute I saw you, it was like un coup de foudre."

Hyslop bit her lip so hard it hurt. "Yes, Hugo," she thought. "You certainly have been struck by lightning, and there's nothing you can do about it." She also thought that his French accent was pretty awful.

Her mother said something which Hyslop could not catch and Hugo stepped towards her. Although Hyslop was unable to make out his exact words, Hugo's tone was familiar. She had heard it all before, in French, in Italian and now in English. Her mother had made a conquest. Hugo had fallen in love with her.

It was a strange development. Hugo was a married man, and although her mother had targeted married men before, this was surely different. Hyslop had never known the wives of any of the Uncles. Now she not only knew Penny, but liked her very much. Hugo was Penny's husband, he was Sandy's friend, Malcolm's friend, Sir Northcote's son-in-law. He was part of the whole community. Turning him into an Uncle would hurt lots of different people. Everything was different here.

Money: that had to be it. With Vanessa, it was always about money. Was Hugo really so fantastically rich? So much richer than the Italian Uncles?

"I just don't want to waste any time," she heard Hugo saying. "I want us to be together."

Vanessa's reply was a low murmur and Hyslop strained to hear. They were standing very close now, drinking champagne with their glasses almost touching.

Hyslop kicked the wall in front of her. It was rather painful as she had bare feet, but she welcomed the sensation of pain as it blocked out the other familiar emotions of fear and insecurity. She did it again, and the pain felt good.

What did Hugo mean, he wanted them to be together? How could such a thing be possible? She caught more snatches of conversation from Hugo, declarations of love that made her feel like vomiting, and mention of a London flat. Her mother's voice was still too low to make out, but she was not rebuffing him, that was clear.

Hyslop had heard enough. She felt physically sick. She crept into her bed and hugged the butterfly book to her chest. She didn't want to put the light back on as they would see it from down below and know she might be listening. In any case, she was too tense to read. She lay on her back, eyes wide open, drumming her fingers on the hard covers of the book.

CHAPTER TWENTY

Zak Watches Hyslop Go Where He Cannot Follow

Zak escaped from the house before his grandmother could give him new chores, or scold him for not doing yesterday's chores. Or even chores from the day before yesterday. Their tiny back lawn needed mowing, and had done for several days, and she wanted him to move some logs into their wood shed. He was not in a particular hurry to get on with either of these tasks. Also, she was probably going to make thin, watery porridge for breakfast and he didn't like it much, so it wasn't worth hanging around.

There was not much to eat in the cupboard, but he found a piece of rather dry bread to chew on. He didn't linger to toast it or spread butter on it. He made his way to the Hemmingswood estate, to the vegetable garden, where he knew there would be raspberries and gooseberries. He crushed some of the berries onto his bread to make it more palatable. He sometimes did this : it was like having really fresh jam. He was still hungry afterwards so he picked some tomatoes in the greenhouse and munched those. They were delicious, so much better than the supermarket tomatoes Granny sometimes bought. Mrs Braithwaite had caught him eating her tomatoes once but she hadn't said anything. She had smiled at him in a friendly way, so he didn't feel that he was stealing. He wouldn't have let Mr Braithwaite or the old man catch him, though. That would be a different matter. There would be shouting and swearing then for sure. And if his father found out he would get a slap. You had to be careful of who was watching; you had to be on your guard all the time.

Zak examined a cucumber plant and wondered if he dare pick one. The cucumbers were more tricky as it was possible that the Braithwaites knew which ones were ripening, and if he picked one it would be missed. There were pepper and aubergine plants too, but he didn't like the taste of those. One of them, he was sure, was a chilli plant, and he had had a very nasty experience once when he had picked a pretty red chilli and taken a bite. He shuddered. He didn't even want to think of it.

As he prowled around the greenhouse, he caught sight of the girl Hyslop striding past the end of the vegetable garden. He ducked down behind a bushy aubergine plant, though he needn't have worried. She wasn't looking in his direction.

She was walking much faster than usual. She did look around her a little bit, but there was no stopping and examining butterflies like she normally did. It was rather too early for butterflies anyway. They were not early risers he had noted. She was moving purposefully, as if her mind were on her destination, not on the insects around her.

Zak slipped out of the greenhouse and followed her at a distance. It was easier to follow her when she was walking fast like this, rather than looking around all the time. Somehow, when she was studying her butterflies, she seemed to be aware of everything and everyone in her vicinity and it was hard to creep up on her.

He kept well back as he watched her stride across the lawn of the big house. Was she going to visit the Braithwaites, he wondered. Her walk was confident: she was not afraid of being confronted.

At the end of the lawn, however, she did not march up to the big house door, but turned right, and he had to wait until she was out of sight before scurrying across the lawn himself. Mr Braithwaite would be safely on his way to work, and he hoped that Mrs Braithwaite wouldn't be looking out of her window. She probably would not shout at him as she was a kind lady, but she would wonder what he was doing on the front lawn.

Cautiously he turned the same corner that Hyslop had, and

followed the line of the wall, guessing that she must have done the same. There was a little door in the wall leading to the estate beyond, and she must have gone through it. Perhaps she was going butterflying in the woods beyond the old man's house.

He opened the door a little and peeped through the crack. To his astonishment she was not heading for the woods, but opening the dilapidated old gate leading to Sir Northcote's house.

Zak frowned. He felt worried. He knew that the old man liked to talk to her about butterflies, but surely she couldn't be thinking of visiting him in his house. No one but Mrs Braithwaite and the potter woman visited him there. His grandmother went in once a week to clean and do the old man's ironing, and he had heard strange tales about the house. It was dark and spooky apparently, and his grandmother was hardly allowed to move or dust anything. She was confined to keeping his kitchen and bathroom clean and making his bed. There were scary objects everywhere, like skulls and stuffed birds with staring eyes, and there were cabinets full of dead insects that Granny was forbidden to touch. There was also a poison cabinet with bottles full of evil looking liquids with skull and crossbones labels on them. "I'm always glad to get out of there," Granny said every week. "The place gives me the creeps."

Part of him wanted to call out and warn Hyslop not to go in. Even as he watched, however, the old man opened his door. He did not smile, but he looked as if he had been expecting her. Somehow that was even more sinister.

Well, it was too late now. Zak closed the little garden door and stood for a while with his back to the wall. She had gone where he could not follow.

"The Camberwell Beauty is one of the most spectacular butterflies to be seen in the British countryside, and one that has always elicited great excitement…"
(from The Butterflies of Britain and Ireland, by Jeremy Thomas and Richard Lewington)

CHAPTER TWENTY ONE

Hyslop Views the Collection and is given a Mission

Hyslop's first impression of Sir Northcote's house was the smell. It was more a mixture of smells really: damp wallpaper, forest floor leaves, old leather, stale Brazil nuts, musty books, decaying vegetables, animal fur and long rainy afternoons. Hyslop liked it.

She followed the old man down the dim passageway into a large, high-ceilinged room. The walls were panelled in dark wood, and there were heavy green curtains at the window, laced with cobwebs, which looked as if they had been there for a hundred years. In any case, the small leaded window panes were so filthy that not much light would have filtered through even if the curtains had been fully open. In such a room could the Sleeping Beauty have been found by the prince. Where she would have lain waiting for that kiss, however, was another matter. There was nowhere to sit down, let alone lie asleep for a hundred years.

"I don't allow the cleaner in here to mess around," said Sir Northcote suddenly whirling round to face her. He said it aggressively, as if daring her to comment. She had no intention of doing so.

To Hyslop the room was just perfect. No one had been in to dust and polish and tidy up for years, possibly decades. Dust lay thick on every surface and spiders had been spinning webs for generations, most of which were dusty too. She wondered if this would annoy the spiders as it would prevent their webs from being invisible to flying insects, which was the whole point of a web. They would have to constantly begin again with new webs. It was clearly a cycle which had gone on for some time. The least movement stirred up dust in the air. Hyslop wondered if she was breathing in air and dust from another era, possibly even from old Queen Victoria's time.

One whole wall was given over to books, leather-bound mainly, and more books were piled up on the floor and on every piece of furniture. In one corner was a trio of stuffed owls which seemed to be glaring at her. In front of them was what looked like a real dead mouse. In another corner, piled high on a table, was a selection of bones. Hyslop wondered if they were animal or human.

Dead flies and bluebottles littered the floor and many of the surfaces. Flies were insects too of course, and it was important that they were studied, but somehow Hyslop could not get excited about flies. Her heart was definitely with the butterflies.

"Sit down, for goodness sake!" barked the old man, pointing to an armchair which only had four books on it. Hyslop pushed them to the back of the chair, and perched herself on the edge of it. She caused so much dust to rise up in the air that it made her cough.

The old man was prowling around the room, frowning and muttering to himself, with only the occasional head slap.

"I don't *do* visitors," he said aggressively. "I don't make tea or coffee or anything like that. Don't be expecting that sort of hospitality here."

"No, thank you," said Hyslop politely, as if she had in fact been offered something to drink. "I don't really like tea or coffee."

"There's a tin of ginger biscuits," he said, looking around him in a vague sort of way. "Somewhere around here. My daughter brought them when I told her you were coming. Insists on bringing me things she's baked. Bit of a nuisance frankly."

"Is this it?" Hyslop leaned forward and picked up a tin from the floor at her feet. It had pictures of chocolate biscuits on it beneath a thick layer of greasy dust and what looked like mouse droppings.

"No, of course not!" he snapped. "That's been there since

Christmas. Possibly the Christmas before that. You don't want stale biscuits, do you!"

"Well, I prefer them fresh."

He narrowed his eyes as if to check if she was being sarcastic. She wasn't, though. She was simply telling the truth.

"Ah!" He pounced on a more shiny looking tin, beside the pile of bones. "Here it is. These are fresh. Penelope made them yesterday."

He handed the tin to Hyslop and as she opened it a delicious smell of ginger and sugar and butter came bursting out, banishing the musty smells around her.

"Can't eat much these days," he said, still wandering around the room. "I tell her that but she keeps baking for me. Help me eat the wretched things, would you!"

Hyslop, who had not had breakfast, was thrilled. She bit into one and had to close her eyes it was so good. She understood why people used the phrase "melt in your mouth" about biscuits, which she never really had before.

"Mmmmm," she said. "That's the best ginger biscuit I've ever eaten."

"Eat the whole tin!" he shouted. "The whole lot! D'you hear! I don't want to be left with them."

If only all adult demands were so easy to fulfil. Hyslop reached for her second biscuit, and bit into it with delight. Crumbs fell onto her lap and she brushed them onto the floor. It wasn't the sort of place where crumbs would be minded.

"Do you want to see the collection then, Hyslop!" he said, glaring at her.

"Of course, that's why I've come," she said, looking up from the biscuits. She was pleased that he had used her name for the first time, instead of calling her "child" or "Miss Smarty Boots." She had told him her name of course, but wasn't sure that he had registered it. "Where are all the butterflies then, Northy?"

She had planned in advance to call him Northy. She didn't want to call him Mr Hemmings, as, according to Sandy, that was wrong.

His correct title was apparently Sir Northcote Hemmings, but she didn't fancy calling him that all the time; it sounded like some strange medieval knight. Sandy called him Uncle Northy as he was her Godfather, but Hyslop had always had bad experiences of Uncles so had decided on plain Northy. Besides, he wasn't a relation of hers, or ever likely to be her mother's lover. She looked at him to see how he would react, but he did not seem to mind. He barely seemed to have noticed. He was preoccupied with opening a cabinet of drawers with a key.

As he fumbled for some time with trembling old man's fingers, Hyslop took the chance to cram another biscuit into her mouth. She felt deliciously full.

At last he pulled a whole drawer out of the cabinet and laid it on the table, on top of a pile of books, in front of her. Hyslop put the biscuit tin out of the way on the chair behind her, closing the lid against dust, and wiped her hands on her T-shirt. Unlike everything else in the room, the slim drawer with its glass top was remarkably dust-free. In it was an array of brightly coloured butterflies, each one with a tiny label beneath it.

"These are from West Africa," the old man said. "My grandfather went out there many times. What they called the Gold Coast in those days. Been there myself. You can see a couple of hundred species in a day if you know where to look."

"What! In one day!"

"Oh yes, there's variety there all right."

"They're so fresh looking," said Hyslop. It was extraordinary to think that these butterflies, in their rainbow colours of red and blue and yellow and green, had been flying around in African forests a hundred years ago. "I don't know any of these species though."

"It would be queer if you did," said Sir Northcote. "You didn't know a Brimstone until a few weeks ago! You've never been to Africa have you? Eh?" His voice rose to a shout. "Have you!"

"No," sighed Hyslop. "No, I haven't, but I would like to go one day. I would like to see butterflies like this and study them."

She stared at the beautiful creatures and felt a great longing in her heart to be in a place where you could see two hundred different sorts of butterflies in one day. She would be like Alice in Wonderland, only it would be much better than that. Alice found some rather nasty things in Wonderland, and there simply couldn't be anything nasty in a place with two hundred species of butterfly in one day.

The old man seemed to be clenching his teeth to stop a swear word from tumbling out, or maybe just his funny Scottish word.

"Can I start by looking at the British butterflies?" Hyslop said after a while. "I mean, these are unbelievably beautiful but I'd like to start with what I know."

"I think that might be best." She had clearly said the right thing, as he nodded his head vigorously, took the drawer away and replaced it in the cabinet. He then took a different key out of his pocket and opened a different cabinet with the same trembling and fumbling. Although it took a long time, Hyslop decided against offering to help him. She wondered about another biscuit but decided she really couldn't manage one.

"The few people I have allowed to see my collection," he said, pausing before he lowered the next drawer in front of her, "the *few* people" he repeated, "have been a great disappointment to me. A *huge* disappointment! 'Which one is the biggest?' they always ask. Or 'How much are they worth?'" He imitated these imaginary people in an unpleasant whiny voice. "Then they always ask to see an Atlas Moth." He spat out the word "Dunderheids!" and placed the new drawer in front of her, with its neat rows of tiny orange butterflies. "Here are some Skippers." He glared at her, his eyes staring out from his head in his angry-old-man-way: "Most people would find these little creatures boring I suppose."

"I don't," said Hyslop. "I don't find any butterflies boring."

"These are mainly from my grandfather's day," he said. "You can tell by his copperplate writing. I was with him when he collected these last two. Fine fresh specimens."

"A boring butterfly would in fact be an oxymoron," said Hyslop. "Just not possible."

"This drawer is the Small Skipper and the Essex Skipper," he said. "You can tell the difference... "

"... by the tips of their antennae," interrupted Hyslop. "Yes, I know."

He pulled up an upright wooden chair and sat down beside her.

"My eyesight isn't so good for close up," he said, slapping his head. "Can't enjoy them all like I used to." His voice became gentle and soft which was unusual, and the slapping stopped. His gnarled old fingers hovered over the glass drawer, above the last two butterflies in the drawer. "Just as well I know them all off by heart."

They sat for some time together contemplating the Skippers. After a while Hyslop offered to put the drawer away and fetch the next one in the series.

"Ah," she said. "Chequered Skippers. They're only found in Argyll in Scotland now."

The old man gave a wheezy chuckle when she said this.

"You have the makings of a true lepidopterist, Hyslop," he said. "Dunderheid!"

If she ignored the last word, it was the nicest thing anyone had ever said to her.

The morning was passed looking at drawer after drawer of British butterflies. Their comments on the collection were interrupted only by the occasional crunch of a biscuit or a gentle head slap. There were all her friends from her wonderful book: Red Admirals, White Admirals, Gatekeepers, Purple Emperors, Small Coppers, Green Hairstreaks, White-letter Hairstreaks, Silver-washed Fritillaries, Scotch Argus, Mountain Ringlets, Browns and Whites and Blues of all shapes and sizes. There were even drawers and drawers of aberrations, and these were what made his collection so famous: butterflies with too much or too little black or orange in their wings, butterflies with mutant markings which made them different from their peers. And there were the beautiful Swallowtails which were only found in Norfolk. Hyslop smiled to herself as she remembered Zak pretending to have found one. There was the dear little Glanville Fritillary, found only on the Isle of Wight, and called after the first ever female lepidopterist, Eleanor Glanville. Now that *would* be something. To have a butterfly called by one's own name!

"In one way it could seem cruel, I suppose," she mused aloud. "All these butterflies killed and pinned. But then again, in the days before decent photography, how else could they be studied? This is a scientific record."

"Yes, it's only stupid, misinformed tree-huggers who grumble about how cruel this collection is!" snarled Sir Northcote. "They don't understand its importance. Dunderheids! It's a collection for posterity, for science. Some of these butterflies are extinct in Britain now. Many of them are one-offs. We need records like this. If we keep killing off butterfly habitats, they'll *all* be gone. We could lose them all!"

Hyslop recognised that he was about to rant. A vein was standing out on his neck, his eyes were flashing, and she knew he was getting angry. He was going to start shouting about habitats in a minute. When he mentioned tree-huggers a rant was always imminent. Quite who these people were who hugged trees was a mystery to Hyslop, but they certainly annoyed the old man.

"I know habitat is essential," she burst in, to deflect him. "It's the most important thing of all. I mean, I know I've found *my* habitat here."

This did stop him from ranting. He stared at her, his mouth slightly open. His teeth were not very nice, but at least it was better than his shouting and swearing.

"It's the place where I feel I belong," said Hyslop. The words tumbled out of her mouth, and only once they were out did she see how true they were: she had not thought that being happy was a possibility for her until she had come to Hemmingswood. "Here, with the butterflies and you and Sandy and Penny, is the first place I've been happy since my Nonna died. I think it's *my* natural habitat."

"Your Nonna?"

"She was my Italian grandmother," said Hyslop. "All my early memories are of being with her and being safe." She paused, and for a long time there was silence, which the old man did not disturb by even the slightest slapping of his head. Hyslop sighed. "She died, my Nonna. They said the angels took her, or it may have been the Virgin Mary. I'm not sure. If you're not a Catholic, Northy, you probably don't believe in all that. I'd like to believe in it, and I sometimes talk to her, and say my Ave Maria and my prayers, but my mother says that religion and God and going to heaven are a load of rubbish. I don't know what you feel about that." The old man still said nothing, and Hyslop continued. "Anyway, after Nonna died my mother came into my life. And lots of Uncles. Uncles I didn't like. I wasn't happy, and now I understand the reason for that: I wasn't in my proper habitat."

Hyslop gave a shudder as she remembered some of the really bad habitats of the past. The old man gave a strange snort and Hyslop looked up at him.

"We all need to find our natural habitat, don't we, Northy?"

"Who were the Uncles?" asked Sir Nothcote, watching her closely. Hyslop knew that all those people who said he was losing his marbles were wrong. He had a very sharp mind. The marbles sometimes got a bit muddled up but they were all there. He was clenching and unclenching his fists, and then he slapped his head really hard. "You don't mean real Uncles, as in relations, do you?"

This was dangerous territory as her mother had forbidden her to talk about their life in Italy, and she knew that she was certainly not allowed to mention the Uncles.

"Um, I do have one real Uncle Carlo. He never liked me much and I didn't like him. I haven't seen him since Nonna died. Most of the others were sort of… well, sort of *friends*," she said vaguely. "Friends of my mother's anyway."

"Very close friends I'd imagine!" the old man slapped his head again, and glared round the room. "Dunderheids!"

Hyslop smiled to hear the Uncles described by his funny word, but decided she should change the subject again.

"I'm interested in how your grandfather killed the butterflies," she said, peering closely at a Scottish form of the Dark Green Fritillary. "I mean you'd have to be careful not to damage their wings. It must be quite difficult to do properly."

For a while the old man was tense and angry looking, then he relaxed his shoulders.

"Yes," he said. "You have to be very careful. There are various ways, but I use a net and then cyanide. You can't beat an old fashioned cyanide killing jar. I don't want you anywhere near that, though. If you broke the glass the cyanide could be deadly. It's not done much nowadays but it's the method I prefer."

Hyslop looked up, startled by his use of the present tense.

"Do you mean you still have a killing jar?" she asked, frowning. "You surely don't kill butterflies nowadays?"

"I don't make a habit of it!" snapped Sir Northcote. "As you know, I try to preserve butterflies, not kill them. Don't get stupid on me!"

"I'm not being stupid, I'm trying to understand," said Hyslop. "Surely the collection of British butterflies is complete. You don't have to keep adding to it, do you?"

"Did I say it was complete!" he shouted. "DID I?"

"Well, no," admitted Hyslop. She wished he wouldn't shout so much. "You didn't actually *say* it was complete, Northy. I guess you're always on the look-out for aberrations. Ones that are different."

"Oh yes, but not just aberrations. There's one last drawer at the bottom," he said, slyly. "Bring it over."

"I checked that already," said Hyslop. "There's nothing in it."

"Bring it over I said."

"Well, I'll bring it over, but… "

"Just bring it!"

Hyslop replaced the last drawer they had been looking at and fetched the very bottom drawer from the British Butterfly Cabinet.

"See! There's nothing in this one," she said, laying it down for him to see.

"Well, I know that," he said softly. "I've known it these last seventy years."

He was looking at her in a very odd way, as if she had missed something obvious, and Hyslop screwed up her eyes and peered again at the empty tray.

"There's just a tiny label," she said. "It's hard to read."

"It's the one species missing from the collection," said the old man. "A species I've been searching for all my life. I'm surprised, Miss Future Lepidopterist Miss Smarty Boots Hyslop, that you haven't fathomed it out."

Hyslop peered at the faded writing on the label.

"Nymph… Nymphalis Antiopa," she read aloud. She stared over at Sir Northcote.

"Of course. The Camberwell Beauty."

It was a butterfly she remembered as coming straight after the Purple Emperor in her book, an exquisite dark butterfly with cream borders on its wings. She recalled reading that the early collectors of butterflies had regarded it as something of a Holy Grail. It was a great rarity, sometimes never seen for years and years in Britain. Lepidopterists all over the country would rush around with cameras and binoculars on even the vaguest rumour of a sighting.

"Yes, Hyslop!" he nodded at her, his eyes shining. She thought he was going to clap his hands he looked so pleased. "Nymphalis Antiopa. Sometimes known as The Camberwell Beauty. Or The Grand Surprise. Or The Mourning Cloak. Call it what you like, my grandfather and I spent years looking for one to complete the collection. I promised him I would get one before I died. And I have not succeeded."

"Well, you're not dead yet."

"I've been searching all my life," he said, his voice quieter than she'd ever heard it. "And I've failed to get one for him. I've failed to complete his British collection."

"But surely… " she frowned. "Surely you must have seen one in all that time!"

"Oh, I've seen them dozens of time abroad," he said, a slapping movement starting up and his voice rising. "Of course I have! But it doesn't count. I have to get a British specimen – one that I find in the British countryside. This collection has to be honest. You can't lie about butterflies."

Hyslop nodded, as she recalled having said something similar to Zak.

"I guess not. You've never found one here in Britain?" she repeated. "In all that time!"

"I think I did see one once," he said. "It was in Kent, in the hot summer of 1976. It flew past so quickly I couldn't be sure. I didn't have my killing jar with me anyway. I was visiting my cousin. We were sitting having a gin and tonic in his garden. He was partial to a few gins before dinner was my late cousin, Southwold, and it suddenly appeared before me. It just *appeared*." He might have been talking about a visitation from the Virgin Mary his tone was so full of awe. "And then it disappeared again."

He stared into the distance and Hyslop imagined the elusive black butterfly soaring past him, out of sight.

"How frustrating!" she said. "Still, at least you saw one."

He came out of his reverie and stared intensely at her.

"The collection has to be completed, Hyslop," he said. "I owe it to my grandfather. Every year I have lived in the hope of seeing one, of capturing one and placing it beside that old label that he wrote. There always seemed to be plenty of time. Each year I hoped for a Camberwell Beauty Summer but it just never happened. And now time isn't so plentiful any more. Not for me."

"Do you mean you think you might die soon?" asked Hyslop. Northy had said one should always be honest about butterflies, but she did wonder if her question was perhaps a little too honest.

"That can't be far off," he said, nodding. "At my age there's no point in pretending otherwise. But before I go, that ghastly son-in-law of mine, Hugo, will cart me off to a fate worse than death, my dear. He's desperate to shove me in a nursing home. A nursing home, I ask you!" He ended on a bellow of rage, and repeated with an even louder shout that made the walls shake: "A NURSING HOME!"

"You don't seem to need much nursing," said Hyslop.

This made the old man wheeze, which she now knew was his strange way of laughing. Wheezing turned to cackling and violent head-slapping.

"You're right," he said. "I don't need nursing." There was a pause, and they both waited for the word to pop out : "Dunderheids!"

"Do you want me to help you?" asked Hyslop. She decided that this was perhaps what he was leading up to. She wanted to make it easier for him before his shouting and head-slapping got out of hand. "Do you want me to promise to try and get one for you if you die before you find one? Or before you're carted off to the dreaded nursing home? Like a sort of secret mission! A sacred quest!"

"Yes, Hyslop," he said, hand poised to slap his head. "Yes, that's exactly what I want you to do. You must be the guardian of the collection and make sure it is completed. That is indeed your mission."

CHAPTER TWENTY TWO

Zak is also given a Mission

For once Hyslop caught Zak unawares. He was poring over a courgette plant in Mrs Braithwaite's vegetable garden. He knew he should be weeding or hoeing, but he wanted to see how each individual courgette had grown since his last visit. They seemed to sneak to double their size in the night, and it was always amazing how many large ones would suddenly appear at once. As a shadow fell over him, he jumped up, thinking it was his father come to scold him for idleness.

He felt a strange sensation surge through his whole body when he realised it was the girl Hyslop. If he had known how to name it he might have called it joy.

"Oh, you've been in there a while, haven't you!" he exclaimed, before he thought what he was saying. "Whole hours and hours!"

Of course he realised he shouldn't have said anything the minute the words were out. That was always the problem with words. The wrong ones came out and caused trouble. It was too late: he had betrayed the fact that he knew where she had been and for how long.

"Where have I been then for hours and hours, Zak?" asked Hyslop softly.

"I... eh... I don't know," he said, looking back down at the courgettes.

There was a silence. They were both good at silences. Some people had to fill in and say something just to end a silence, but he knew that he and Hyslop weren't like that. On the other hand, if he distracted her by mentioning a butterfly, maybe she would forget about the question she was asking him.

"There's a Cabbage White," he took the opportunity to point out a white butterfly with black tips on its wings. "Cause a lot of damage, don't they?"

"As I told you before, it's a Large White," she said. Those eyes were boring into him again. "Where is it you think I've been? For whole hours and hours?"

Zak wondered what it was best to do. She had told him not to lie about butterflies, and that if he did she wouldn't let him follow her or spend time with her again. Did she mean that he was not to lie to her at all, about anything? It went against all he had learned in life so far. Lying was what you had to do so as not to get into trouble. It was what you had to do to keep people from getting angry or suspicious or nasty. His feelings for the girl Hyslop were so strong, however, that some deeper instinct made him decide that it was best to be truthful with her. Even if she was angry with him afterwards, he would tell her how he knew where she had been.

"I followed you," he mumbled. "I followed you this morning and I watched you go into the old man's house."

He did not dare meet her eyes.

"Well done, Zak," she said. "You told me the truth."

When he looked up, he found that she was no longer looking at him, but had opened her precious book again. She seemed to carry it around with her everywhere.

Her words echoed round and round in his head. She had said : "Well done." She had used his name. She did not seem to be worried about what he had said, and had just returned to her book with no sign of anger or irritation. It was as if he had been holding his breath underwater and had surfaced and was able to breathe again. He had been truthful and it had been the right thing to do. Telling the truth to his father or grandmother was not a good thing. If they asked what he had been up to he could never tell the truth and say that he had been sitting looking at plants for a whole hour. There would be trouble if he did. He always had to lie and say he had been weeding, or going on an errand for Mrs Braithwaite. It was the same at school.

If Miss Carradine asked why he had not done his homework, it was best not to tell the truth and say that he didn't want to do it because it was boring, or because he didn't understand it. Instead he had to pretend to have done it but left it at home, or say that his grandmother had been ill and he was looking after her. That was always a good one. Adults felt sorry for him because his mother had died, so if he pretended that Granny was ill there would be a sympathetic nod and no more said on the subject. With the girl Hyslop, however, none of the normal rules applied. She had not questioned him on why he was following her; she just seemed pleased that he had not lied.

After a while she turned the book round and showed him a picture of a dark butterfly, almost the black-red colour of her hair, with blue spots and creamy yellow at the edges of its wings.

"I want you to look at this," she said. "Look at it *very* carefully."

Zak humbly took the book from her and looked at the picture.

"Have you ever seen this butterfly before?" she asked. Her tone had an edge of warning: "Think before you speak, Zak."

Zak shook his head.

"No, never one like that," he said.

"Well, I didn't think you would have done," she said. "The last one of those seen anywhere near here was in 2006. Do you know what it is?"

Zak looked at the name under the butterfly picture and his mouth tried to form the long words. He desperately did not want her to know how poor his reading skills were.

"It's a Camberwell Beauty," said Hyslop, coming to his rescue. "Nymphalis Antiopa. Sometimes called a Mourning Cloak because that's kind of what it looks like."

"Oh," he said.

"I want you to look at that picture really hard, Zak," she said. "I want you to memorise that butterfly. And I want you to look out for it in the woods and garden and the fields around here."

Zak stared intently at the picture. He almost felt his eyes burning with the intensity of his looking.

"It's a very important insect," she said. "It's very rare, and doesn't often come to our country, but Northy wants me to look out for one."

Zak was astonished to hear her call the old man Northy, but he said nothing, and kept his eyes on the picture of the butterfly. He did not want to forget a single detail.

"If you ever find one, you must come and get me at once," she continued. "It doesn't matter where I am. Just come and find me."

He looked into her eyes and felt slightly dizzy.

"If you find one," she said, "if you can get one for me, you will make me very happy, Zak."

Her face creased into a smile. It was a quick smile, it hardly lasted a second or two, but he had caught some of its magic, and it almost made him drop the butterfly book. He closed his eyes for a moment and tried to imagine how bright her smile would be if he could find a Camberwell Beauty for her. He could hardly breathe.

"I'll look out for it," he whispered. "I'll look every day for the Beauty."

CHAPTER TWENTY THREE

Moths on the Patio

When her mother sent her to bed at a strangely early hour, Hyslop did not mind at all. Vanessa had been to the supermarket for once, but had bought nothing very substantial for supper. Bags of crisps and nuts lay unopened on the kitchen table, waiting to be decanted into little bowls, and the fridge was full of wine. Clearly she was expecting someone. Hyslop decided that one bag of salted peanuts wouldn't be missed and she sneaked it upstairs with her.

She lay on her bed with the window open, her book propped up against her knees, and the bag of peanuts beside her. They were deliciously satisfying even if they did make her fingers salty and greasy, and she was hungry as usual. Carefully she opened the pages of her book with a handkerchief, so as not to mark them.

It was no surprise this time when she heard Hugo's voice downstairs and his loud "Darling!"

She hummed to herself and opened her book at the section about the butterfly she had been told to look out for: "The Camberwell Beauty is one of the most spectacular butterflies to be seen in the British countryside, and one that has always elicited great excitement… "

As the voices and laughter downstairs drifted out onto the patio, Hyslop hummed even more loudly and continued reading: "British specimens came to be regarded as the greatest of all prizes among early dealers and collectors… " The words in the book and her tuneless humming blocked out the laughter from outside. Hyslop closed her eyes and tried to lose herself in a fantasy of finding a Camberwell Beauty for the old man. The trouble was that finding the butterfly, near impossible as that would be, was only the first stage. She would somehow have to get near enough to it to catch it without damaging it. It would be sad, quite unbearable, to capture such a rare and special creature and then have to kill it. She was not sure she could do such a thing, even for the precious collection. Northy would have to teach her about killing with his cyanide jar. Part of her was curious about how it worked, yet she still recoiled at the thought of the deed itself. She wondered if a net was needed too. The main point for those early collectors was not to damage the wings. It was such an extraordinary mission to have been given, a privilege of course, but also a heavy obligation. There was no point in worrying about it too much, she decided, as it was scarcely likely to happen. If Sir Northcote and his Victorian grandfather had failed in two lifetimes of searching, probably with servants helping, it was unlikely that a small girl, who had only just discovered the joys of butterflies, would succeed.

Sometimes in an indistinct background murmur, a phrase or a sentence stands out.

"And of course I have a flat in London," she heard Hugo's voice say clearly. Hyslop stopped humming and put the book down, listening despite herself. "A very beautiful flat in Chelsea."

"I have missed London all these years," she heard her mother say. Hyslop knew that this was a lie. Her mother had been born in London, in a poor part of the city, somewhere south of the river Thames and had always tried to forget her roots, and reinvent herself in French or German or Spanish or Italian. Hyslop turned her bedside lamp off and mouthed the word: "Liar" into the darkness.

"Come to the flat," Hugo's voice was thick with emotion. Hyslop screwed her face up in disgust as she imagined him closing in on her mother and getting ready to kiss her. "Come and stay there, Vanessa!"

There would be a declaration of love next. Hyslop closed her book and made her way over to the window.

Her mother and Hugo were standing very close together. There were little bowls of nuts and crisps on the table and a bottle of wine. There were candles everywhere too, which flickered and danced. Her mother was barefoot as she usually was on the patio, which made her seem even tinier beside the huge bulk of Hugo.

Hyslop looked out into the darkness beyond the patio, distracted by a movement in the distance. Was someone else out there?

Her mother's voice was low and difficult to make out, but Hugo's voice carried more clearly and she could make out snippets: "… life here is meaningless… " "… been like this for years… " "… life is short, no point in wasting time… " "… I *know* you feel the same way too, I know you do… "

"You know nothing, Mr Hugo Braithwaite," whispered Hyslop softly. The man was mistaken if he thought he knew what Vanessa felt about anything.

Whatever her mother felt, however, the whole thing was going to end in an embrace. Once again, Hyslop was distracted by a movement in the shadows beyond the patio. Surely it wasn't that boy Zak Judd again. Did he watch her and follow her around at night too? He would not be able to see her standing in her darkened room. Or could it be the old man out looking at his moth traps?

Hyslop had a strange sense that she wasn't the only one watching the couple on the patio, and she put her hand on the glass of the dark window pane. A dark coloured moth appeared almost at once, climbing up the window on the other side of the glass. Sir Northcote had a moth collection too, which he had promised to show her one day, after she had done more field work on butterflies. He had given her a moth book, beautifully illustrated like her butterfly book, but she had only flicked through it.

"I don't know your name, moth," she whispered. "But one day I will."

As she looked on, a fawn coloured moth appeared and walked up her hand on the other side of the glass, soon joined by a stripey brown one. Hyslop kept her hand there and watched them in fascination.

"My goodness, what on earth was that?" she heard her mother's voice, and saw the couple on the patio spring apart. "There's something in my hair! Aaah, is it a bat!"

"No, it's all right," Hugo said. "It's only a moth. God, there are two or three of them! Hold still, I'll swat them away."

"Moths!" cried Vanessa. "I don't think so. They're squeaking at me!"

"I've never seen the wretched things behave like this," Hugo was swiping at the moths in Vanessa's hair, but as he did so several more descended around his own head. His swearing and cursing were worse than anything Sir Northcote had ever said, even in one of his more noisy outbursts.

Hyslop watched without expression as more large brown moths circled ever closer round her mother and Hugo. He was batting vainly at a dozen fluttering creatures with his hands, but the more he did so the more it seemed to attract others.

"I've never seen so many!" cried Vanessa. "It's disgusting! Let's go inside."

"The ghastly things have probably been encouraged by my idiot of a father-in-law!" Hugo was surrounded by moths now. "Good God! You're right, we can't stay out here. Let's get back inside!"

With hands flapping and swatting at the myriad wings, Hugo and Vanessa ran indoors, slamming the patio doors behind them.

Hyslop stared out into the night, her eyes scanning the dark horizon. She took her hand from the window pane and nodded.

CHAPTER TWENTY FOUR

Coil Pots and a Disloyal Thought

Hyslop left the cottage before her mother was awake. All was quiet downstairs, though some of the lights had been left on, and the crumpled body of a dead moth lay on the bottom stair. She was not sure if Hugo had stayed the night and she didn't want to find out. She peeped in at the kitchen at the bowls of nuts, the two empty bottles and the wine glasses and decided that she didn't fancy hanging around for breakfast. A nasty smell of alcohol and cigarette smoke lingered. There were disadvantages in not having maids after all. At least in Italy, at horrid Uncle Massimo's house, Carla would have tidied up the previous night's wine glasses and mess, and would have some fresh bread and jam ready for Hyslop.

Today she was going to spend the day with her Godmother, just the two of them in the pottery. It looked as if it was going to pour with rain at any moment, so Hyslop knew she would not be missing seeing any important butterflies. She did not care if Zak Judd was following her or not, and did not bother to look out for him. If he wanted to lurk in bushes spying on her then he was going to get very wet. Besides, she had given him an important mission, and had nothing else to say to him for the moment.

The two Bernese Mountain Dogs, Sasha and Skye, came bounding out to greet her as she approached Sandy's house. Any worries and fears about Hugo and her mother were dispelled at once as she buried her face in the dogs' soft black fur, and enjoyed the boisterous pawing and licking that followed.

"Sorry, Hyslop!" called Sandy, though she was beaming proudly at the excited dogs. "Come on, girls! Let poor Hyslop come in!"

Hyslop asked if the dogs had been walked.

"They've had their early morning run round the woods," said Sandy, "so they'll be fine for a few hours. I thought we could have a session together, finishing that coil pot you began last time, then we could take them for another walk if you like. Looks like rain at the moment, but I'm hoping it will be fine later in the day. I'm not sure what time your Mum wants you back?"

It amused Hyslop to hear Vanessa called "your Mum" and the implication that there was a set time that she was wanted back home was equally bizarre.

"No particular time," she said. "I'm on my own today."

"Good," Sandy rubbed her hands. "I've got a delicious picnic lunch for us to have, indoors if necessary. I'm not much of a cook," she laughed, "not like Penny and Ilga, but I do pack a mean picnic!"

Hyslop assumed that a "mean" picnic was actually a good picnic. It must be some sort of English slang.

"If it's really wet, we'll just eat our picnic here. I've got some brioches to keep us going until then," said Sandy, producing a packet. Hyslop eyed them hungrily but said nothing. Instinctively she knew that Sandy was aware of how little food Vanessa provided.

Sure enough, once they were settled in to the pottery, four brioches were placed on a plate beside Hyslop with no further comment and Sandy merely nibbled at a dry biscuit at the other side of the table. A tall glass of lemonade was also supplied.

"OK, let's leave the throwing until you're a bit more used to working with clay," Sandy said. Such a statement made Hyslop feel flutterings of happiness, as it implied an unlimited number of future visits. "You can paint that little coil pot you began last time," Sandy tossed the ragged old shirt at her. "Pop this on, sweetie. And when you've painted pot number one you can start making number two. With pottery, as I explained, there are so many stages that you're always in the middle of various different things at once."

Sandy supplied Hyslop with a set of tiny ceramic tiles, each painted with a different glaze, for her to choose a colour. There was no point in looking at the colours in their jars as they came out quite differently when they were fired. There was a dark green one which Hyslop liked. It would match the green tiles on the little fireplace in her bedroom.

"That clay there is fine for you to do your next coil pot with," said Sandy, picking up a huge lump of clay and placing it on a wooden board next to Hyslop. "I'm going to have to prepare mine though."

Hyslop watched in fascination as Sandy kneaded her clay as if it were dough. It brought back distant childhood memories of Nonna making pizza, lifting and kneading the floury dough with her gnarled old hands. Hyslop closed her eyes at the sudden sharpness of the memory. She realised that she wasn't having to conjure up Nonna when she was with Sandy or Northy. In fact, she felt guilty at how little she was thinking of her life with Nonna now that she was in England.

"It's like making bread," said Sandy. "Have you ever watched your Mum make bread?"

"No," said Hyslop. The mere thought of her mother's long painted fingernails in either clay or dough was too extraordinary to contemplate.

Sandy threw her head back and laughed: "No, I guess that was a stupid question. Even if you did hit hard times in Italy, I don't suppose Vanessa would get round to bread-making! I bet her smile would charm the last loaf out of the local baker!"

Hyslop frowned, as she remembered the letter she had written to Sandy, explaining how poor they were in Italy. It was still not clear to her why her mother had made her write such a pack of lies, but she knew she had to be careful what she said.

"Was it really awful in your little cottage with no electricity?" was Sandy's next question, and Hyslop decided it was time to change the subject. It was all right to tell things to the old man as everyone thought he was mad, but it was more dangerous to confide in Sandy, as she was, after all, her mother's old friend.

She shrugged and mumbled about how you can get used to anything after a while.

"Why do spell your name Xandi?" she asked, hoping to deflect attention away from life in Italy. Also, it was something she was genuinely curious about.

Sandy looked pleased that Hyslop had asked a question.

"Ah, yes," she said, her eyes twinkling. "Well, it goes back to when I was at school, Hyslop. I guess that's why your mother thought I still wrote my name with that silly spelling. I used to think it was very artistic and a bit different I suppose. Xandi with an X – it was meant to look mysterious. I told people that my name began with a kiss. Frankly, it was just me being pretentious! Me being young!" Sandy laughed at the memory, and Hyslop realised that she was laughing at herself, which was a strange thing for an adult to do. "Your Mum used to be called Nessie then, but I don't think anyone calls her that now."

"No," Hyslop shook her head. She had never heard her mother called anything other than Vanessa. It was amazing what she was learning from Sandy, though. For the first time in her life, she was encountering someone from her mother's distant past, someone who knew exactly how old Vanessa was, and who didn't know all the different cover stories in various languages that she spun around her whenever they moved.

"Yes, that's a good shade of green," Sandy seemed to approve her choice of glaze.

"It's going to match the fireplace in my bedroom," said Hyslop. "Then I'd like to make one for Malcolm. He lets me look up butterflies on his laptop, so I want to make a coil pot for his pencils. He says he's always losing them."

"For Malcolm, eh?" said Sandy. "Well, he *will* be honoured."

"Don't tell him, though," said Hyslop. "I want it to be a secret."

"Your secret's safe with me," said Sandy. "But what about your mother? Don't you think she might like one?"

"No," said Hyslop in a matter of fact tone. "She wouldn't."

"Maybe for her make-up brushes?" said Sandy, and Hyslop detected a mischievous glint in her eye as she said it.

"She doesn't like my stuff much," said Hyslop, and she watched the twinkliness disappear from Sandy's face. "I know some mothers like their children's artwork and stick their pictures on their fridges and walls, but my drawings and craftwork used to always get torn up, so I don't show her anything I make now."

Hyslop felt a perverse pleasure in giving glimpses to Sandy of how her life with Vanessa really was. She was still not talking about any of the taboo subjects, so technically she was not disobeying her mother's commands.

"I see," said Sandy after a while.

They both worked in silence after that. Hyslop painted her first coil pot, and Sandy finished kneading her clay then took it over to the blue contraption which was called the throwing wheel.

"Well, I was going to make you and Vanessa a mug each," said Sandy, "but from what you say about your mother's fine taste," she paused, and the laughter returned to her eyes, "I don't think she'll appreciate a ceramic mug. So I shall just make one for you instead. Now do you want a big fat round one, or a tall narrow one?"

"I should like a fat round one, like yours," said Hyslop at once. "And what colour will it be?"

"You choose from the glazes," said Sandy. "I can even put a little butterfly on it if you like."

Hyslop felt a fluttering zig zag of happiness, and with it came another emotion, a thought that she knew she ought to banish, but somehow couldn't, a thought that could only be whispered deep deep inside her: how happy her life could be if only Sandy were her mother instead of her Godmother.

Her face must have betrayed something of the turmoil of emotions she was feeling, as Sandy looked concerned.

"It's all right, Hyslop," she said. "I won't do a silly butterfly. I'll make it as accurate as I can. I know how important they are to you."

Hyslop looked up earnestly: "Thank you, Sandy," she said. "I can't stand it when people make butterflies all pink and glittery and silly. It takes away their dignity I think!"

Sandy burst out laughing. "Oh, Hyslop," she said. "No wonder Uncle Northy has taken such a shine to you. Now don't you worry, I shall do my best to preserve the dignity of butterflies at all times."

Normally Hyslop hated adults laughing at her, but with Sandy it was different. It was the kind of laughter that drew you in, like a big fat hug, not the kind of laughter that pushed you away and mocked you.

"I'm happy here with you, Sandy," she thought. "So happy that I don't want to move away again. Ever."

CHAPTER TWENTY FIVE

Clouded Yellows and a Slap

Hyslop sat curled up on the tiny sofa in the front room of the cottage, reading her butterfly book. She was getting to know it as well as her beloved Narnia book. Her mother was out having drinks with Penny and Sandy and Ilga, having what she called a "girlie" evening, though none of them were exactly girls any more. It probably just involved sitting around a table drinking large amounts of wine.

The pictures in her book were glorious. They showed details of both upperwings and underwings of all the British butterflies, and also enlarged drawings of many of the eggs, caterpillars and chrysalises. Her fingers traced the lines of each butterfly as she turned the pages, and she sat muttering Latin names aloud like magical incantations. She loved the book so much she rarely let it out of her sight. During the night it was by her bed so that at any moment she could reach out and touch its comforting hard cover.

She mused on the number of butterflies with regal names: the Purple Emperor, the Duke of Burgundy, the Queen of Spain Fritillary, the Monarch. She wondered if they had been given these names because people were so awed by their beauty. Even the Painted Lady and the Red Admiral sounded like characters from a Victorian drawing room. Sometimes Hyslop would study the book seriously as if studying for an exam. She stored up information about their wing patterns, their life cycles and their food-plants, so that she would never appear as ignorant as she had on that first day in the garden when she had not known what a Brimstone was. It was much more rewarding than doing well in a class test when she impressed Sir Northcote. He didn't give praise easily but she would know when she had astonished and delighted him with a detail or a Latin name. The ultimate reward would be his strange wheezing chuckle, or a gruff "Who's a Miss Smarty Boots then?"

At other times she just read the stories in the book for pleasure. There was an amazing account of a nineteenth century vicar who had witnessed the arrival of a great yellow patch out at sea, which turned out to be composed of thousands of Clouded Yellow butterflies flying from Europe towards the cliffs of Cornwall, just skimming over the waves. Hyslop groaned with longing. What an incredible sight that must have been. She closed her eyes and pictured the wonder of it. How could such fragile little creatures brave the storms of the open sea to come to England?

Her concentration was interrupted by the sound of a door slamming. She whirled round.

"Hello, daughter!" said Vanessa from the doorway. She had been drinking, and her face was pinker than normal. Hyslop was wary: the normal rules of gauging her mother's moods did not apply when Vanessa had been drinking. She wished she had had the sense to be safely upstairs in her room.

"Reading about insects, are we?" Vanessa's mouth turned up in a sneer. Hyslop said nothing. It was best not to antagonise her mother when she was like this, and saying anything at all could prove dangerous.

"Got quite in with the old man I hear," said Vanessa, teetering over in her high shoes to where Hyslop was sitting. "As well as Sandy and Penny. They talked about you the whole night long! Thank God Ilga was there to talk about more interesting topics. Otherwise I'd have been bored to death." She narrowed her eyes at her daughter. "Quite a little manipulator, aren't you? Do you think you've got them all wrapped round your little finger with this butterfly rubbish?"

Hyslop remained silent.

"Well, you could answer me when I ask you a question!" said Vanessa, her tone turning from sarcasm to anger.

"What was the question?" said Hyslop as blandly as she could.

"I think you know quite well what I said." Vanessa was seeking confrontation, which was the very thing Hyslop wanted to avoid. Slowly, not meeting her mother's eyes, she stood up. She wanted to be upstairs on her own.

"All this insect rubbish!" cried Vanessa. "How is it going to help you make your way in life, eh?"

Again Hyslop said nothing. She closed her book gently and kept her eyes lowered.

"Where do you think I'd be if I'd spent my life looking at *insects*!" Vanessa was working herself up into an even angrier state, and specks of spittle flew from her lips. "In the gutter, that's where, Hyslop! In the gutter *with* the nasty little creepy crawlies."

Hyslop stood still as a statue.

"All these nice things you have," said Vanessa, "all these nice people fawning over you. It's all thanks to me! *Me* and no one else. Just remember that."

She kicked off her shoes and threw her expensive Italian handbag onto a chair.

"You think you're little Miss Popular round here, don't you?" she continued. "With Sandy and Penny and the old man. And some of the others." She put her hands on her hips and glared at Hyslop. "Think you've found a little paradise here, do you, where you can manipulate people!"

"I'm not trying to manipulate anybody," said Hyslop in a neutral tone.

"Oh, really! Well, you're wasting your time anyway. It's Hugo that calls the shots round here, I can tell you!" Her mother pointed a wavering red-tipped finger at her. "The others don't matter in the slightest!"

"They matter to me," said Hyslop, tucking her book under her arm and walking towards the stairs.

"Don't you walk out when I'm talking to you!" hissed Vanessa.

"What is it you want?" asked Hyslop.

"What is it I want? I want you to show me some respect, that's what!" Her mother's face was not so beautiful when it was pinched into its drunken snarl. Hyslop wondered if Hugo would be attracted to her if he could see her like this. "RESPECT! That's what I want, Hyslop. Not too much to ask from my own daughter, is it! Mmmmm! How much fun do you think it is for me, having to work on new people all the time? Eh! You have no idea, do you! No idea of how much work, how much *hard* work I have to do to keep you in luxury, so that you can sit around and read about stupid butterflies!"

"No, I don't think sitting around talking to people and drinking wine is hard work," said Hyslop quietly. The words seemed to fly out of her mouth by themselves, and for a moment neither of them could quite believe they had been said. The silence was like the moment after the lightning flash, waiting for the thunder to start. As Vanessa took in their full import, she made a hissing sound, then leaned forward and slapped Hyslop hard across her face. She snatched the butterfly book from her daughter's grasp and hurled it with all her might across the room, so that it smashed into the glass doors leading out onto the patio, and flopped onto the floor.

"You ungrateful little witch!" she shouted.

Hyslop put her hand to her cheek and felt the heat from it. It felt as if it had been set on fire. Without a word, she walked over to the where the book lay upside down and broken-looking, and picked it up. The damage was not as great as she had feared : the spine of the book was slightly damaged, but it was still in one piece. The cover had half come off, and there was a tiny tear in it now. Hyslop carefully replaced it.

For a moment mother and daughter stood and surveyed each other. Vanessa's eyes were still flashing and her cheeks were flushed with anger and alcohol. Hyslop's face was devoid of any expression at all.

Eventually, with a curse, her mother stomped off to her bedroom and Hyslop heard her crashing around noisily.

Hyslop went upstairs and lay on her bed, examining her book for any more damage. She smoothed the covers which were marked and crumpled. It would never be quite the same again.

Tunelessly humming to herself, Hyslop turned back to the page where she had been reading about the Clouded Yellows. She put a hand to her cheek, and her humming grew louder as she read on: "… immigrant butterflies often arrive in mint condition, having perhaps flown hundreds of kilometres… It is when butterflies pursue, court, or reject mates among tangled vegetation, or when females scrabble around for egg-laying sites, that the scales fly, and the butterflies lose the pristine appearance of the new arrivals."

CHAPTER TWENTY SIX

Zak Gets Some Good News

Zak had been kept in for most of the morning by his grandmother who made him mow their tiny back lawn and clean the car, whilst she kept up a constant background chorus of scolding and criticism. The jobs themselves wouldn't be so bad if she would just leave him alone, but she had to stand near him, pointing out how he was too slow, not thorough enough, or doing something wrong. There was nothing he did that merited praise. Her only form of praise was temporary silence. Zak kept himself focused on the task at hand, and tried to pretend that he was deaf.

Every so often a phrase would penetrate his efforts at not hearing: "Wait till your father sees the way you've cut that bleedin' lawn!" "A dog's hind leg would be straighter than those lines!" "Put some elbow grease into your polishing, boy!"

He tried several times to finish, but each time his grandmother's critical inspections made him redo a bit here, polish a bit more there, until he was red in the face and hot. He did not attempt to answer her back, though. It was never worth it, and it would only result in his grandmother shouting and getting mad at him. That would mean more time wasted when he could be watching Hyslop.

Finally, after he had obediently done whatever she asked without answering back for nearly two hours, he declared that he needed a cold drink.

"Well, it'll have to be tap water," she said, waggling a gnarled old finger at him. "And you can get it yourself, Zachary. I'm not one of them mugs who spends hard earned cash on fizzy drinks and expensive fruit juices. Load of old rubbish! If you're properly thirsty, then water will do. When I was young, there was none of this cans of this and bottles of that. We had to make do… "

She was suddenly distracted by the telephone ringing, and went indoors, grumbling but still keen to see who it was. Zak decided to forget about the tap water and set off for the Braithwaites' estate as fast as he could. When the phone rang in the morning it was often someone who happened to be in their area trying to sell windows or kitchens, and these people always made his grandmother cross. She would return to him to regale him with a word by word account of what she had said, and what the man had said, and then what she had said in return. He had no desire to hang around to listen. In any case, he would be able to get a drink of water from the tap near the greenhouse.

He ran as quickly as he could, and in a short time he found himself at his usual destination: the vegetable garden. He glanced around but there was no sign of anyone, and he drank some water straight from under the greenhouse tap.

On such a hot day, the girl Hyslop could just about be anywhere. There were butterflies flying, so she would probably be out with her book. She could be in the main garden, in the fields or in the woods. Zak tried to place himself in the mind of a butterfly. Where would he go on such a hot day if he had wings to fly?

He frowned at the effort. It wasn't at all easy, because of course different butterflies went to different places. Here in the vegetable garden there were lots of white butterflies that the girl Hyslop told him shouldn't be called Cabbage Whites, but he did anyway. Over the bramble patches in the woods were the brown ones with the spots, and in the fields there were lots of chequered black and white ones. She had seen all of those many times, though. What he needed to do was to get himself into the mind of that red-black butterfly she wanted to see, the special one that she had told him to look out for.

Zak couldn't remember the first part of its name, but he knew it was some sort of Beauty. He couldn't recall ever having seen a black butterfly, so he didn't know where to look. It probably didn't like to eat cabbages and nasturtium leaves so the vegetable patch wasn't the best place. The trouble was, what *did* it like to eat? If it was that easy to find, surely Hyslop and the old man would have found it by now.

He remembered Hyslop saying that some butterflies weren't even born in England, but flew from across the sea, and he suspected that The Beauty was one of those. None had been seen for years apparently, so there really was little chance of seeing one. He kicked a stone in frustration and then stooped to pick a weed from the edge of the lettuce row. There was so much chickweed that it made little difference just plucking out one random plant but it meant that he could now say, with some degree of honesty, that he done a bit of weeding. His father and grandmother always wanted him to account for his time. They wanted to know what he had done in the whole hours he was on his own. It puzzled him sometimes. He had no interest in knowing what *they* had done when he wasn't around. Why couldn't people just leave other people alone?

Such thoughts did not apply of course when it came to Hyslop. He would always be interested to know what she had been doing in the whole hours of the day or night, when he wasn't with her. He closed his eyes and pictured the girl Hyslop's shiny red-black hair and her oil-black eyes. He had never felt such a longing to see anyone before in his life. The hours and minutes away from her felt like time wasted.

When Zak opened his eyes he saw a black butterfly. For a moment he did not react, then, oddly enough, his legs reacted before his mind understood why and he began to run. It was a large dark-winged butterfly and not like any he had ever seen before. The brief glimpses he had of its wings seemed to show the creamy yellow borders he remembered from Hyslop's book. Could this really be The Beauty? Zak ran faster than he had ever run before, even when being chased by Tristan Pringle's gang.

It dipped and soared, and sometimes did little circles in the air, always just too far ahead of him. He could never see it properly to ascertain if it was the butterfly in the book, but he could see it shining purply black in the sun. For a moment it landed on a plant just a few yards in front but when he ran towards it, as if to tease him, it flew off and then soared high up towards the trees and away. He lost sight of it altogether, and wondered whether to head off for the woods after it.

"Hello, Zak." Suddenly the girl Hyslop was there ahead of him.

"I saw it!" he cried, slightly out of breath, his eyes shining. "I saw the Beauty! It was here a minute ago!"

Hyslop frowned.

"I'm not lying," said Zak, as he could see what she was thinking. "I'm not. Honest."

She looked right at him with her spooky eyes.

"No," she said. "I can see that you are not telling a deliberate lie." How on earth could she see that, he wondered. "But I think that you are probably mistaken. Where was it?"

He felt a little stab of happiness like a physical pain. She had believed him.

"It flew over there, towards the woods," he said. "I can show you."

They fell into step together and walked for some time in silence.

A fluttering dark butterfly appeared suddenly from behind a tall hedgerow.

"Ah!" cried Zak. "Look, there! Is that it?"

"No," said Hyslop. "That's a Red Admiral."

Sure enough, the butterfly stopped and landed on a nettle just beside them and he could see that it was a familiar red and black one that he had often seen before.

"Oh," he said. "No, that's not what I saw earlier."

"It can be hard to tell what they are when they're flying," said Hyslop.

Zak was puzzled. He had been so sure earlier that he had seen the Beauty, but now he began to have doubts. They were tricky things, these butterflies. How were you meant to memorise all their different wing patterns, and what they looked like when they were flying? It was too much information to hold in your head at once. This red and black one, however, this Red Admiral, was certainly one he had often seen before. Perhaps he had imagined The Beauty because he wanted to see it so much.

For some time they gazed at the butterfly together. Hyslop seemed entranced by it, and Zak sneaked little sidelong glances at Hyslop who was much more interesting than any insect could ever be.

"By the way," she said after a while. "I have checked with Sir Northcote and he says it's all right if you come on the Emperor trip with us."

She looked at him again, and her eyes almost seemed to be laughing at him. Zak found himself unable to speak.

"That is if you want to come," she added.

"Yes," he said quickly. "Yes, I want to come."

CHAPTER TWENTY SEVEN

Hugo meets a Hornet

"Oh, Sands, I think I get worse every week!" Penny turned a rather wonky looking bowl round and round in her hands. "Not sure it's worth painting this one."

Sandy raised her eyebrows and smiled: "I've seen worse, Pen."

Hyslop liked it best in the pottery when she had Sandy to herself, but at least Ilga wasn't there, and neither, thankfully, was her mother. Penny was having her weekly pottery class, but said she would have to rush off soon. Penny tried hard to be friendly, but there was something reserved, something held back, that Hyslop recognised only too well. Penny gave little snippets of herself to others, and kept most of herself private, and this Hyslop suspected was because she was unhappy inside. All her bright smiles and jolly comments could not conceal it from one who was used to concealing her own emotions. Hyslop also felt uncomfortable in Penny's presence because she knew that her mother was plotting something underhand with Hugo, perhaps marking him out as a future Uncle, and that did not bode well for either Hyslop or Penny.

It was difficult, therefore, to meet Penny's eyes and accept her friendly overtures.

Sandy's open nature was laid before all of them like a butterfly with wings outspread in the sunshine. Sandy may have had troubles in her life, but she did not seem weighed down by secret sadness. Hyslop felt sure that Sandy could just get up in the morning, stretch out her arms and be herself, not fearful of displeasing people, not to blame for someone else's violent mood swings. Hyslop longed for such freedom, to fly away from the constrictions of her mother's control. Yet, how was such a state to be achieved? Vanessa was never going to change.

"You OK, Hyslop?" Sandy plonked a glass of lemonade and a little plate with some chocolate squares on it in front of Hyslop.

"You have to try some of Penny's wonderful chocolate tiffin. I only allow myself one piece or I'll explode out of my jeans, but you're a growing girl, so do eat it up on behalf of all of us. Have it now before you get clay over your hands."

Hyslop, hungry as usual, took her first piece. It was chocolatey, crunchy, biscuity, buttery, sugary and slightly salty all at once. She glanced down at the three remaining pieces on the plate and felt a shiver of delight. The only question was whether another three pieces were going to be enough.

"Mmmmm," she said, the tiffin giving her courage to look Penny in the eye. "This is the best thing I've *ever* tasted."

"Oh, Hyslop," said Penny with her sad smile. "I shall make you some to take home next time."

As Sandy and Penny fell into conversation, Hyslop took her second piece. She knew by now that with no Vanessa around, there would be no criticism of her table manners or comments about greediness and chocolate giving you spots, and there would be no problem if she made crumbs. The second piece was just as heavenly as the first. She decided that it was sometimes good to feel really hungry as things tasted so wonderful when your tummy was rumbling and empty.

Penny beamed over at her as she took her third piece.

"How lovely to see a good healthy appetite!" she said. Hyslop felt a slight pang of guilt, as she wondered if Penny would be so pleased with her appetite if she knew that her mother and Hugo were seeing each other in the evenings. She assumed that Penny didn't know anything about it, but then again, adults were so complicated that you never knew what was normal and what was not in their world.

Sandy brought out the first completed coil pot, the dark green one that Hyslop had made for her bedroom, and also the biscuit fired one, destined to be Malcolm's pencil pot, which she was to paint. Hyslop surveyed them both with delight.

As she decided that even she could not manage a fourth piece of tiffin without a pause, she heard Penny sigh: "Ilga seems to have given up our little pottery class, Sands. What's she up to today?"

"I hardly see her," said Sandy. "She always seems to be driving Nessie around somewhere these days. Today though I think she's with a client in London. Some rich banker's wife who wants to change her whole kitchen though it's only two years old and I don't think the woman ever cooks anyway!"

Penny laughed. The three of them settled down into a quiet and peaceful rhythm of shaping clay, painting clay or occasionally commenting on what the others were doing with their clay.

"If you want a really deep shade of blue with that glaze you've chosen," Sandy bent over Hyslop's pot, "you'll have to give it lots and lots of coats. Lay it on as thickly as you can."

Hyslop felt pleasantly full of chocolate tiffin, and enjoyed painting the coil pot for Malcolm. When Penny had to leave early, she even felt sorry to see her go.

"Thanks again for the tiffin, Penny," she called after her.

She and Sandy looked over the table at each other, and Hyslop felt a connection between them, an invisible silken thread. Neither of them said anything, but Hyslop was sure that Sandy felt it too.

For some time they worked in companionable silence and for Hyslop this feeling of connection, of being with an adult who was not going to find fault or sneer, an adult who was, moreover, a sort of relation, made her feel warm inside. If only she could stay forever with these safe, kindly people who fed her delicious food, and never got cross with anything she said or did.

"I'm going on a trip with Northy," she informed Sandy. "We're going to Bernwood Forest."

"Ah, the Forest of the Emperor," said Sandy. "Yes, dear Uncle Northy – he took me there with my father when I was about your age. My father and Uncle Northy were best friends. Daddy and I weren't really that interested in butterflies, I am ashamed to admit, but even we found the Purple Emperor rather special. We went a few times without seeing any, but when we finally saw one it was well worth the wait."

"Is your father dead now?" asked Hyslop. She liked hearing about other people's families.

"Sadly both my parents are dead," said Sandy. "I was very close to both of them, but especially close to my father. When I was left on my own, and frankly feeling pretty sorry for myself, not coping at all, Uncle Northy suggested I come and live here near him and Penny. He encouraged me to set up my pottery. It was something I had only dabbled in beforehand."

"He likes to encourage people, doesn't he?"

"Well, yes, if he thinks they've got a talent, he does." Sandy nodded. "I had no confidence in my work until I started here. He made me believe I could make a living as a potter. And he encourages you, Hyslop, because I know he thinks you could be a proper lepidopterist."

"Did he really say that?"

"Hi Sandy!" a voice boomed into the room as the door burst open.

Hyslop jumped in her seat and frowned as she saw that it was Hugo. What could *he* possibly want?

"Why, Hugo!" said Sandy. "This *is* an honour. I don't know when you last visited my humble pottery!"

"Looks like you're busy," said Hugo, though he was not looking at Sandy at all, but round the room as if he was searching for something. Or someone.

"Are you looking for Penny?" asked Sandy. "She left about half an hour ago."

"Umm… no," said Hugo. "No, I was actually looking for Vanessa." He paused. "Bit of… um… business stuff to discuss with her. Do you know where she is, Hyslop?"

Hyslop scowled and said nothing. Hugo had never addressed her directly before.

"Hyslop's been here for the last hour or so," said Sandy hurriedly. "But I think Vanessa was going in to the village last I heard. She had to go to the Post Office to post a few bits and pieces, and to sort out new passport forms or something."

"Oh," said Hugo. "When was that?"

"Well, I'm not sure," said Sandy, looking at Hyslop who was now hunched over her coil pot, and pointedly not looking at Hugo at all. "But I know she went on foot because Ilga's busy today and my car's being serviced. So if you took the car into the village you might catch up with her."

"Excellent!" Tension disappeared from Hugo's face and he smiled happily. "Well, enjoy your potting, you two!"

He turned to go and as the door closed behind him he gave a sudden yelp.

"What the devil was that!" they heard him shout, and this was followed by some rather nasty swear words. Much worse than Northy, Hyslop noted.

"Hugo!" Sandy rose to her feet as Hugo burst back into the room, rubbing his arm. "What happened? Are you all right?"

"Of course I'm not all right!" Hugo was staring down at his forearm, looking furious. "I've been stung by a ruddy great wasp. In fact it was bigger than a wasp. The biggest I've ever seen. It was a hornet, I'm sure of it. Probably a queen hornet!"

"Probably not," murmured Hyslop.

"I've got some stuff you can rub on it, hang on a sec," and Sandy rushed to the other side of the room and began rifling through a drawer. "I know there's a tube somewhere. Now, are you sure it was a wasp and not a bee?"

"Hurry up, could you! I'm in absolute *excruciating* agony! As I said, it was a hornet – a *huge* great thing!'"

Sandy raised her eyebrows to Hyslop but said nothing. She found a small tube of some sort of salve and took it over to Hugo.

"Here, let me put a blob on it," she said. "Now rub it on gently."

"D'you have a nest of them near here or something?" Hugo sounded accusing as well as angry, as he rubbed the white ointment onto his arm. "Oww! It still hurts. The pain's getting worse by the minute. I'd have thought we had enough insects round here without people encouraging wasps and hornets to build nests. I'm going to put a stop to all these vermin around the place, I'm telling you, Sandy, whether any of you like it or not!"

With that, and with a string of swear words, still rubbing his arm, he stormed off.

"Pardon me, Hugo," said Sandy, addressing the door which Hugo had just banged behind him. "Well, of course I breed them here on purpose just to sting you!"

Hyslop looked up, and to her surprise her Godmother winked at her and they both returned to their work.

CHAPTER TWENTY EIGHT

Zak Finds that Happiness Can Have a Nasty Smell

When Zak Judd woke up on that hot morning in late July he felt at once that something was different.

His first instinct was to spring up from his bed and be ready to defend himself, but then he decided it might be safer to play dead until he had worked out what it was that was different. He opened his eyes very slowly. There was a knack to doing this. It was important to ascertain first of all that no one was watching, so he peered through the bottom tenths of his eyelids, giving sleepy breathing noises to pretend he was still asleep. They were not very good sleepy noises. They were rather exaggerated, a sort of imitation of his father's snores after several pints of beer. He was not sure why he did this, but he felt that it was safer to feign sleep until he knew what was happening. All seemed to be safe on this occasion: he opened his eyes fully and no one was there. His messy room with its peeling flowery wallpaper looked the same as always. There was the damp patch on his ceiling still in the shape of a whale. There was the broken chair in the corner, and the cardboard boxes for his clean and dirty clothes. He wondered if he just felt this way because it was the summer holidays and there was no school for weeks ahead. Or perhaps it was because so far neither his grandmother nor his father had burst into his room to shout at him.

All of these were good things, but not enough to explain why he felt slightly dizzy and strange. It wasn't in a bad way. He didn't feel dizzy as if he was going to be sick. Zak sat up in bed to see if that would help him fathom it out. The light was streaming in through the gap in his curtains but it was the middle of summer so it might still be quite early. He had no clock in his room and wasn't good at telling the time anyway. There was no sound of his grandmother crashing around downstairs, so it was probably before seven.

Suddenly the strange feeling became clear, because he realised that it was the opposite of when he felt scared about the day ahead. Most days were bad, but some days were particularly scary, like when his father had been drinking heavily, or when he was cornered by Tristan Pringle and his gang. Some days when there were too many chores to do, and he knew he was going to be bullied at school, he would wake up feeling tired of the day before it even began. He would want to curl up in his bed and just stay there. Today, however, he had woken up early and wanted the day to begin at once. The strange sensation he was feeling was *looking forward to something*. He had heard other kids at school use that expression: looking forward to something meant that they were excited about a day out or a treat they were going to get. Those kids in his class were always getting treats and they were always looking forward. Zak had tried to understand their feelings. Perhaps it was as if you were on a path, heading through the woods, and you knew that just ahead of you, just out of sight through the trees, someone had left you a wonderful present and it would be sitting there waiting for you, all shiny and wrapped up with your name on it. His grandmother, on the other hand, seemed to be always looking *back* to something. She preferred looking back to where she'd come from, rather than forward to the road ahead. Her whole conversation seemed to consist of how much better things had been in the past, before his father met his mother, before he was born. Especially before he was born. She must have had nice presents left in her path then, and now they were all too far away in the past for her to ever get back to them, and there was nothing much ahead of her any more. No wonder she was always in a bad mood. No one had ever left stuff out on the path ahead of Zak before, nothing worth rushing to get to, but today there *was* something good, something waiting for him just ahead.

Today he was going to see The Emperor.

He was going to be with the girl Hyslop *all* day.

His father often drove the old man around in the ancient Mercedes that Zak had to help polish. Now there was a job he hated. However hard you scrubbed and rubbed and dusted, it was never enough. There was usually a smack from his father at some point. Only once had Zak accompanied his father and Sir Northcote on an outing. It had not been a happy occasion. Zak had spent most of it staring miserably out of the car window. No one spoke much, apart from the old man shouting his strange word in the funny accent, and swearing all the time. His father and his grandmother said swear-words too, though never in front of the folks at the big house. They cursed and said the bad words in a different way from the old man, like when they were angry at something or someone, usually him. Zak knew that if he swore like the old man did, his father would smack him one. Maybe the old man had been too posh to have been smacked or told off when he was a kid and no one had told him it was bad to shout swear words. Maybe he just didn't know. Or maybe if you were posh and rich you could say whatever you liked and it wasn't considered rude.

Today, however, and this was the shiny, exciting thing just ahead on Zak's path, the girl Hyslop was going on the trip, and she had said that he could join them. The girl Hyslop was ahead of him and behind him too. She was everywhere: she *was* his path. He could look back and comfort himself with thoughts of the smiles she had given him, with memories of her spooky eyes and her wonderful hair. He could relive the best bits of her telling him about butterflies, even when she used big words that he did not understand. He could look forward to smiles in the future. Today they were driving to a wood a whole hour away and they were going to look for The Emperor. Perhaps the Beauty would turn up too, and he would be the first to see it. Oh, how Hyslop would smile at him then. All sorts of wonderful possibilities lay ahead of him, mysterious parcels wrapped up and strewn on the path, things he could look forward to.

Zak jumped out of bed. His dirty clothes lay on the floor all around him. He looked in one of the cardboard boxes and found one clean T-shirt, and put it on. He even thought about having a shower, but then decided that you didn't need a shower if you were wearing a clean T-shirt. Anyway, his grandmother would be suspicious if she heard him in the noisy shower that was always more cold than hot. She might discover that he was keen to go on this trip, looking forward to something, and then she would stop him.

The thought of his grandmother finding chores for him to do that would prevent him from accompanying Hyslop on the Emperor trip was terrifying. Zak put his jeans and his dirty old trainers on and crept out of his room. No one was stirring and he decided it must be really early. The birds were singing in a very early morning kind of way and the lazy butterflies were not up and about. He found a packet of biscuits on the kitchen unit with two biscuits in it and stuffed it in his pocket. It was best to get outside as quickly as he could. He would hide until his father appeared and then join him once they were out of sight of his grandmother.

He sat on a tree stump some distance from their cottage, and munched the biscuits. They were rather stale and he ate them because he was hungry rather than for enjoyment. He had no idea how much time passed, because time was difficult to measure. The woods were full of birdsong from all different sorts of birds. The birds didn't need to be able to tell the time, and they got along fine. He sat staring into space, thinking of the day ahead, thinking mainly of the girl Hyslop, until he heard the cottage door opening and his grandmother calling his name. She sounded cross as usual. He stayed out of sight, pouring the last crumbs from the packet into his hand and eating them all up. She was going to be mad at him for taking the biscuits so he was certainly not going to show himself. Luckily she never ventured outside in her dressing gown, so she was unlikely to come looking for him. He imagined the swearing and cursing that would be going on inside the cottage.

After some time his father came out of the door, slamming it behind him, and walked swiftly along the path in Zak's direction. Zak stuffed the empty biscuit packet into his pocket.

"What you doing here?" his father scowled at him. "Didn't you hear your granny calling?"

"Got up early so I'd be ready to go with you," said Zak.

His father narrowed his eyes suspiciously.

"She's got jobs for you to do," he said.

Zak said nothing. He looked up pleadingly. He knew that his grandmother had been angry with his father for drinking too much beer the night before, and there had been raised voices, so things could go either way for Zak. Sometimes his father took his side against his grandmother, and sometimes he shouted at him to do what he was told when she gave him orders.

"Oh, let the old witch do 'em herself." His father thrust a polythene bag at Zak. "Here, take that if you're coming."

Zak realised he was not being sent back. He hurried along carrying the bag, having to run to keep up with his father's long strides. It was not long before he became aware that the polythene bag smelt very unpleasant.

"What's in here?" he asked, hoping it wasn't lunch. It smelt revolting.

When his father told him, Zak almost dropped the bag. He screwed up his nose and swore aloud.

"Why are we carrying dog… " His father gave him a sharp cuff on the side of his head.

"Don't you call it that!" he said angrily. "Not in front of the old man and that foreign girl. Posh folk don't use words like that." His father paused, as they both contemplated the fact that the old man did, in fact, shout swear words, and that Mr Braithwaite often cursed in his posh voice too. "You're to call it dog poo. That's the word that lot use."

"Dog poo," said Zak obediently. He would have called it anything in order to be able to tag along.

He wanted to ask why they were carrying a bag of dog dirt with them. It was just as smelly whatever name you called it.

His father, however, was in his morning-after-drinking mood so it was best not to ask irritating questions. He decided to do as he was told, though he kept the bag as far away from his body as he could. In his looking forward to the outing, Zak had not anticipated a smelly bag of dog's doings, but it did not spoil his feelings of hope. He was sure that the other things ahead of him on his path were better, and he looked forward, and kept looking forward, as he ran after his father.

CHAPTER TWENTY NINE

Journey to the Forest of the Emperor

Hyslop got up, as usual, before her mother. It was not difficult as Vanessa did not generally emerge before eleven, and she was careful not to make any noise as she crept downstairs. Two wine glasses and an empty bottle of red wine showed that Hugo had been to visit the previous night. She opened the fridge and the larder but there was nothing much to eat. There were three bottles of wine, two bottles of champagne and a little pot of olives. There was a carton of milk but when Hyslop took the top off to have a sniff, it smelt sour. Vanessa drank her coffee black, so rarely thought to buy fresh milk. Although Hyslop was not fond of olives, she took two or three and grimaced as she swallowed them. Adults did eat some funny things, or at least her mother did. There was also Penny's jam but no bread to spread it on. She wished she could eat at Sandy's house. She closed her eyes and imagined the delicious treats that there would be in Sandy's big white fridge, and the bread bin full of fresh bread and croissants.

As she passed the vegetable garden it occurred to her that she could pinch some tomatoes from the greenhouse. They were not as good as the glorious fat tomatoes in Italy, but they were sweet enough to take away the taste of bitter olives. She ate several and they helped fill up the empty feeling inside her. She felt slightly guilty at eating Penny's tomatoes, but then she decided that they were also Hugo's tomatoes, and this thought made her eat two more in defiant succession.

As she reached Sir Northcote's house, the Mercedes was coming along the road slowly towards his gate. Zak's father, Jack Judd, was driving. He was a surly looking man, but Hyslop decided that she would ignore him as much as possible. She did not want anything to distract her from the joyous day ahead, the day when she might be seeing a Purple Emperor. She strode up to Sir Northcote's front door and knocked his lion's head doorknocker loudly.

She heard some muffled shouting from inside, then the old man opened the door, his wispy hair standing on end, his eyes staring wildly. Hyslop was used to his expressions by now, and half expected the glare to be followed by head-slapping and cursing. He was a bit like a dog which barked furiously at visitors but was really quite harmless when you got to know him.

"You're here, are you!" he said. He started to say his funny word then stopped.

"I'm really looking forward to today," she said. For a moment Sir Northcote looked so wild eyed and strange she wondered if he remembered about their outing. Then she saw him slap his head once and nod at her.

"Has Judd brought the car round?" he demanded. At that moment the car stopped in front of his gate and he turned his glare towards it instead. "There he is. Jolly good!"

The old man disappeared into his house and emerged, to Hyslop's joy, carrying what looked like a picnic basket. In fact he seemed to be laden down with all sorts of interesting things.

"Can I help carry something?" she asked, hoping he would let her take the picnic basket and she could have a peep inside.

"You can carry these," he said, handing her some binoculars. He seemed to be carrying two pairs. "In fact, you can keep them. They're close focus binoculars for butterfly spotting. I have several pairs and I don't need all of them. No one else will want them!"

Hyslop gasped as she realised that the binoculars were a gift.

"Northy!" she cried, taking them in delight. "Oh my goodness! Thank you!"

"Well, if you're serious about becoming a lepidopterist," he raised his voice to its customary shout, "*serious*, and not playing the fool, you'll need them!"

Hyslop took off the lens caps and focused the binoculars on a nearby shrub. The old man showed her how to adjust them and at once the leaves of the shrub became so clear and defined she could see every detail, every vein, every blemish.

"You'll need those for spotting the Emperor," he said. "They're often high up in the trees." He gave his head a hard slap. "Dunderheids!" he added.

At this point Judd approached, muttering something that sounded vaguely like "Sinothctt," and the old man barked "Judd!" back at him.

Zak appeared behind his father and Sir Northcote scowled.

"Is the boy coming?" he shouted. "Hmmm! That boy!"

"Not if you don't want him, sir," said Judd.

Hyslop saw the light go out of Zak's eyes. He opened his mouth to say something, then closed it again, giving Hyslop an anguished look. She had so often had her own hopes crushed and stamped on by her mother, and she knew what he must be feeling.

"I said he could come," she said, with authority in her voice. "We will need an extra pair of hands to carry stuff. There's the picnic basket and the binoculars, and you will need your walking stick, Northy. And... "

"And there's the dog... poo!" interrupted Zak, producing from behind his back a rather nasty looking plastic bag.

"You brought that, did you!" cried Sir Northcote. He narrowed his eyes at Zak, his tone accusing and angry.

"I thought that I had to... that I was supposed to... "

"All right, boy!" shouted the old man. "Just keep it away from the picnic basket, could you!" He slapped his head several times and shouted "Dunderheids!" at the top of his voice in a particularly Scottish accent.

Hyslop realised that Northy was about to start a head-slapping rant, that Judd would stand stupidly in one place until given an order to move, and that Zak, awkwardly holding his smelly burden, was looking at her and only her. She took charge of the situation at once, organising where things should go in the boot of the car. She picked up the picnic hamper and looked inside. There was food enough for all of them, delicious treats that no doubt Penny had prepared. Zak's smelly bag was strapped to the roof rack. She told Northy to get into the front of the car, checked that he had his safety belt on, and instructed Judd to get into the driver's side, ascertaining that he knew exactly where they were going. It was an extraordinary feeling to be in charge. Sir Northcote, despite his noisy ranting, was quite happy to be organised; Judd would follow orders without comment; and as for Zak, well, he would do whatever she told him to do.

She sat in the back of the car with Zak and allowed him to stare at her for the duration of the journey. Sir Northcote's hearing was not good enough to allow for conversation from the front of the car, so, apart from his random mutterings and swear words, there was no real communication between any of them until they got to the Forest of the Emperor.

CHAPTER THIRTY

The Perfect Day

For three out of the party of four, the day of the Emperor was a perfect day.

The exception was Judd, who announced that he would stay and look after the car, which meant of course that he fell asleep in the sun with his mouth open, shedding his hangover with every snore. No one consulted his opinion, but he surely would not have counted this day as particularly interesting or eventful if he had been asked. In later life, he would not be able to remember it at all.

In later life, Hyslop would see more amazing and more numerous butterfly species, and Sir Northcote had, in the course of his long life, seen more amazing and more numerous butterfly species on many occasions. The butterflies on this day, however, were unspoiled by the tragedy that was to come. Locked forever in a memory of high summer sunshine and birdsong, they were pure and brave and beautiful. Meadow species, nymphalids and blues danced in the sun above the grassy clearings in their hundreds. Even Sir Northcote was astonished at their numbers. Red Admirals and Painted Ladies bustled about everywhere, and high in the treetops Hyslop was treated for the first time to a spectacular display of aerial acrobatics by White Admirals. She picked them out with her new binoculars, and gasped with joy at their soaring and swooping. They were the most graceful gliders of the butterfly world. There were Silver-washed Fritillaries too, their underwings water-colour-washed with green and silver, zig zagging amongst the brambles.

Bernwood Forest itself, one of the loveliest butterfly woods in the country, was majestic and ancient, a forest fit for an Emperor.

One would not have been surprised to see an eccentric Victorian collector with net and killing jar emerge from the forest. One would scarcely have been startled, indeed, to have encountered a prehistoric caveman. The trees were tall, many of them twisted and gnarled with age, and they exhaled dignity and history with every rustle of their leaves. This was not a forest where man was in charge, chopping and felling and pruning: this was a forest where nature ruled.

"What a beautiful, beautiful place!" exclaimed Hyslop. "Oh, look at the trees, Northy!"

Sir Northcote, moved by Hyslop's joy, was strangely quiet. He barely muttered or cursed or slapped himself the whole day long. His voice was gentler than normal too, as if someone had turned his volume down. Occasionally he would point out a path they might take, or a tree that might be good for Purple Emperors, but sometimes Hyslop took the lead. When she stopped to stare, they all stopped. Some little way behind Zak followed, still carrying his smelly burden.

"The White Admirals are amazing fliers, aren't they?" Hyslop was peering through her new binoculars at a pair high up in the trees. "They just seem to belong here somehow. It's hard to imagine them as caterpillars, crawling around, when they were clearly designed to be such stars up in the air."

"Oh yes," agreed the old man. "Beautiful flyers. Nothing like them for gliding. We're getting quite an air display today. Never seen so many out and about. Now the Silver-washed Fritillaries can glide too, but they're more bouncy." He seemed about to shout a swear word but stopped. "Bouncy like Tigger I always think."

Hyslop frowned and put her head on one side to consider this.

"I never think of tigers as particularly bouncy creatures," she said.

"Not tigers!" Northy raised his voice slightly. "I said Tigger!"

"What do you mean 'Tigger'?"

"Goodness me. Surely you know who Tigger is! Don't you read, Hyslop!"

"I like reading very much," said Hyslop, "but I don't know who this Tigger character is."

"Didn't your mother ever read to you?" he said. Then he stopped and shook his head. "No, I don't suppose she did. I just thought all English children would know Winnie the Pooh!"

"Well, I'm half Italian and I've never heard of her," said Hyslop.

"No, it's not a her," said Sir Northcote. "Winnie the Pooh is a bear. A bear of little brain. I shall find my old books for you when we get back. You have to read them. I bet even *you*, boy, have heard of Winnie the Pooh!"

He glared back at Zak. The boy looked startled at being addressed, but shook his head in a puzzled way.

"Never heard of Winnie the Pooh!" the old man shouted again. "*Neither* of you! What is the world coming to nowadays!"

Zak had no idea what was expected of him. Clearly there was a bear, a stupid bear if he had understood correctly, that he was meant to have known about. He knew what poo was now, and he wrinkled his nose at the thought of what was in his plastic bag, but thought it rather an odd name for a bear, even a stupid one. Zak sighed. The world was full of unfathomable mysteries.

He trailed behind them, enjoying the effects of the sunlight on Hyslop's wonderful hair. She was so preoccupied with butterflies, and with gazing through her new binoculars, that she was unaware of anything else. He could look and look for as long as he wanted.

"You're still with us, boy, are you?" the old man said, after a while. "Get the dog dirt out of the bag, would you and put it on the ground over there."

Zak humbly did as he was told. Hyslop could see that he was baffled by the task, and, taking pity on him, she explained to him that the Purple Emperors they were seeking were attracted to dog and fox droppings.

"They love a rotting carcass too," said Sir Northcote. "and some people bring banana skins and Stilton cheese but I've never found them much use. I do have some fish paste in my pocket, though.

Here, boy, spread some of that over there on the grass too. It's all a matter of luck and patience I'm afraid."

"For such beautiful creatures they do have an odd taste in food," laughed Hyslop.

Zak said nothing at all. His unpleasant task was lightened by the sound of the girl Hyslop laughing. It was better than all the birdsong of the forest.

They waited by the dog droppings for some time, and Hyslop scanned the treetops constantly with her binoculars. There was no sign of the elusive Emperors anywhere. The sun was beating down on them now almost as strongly as an Italian sun, but there were no visitors to the revolting feast apart from some flies.

"Shall we break for some lunch," said Hyslop at last. She said it as a brisk command, not as a question. "I'm pretty hungry."

"May as well," said the old man. "Though I'm never hungry these days. Old age takes the appetite away. Penny has packed a fair old picnic as usual. You young 'uns can eat up. Far too skinny, the pair of you."

"Zak, here, I have some hand-wipes for us to wash our hands before we eat." Hyslop handed some to Zak and took charge of the hamper.

Zak was thrilled at being included in the picnic, and he ate wonderful sandwiches and home-made cakes and biscuits that were better than anything he had ever eaten before. It wasn't stuff that had been bought in packets at the supermarket. It wasn't like anything his grandmother ever produced. The best part of it all, of course, was sharing with the girl Hyslop. She would hand him a sandwich or a cake and treat him as if he were her equal, her friend: "Try this, Zak, it's pastrami and cucumber on rye bread I think." He wanted it all to go on forever. He wanted to make time, whole hours of time, stand still. He was speechless with happiness.

"Oh well, it's been a lovely day, Northy," sighed Hyslop, when she was too full to eat another morsel. "Even if we haven't seen any Purple Emperors, we have seen so many other species. Such huge numbers and such fresh specimens. And those White Admirals! It's really been the best day of my life. I feel like a proper lepidopterist."

Sir Northcote made a happy snorting noise that turned into a wheeze.

On the way back to the car he pointed out a Marbled White with more black than usual in its wings, and they all stopped to admire three basking Small Tortoiseshells on the path in front of them. At least Hyslop and Sir Northcote did, and Zak, as usual, stopped to admire Hyslop.

As they approached the car, where Judd lay snoring on the driver's seat, with the door open, Sir Northcote suddenly hissed at them all to stop.

"There!" he shouted, spittle flying from his mouth. He pointed his stick at the car in a state of agitation.

Hyslop was puzzled. Surely they could all see the car. It was exactly where they had left it.

"There!" he shouted, pointing at the wing mirror on the passenger side of their car. "It's an Emperor!"

"It's just my Dad," said Zak.

"Oh!" Hyslop suddenly realised what Northy was pointing at. There, settled on the car mirror, was a large butterfly with the unmistakeable underwings she had memorised. It was a Purple Emperor. She got her binoculars out and gazed with greedy joy at its beautiful markings.

"Can we go closer?" she said, after many minutes of looking and looking.

"Yes, it won't mind," said Sir Northcote, with a tenderness in his voice that astonished Zak so much he forgot to stare at Hyslop, and stared at the old man instead. "They are attracted to shiny silver things sometimes. I've seen this happen once before."

This was the joy of butterfly watching, unlike bird-watching. You didn't have to be quiet, or observe from a hide. Unless you let your shadow fall on the butterfly, most of them would stay where they were and allow themselves to be looked at. In this case, scarcely daring to breathe, Hyslop was able to stand a few feet from the glorious insect and study its markings for a full ten minutes. Then, very slowly, the butterfly opened his wings and the sun caught the beautiful purple sheen on first one side, then the other as he moved around the wing mirror. Even Zak stood staring at the lovely creature, as if hypnotised. It was like the picture in Hyslop's book: one wing was black and white and the other purple and white. It was a trick of the light, and it kept changing.

"Hey, look at his wings!" he said, pointing at the butterfly. "He's a fine one!"

Sir Northcote and Hyslop turned to look at him. The old man nodded at him approvingly.

"Yes, Zak," said Hyslop, smiling at him. "Yes, he's very fine."

Zak knew that even if he had nothing to look forward to on his path of life ever again, he would have this moment, this shared joy in the Emperor, the acknowledgement from the posh old man, this smile from Hyslop, the way she used his name, this incredible moment, to look back on. Looking forward was a difficult business as people could take things away that were lying on the path ahead, but no one, not his grandmother at her angriest, his father at his drunkest, or Tristan Pringle at his nastiest, no one could ever take this moment away from him.

The Purple Emperor stretched his wings and flew away.

CHAPTER THIRTY ONE

A Discovery on the Internet

Hyslop had given up expecting breakfast in the cottage. She had given up expecting anything much from her mother, and it was always easier in life when you expected nothing. It was easier to take your hunger elsewhere, and she found she was always hungry. She had an excuse to go and see Sandy because there was a new firing from the pottery kiln this morning and the coil pot Hyslop had made for Malcolm was ready to pick up. She was hopeful of getting something to eat there as well as a smiling welcome. There had been no supper the night before. Her mother, dressed up and with the shiny high heels that meant she was going out, had left, saying she was off to London, and had not returned home all night.

When Sandy saw her approaching out of her window she opened the door and let the dogs out.

"Brace yourself, Hyslop!" she called as the dogs bounded towards her and enveloped her in a boisterous excited welcome. "I was just about to feed them, but you can do that if you like. You're a bit earlier than I'd expected, so why don't we have some breakfast here first?"

"Oh, well, if you're sure that's OK," said Hyslop. She knew it was polite to look hesitant and surprised when you were offered food, so she tried to do so.

Hyslop fed the two dogs. They seemed to be as hungry as she was, and she watched them wolf down their food as if they were having a race to finish. She turned round to see Sandy putting two croissants on a plate for her, then adding a third.

"D'you want some butter or jam or both?"

"Both please," said Hyslop, sitting down.

"I'm guessing that Vanessa isn't much of a one for breakfast," said Sandy, bringing a pot of homemade raspberry jam and a butter-dish over to the table. "Is she up yet?"

Hyslop wondered what to say, and also wondered if it was polite to reach for her first croissant immediately or to wait for a moment until Sandy began eating too.

"She seems to live off black coffee and cigarettes," said Sandy. "It keeps her nice and slim, but you're a growing girl, sweetie, so you need your fuel." There was a long pause before Sandy said: "I saw Hugo take her out somewhere last night. Just happened to be driving back and met them pulling out onto the main road in his car. Probably taking her to the station I guess." Sandy stirred her coffee continuously with her spoon, and looked down into the mug, inhaling the steam and the smell. She nodded gravely at Hyslop: "Look, don't feel that you're all on your own if your mother goes out. You know you're always welcome here, Hyslop. Any time. For a meal, to do some pottery, to see the dogs, or just… well… just for a break."

There was a pause, as the word "break" hung in the air between them. For why should Hyslop be in need of a break? Surely it was not normal for a child to need a break from her mother.

"Well, anyway, once you've finished eating we'll go and see my kiln," said Sandy. "It's still exciting for me after all these years to see how the night's firing has gone. As you know, not everything turns out fine."

The coil pot, however, turned out not just fine, but even better than Hyslop's first one. The glaze was a deep blue, the colour of an Italian sky, and she hoped Malcolm would like it.

She left Sandy's with an invitation to return for lunch, which was to be spaghetti with meatballs, followed by maple syrup ice cream, and set off for Malcolm's workshop.

She had visited before to use Malcolm's computer, and she knocked on his door more confidently than she had the first few times. She was starting to get used to calling in on people who were pleased to see her and it was a good feeling. It was a feeling of freedom.

"Come in!" called Malcolm, in a slightly irritated tone.

Hyslop opened his door and stood there, unsure whether to go in. She had learned to identify shades of crossness in adults and although his did not sound like nasty crossness, she wanted to make sure.

"It's me," she said.

"I can see that," said Malcolm. He seemed to be planing a piece of wood. "Hello, Me."

"Are you busy?" said Hyslop.

"It would be a poor show if I wasn't busy, Hyslop," he said. "I'm always busy."

Hyslop still hesitated by the door.

"And I hate being interrupted while I'm busy," he put down his tools and stared at her over his glasses. "Except by certain people."

"Who are those certain people?"

"Well, my list of certain people is pretty short. Today, in fact, there's just the one name on it," he said. "And that's Hyslop d'Agostino. So, if you answer to that name, come in, and if you don't, then close the door behind you on your way out."

Hyslop skipped into his workshop, breathing in the smell of wood and polish and sawdust.

"I've got something for you," she said. "Something for you to put your pencils in."

She handed Malcolm the coil pot and he took it wordlessly, pushing his glasses up his nose to look at it properly. He spent a long time examining it, turning it over and taking in every detail. He held it up to the light and turned it round and round with his rough workman's hands.

"I made it," said Hyslop.

"Well, I liked it a lot before you said that," said Malcolm. He nodded his head at the coil pot, as if addressing it directly. "But now I like it even more."

He gathered up two stubby pencils that were lying on his workbench and put them in the coil pot.

"Perfect fit. Thank you very much, Hyslop," he said. "Well-made, very useful, and much appreciated."

He picked up his plane and began working again. Hyslop watched him in silence.

"I'm guessing you might be wanting to use the computer upstairs," he said after a while. "Miss Hilds and Miss McKenzie are up there sunning themselves. They find me a bit boring when I'm working. Do me a favour and give them some attention when you're up there."

"All right," said Hyslop and went upstairs, up the thin wooden staircase to Malcolm's office above his workshop. That was another good thing round here: adults kept suggesting that she should do things and they were always things she really wanted to do anyway, not things that were hateful or scary, like with the Uncles.

There were the two cats, lying stretched out on a rug below the skylight window, where the sun streamed in. Miss Hilda stood up and arched her back and Miss McKenzie stretched out her paws in front of her in a feline greeting. Hyslop spent a long time stroking them, rubbing them behind their ears, enjoying their gentle purrs as much as she had enjoyed the rough affection of Sasha and Skye.

She alternated between giving the cats her attention and looking at butterflies on the internet. There was so much to learn if she wanted to be a lepidopterist. Sir Northcote told her that he was still learning all the time, so she reckoned it would take about fifty years at least. She looked at various species in turn, reading about where they had been seen recently, and in what numbers. She looked at hundreds of photographs that people had sent in of butterflies they had seen in their gardens.

"Camberwell Beauty" she typed in. She looked at image after image of the fascinating insect. It was a rare visitor to Britain, yet seemed to thrive in colder parts of the world like Scandinavia. It was the official state butterfly of a place called Montana apparently, where it was known as The Mourning Cloak, and often emerged in spring whilst the snow was still on the ground. Now that would be an amazing sight indeed: dark wings fluttering above the white snow. Why did they have to be so rare here in the UK, she wondered.

As she surfed from site to site, greedily devouring information, she came upon a site which gave up-to-date information about Camberwell Beauties in England. To her joy, fingers trembling with excitement on the keyboard, she discovered that there had been a possible sighting in Buckinghamshire the previous week. A dark butterfly had been seen in a suburban garden and there was a fuzzy photograph. This was where she could be useful to Northy. She couldn't wait to tell him!

She stood up and looked out of the window. It was not long before she spotted Zak, some distance off, sitting on a tree stump. He must have followed her. Hyslop yawned. She had no use for him at the moment. She wondered whether to stay with Malcolm for a bit longer, looking at butterflies on his computer, or to head back to Sandy's for spaghetti and ice cream before giving Northy the news about the Camberwell Beauty sightings. There were so many possibilities: different places where she could find a welcome, people who would give her things to eat, kindness and generosity, and freedom to wander. It was like emerging from the darkness into the light.

She raised her arms and stretched, rather in the style of Miss Hilda McKenzie, who was purring beside her with outstretched paws. She almost felt as if she could purr herself.

"… the caterpillars of large blues live like cuckoos inside red ant… nests, eating the ant grubs or… being fed directly… by the worker ants, who are tricked into mistaking the intruder for their own brood… a large blue generally destroys its host ant colony."
(from The Butterflies of Britain and Ireland, by Jeremy Thomas and Richard Lewington)

CHAPTER THIRTY TWO

The Story of the Large Blue

The girl Hyslop had spent what seemed to be a whole hour at the potter's house, then even longer at the furniture maker's workshop. Zak had no idea what she was doing in either place but he was happy to wait for her. He didn't mind when she was in someone's house, in an enclosed place. At least he knew where she was. His great fear, a terrible dread that had begun to grip him, was that she would go away with that mother of hers, somewhere far away like Italy, and not come back. The thought of how empty his life would be, with only the vegetables to console him, was unbearable. With Hyslop around there was always something ahead, something to look forward to every day.

In the meantime, as he sat on the tree-stump waiting, he could look back to the Bernwood Forest trip. He could look back to the magical moment when they had seen the Emperor on the car mirror, when he had exclaimed what a fine butterfly it was, and how Hyslop had used his name, and smiled at him. He closed his eyes to recreate the scene in his mind and that was his mistake. When you closed your eyes, you could be caught out.

"Boy!" It was the cross voice of Sir Northcote. He should have been more vigilant and he could have avoided seeing the grumpy old man. Zak jumped up.

"Your father wants you!" Sir Northcote pointed his stick at him. "You've to help clean the car." The stick came dangerously close to his head and the old man said his funny word along with a few swear words.

There was nothing he could do but obey. Zak took one last

anguished glance back at Malcolm's workshop door then set off slowly, shoulders slumped, towards the trees, on his way to the garage behind the big house where he knew his father would be washing the Mercedes. He kicked a stone in frustration.

"Come back a moment. I need to ask you what you mean by hanging about here anyway?" The old man sounded very cross indeed. "Are you following Hyslop around? Hmm! Are you bothering her, boy!"

"No, Northy, he's not bothering me," Zak whirled round at the sound of Hyslop's voice. She had just come out of Malcolm's workshop. "I'd let him know if he was bothering me. Really, he's fine, so don't worry about me."

The old man said a few more swear words and then his Scottish word, but Zak ignored that. The girl Hyslop had defended him and that was all that mattered. He stopped to look at her, and there she was, the sun behind her making her hair look on fire, all dark and red and golden at the same time. She looked very fine indeed.

"See you, Zak," she said, half raising a hand in a farewell gesture, and Zak's shoulders went back like a soldier's. She had used his name again. He ran off through the trees towards the garage, and knew that he had enough stuff to look back on to keep him going through the car cleaning and beyond. And he could also look forward to seeing her again tomorrow…

"I was looking for you," Sir Northcote pointed his stick at Hyslop now. "I've just seen that ghastly mother of yours outside Keeper's Cottage!"

Hyslop's eyes opened wide. No one had ever been so openly rude about her mother before.

"She had no idea where you were when I asked," he said. "Looked like she'd been out all night. I know what's going on round here, I tell you!" He shook his stick violently. "People think I don't know, but *I* know what's happening!"

His voice grew louder and louder and spittle was flying in every direction, then he turned towards Hyslop, and it softened again: "It's not your fault, Hyslop. Not your fault." Then his eyes glared angrily around him and he looked quite mad again: "Something has to be done about all this! Something *has* to be done!"

"Never mind that for now, Northy," Hyslop decided to try and calm him down. "I was looking for you too. I've found some interesting information on Malcolm's computer about Camberwell Beauties."

"Oh!" He put his stick back on the ground and stared at her.

"Yes," said Hyslop. "There has apparently been a sighting of one in Chesham in south Buckinghamshire. That's not too far from here I think?"

She described what she had learned on-line and the old man listened intently.

"If only I could bag one before I pop my clogs," he said. "My grandfather's collection would be complete and I could rest in peace. You understand that, Hyslop, don't you? You understand the importance of this?"

"Well, I do understand, Northy," she said. "Of course I do, but I also want you to understand that I'd find it hard to kill a Camberwell Beauty even if I was lucky enough to see one. Not sure how it could be done. I don't carry a killing jar around with me. Besides, I want to get into conserving butterflies, not killing them."

"Good girl, that's what I want you to do," said Sir Northcote. "Lots of work to be done on conservation. A life's work if you like. Don't you worry about the killing bit. That sort of thing can be taken care of." He glared around him and headed off towards the trees, slapping his head and muttering "Dunderheids!" over and over again.

"Where are you going?" Hyslop had to run to keep up with him, and she wondered, as she often did, why he needed a walking stick when he could move so quickly.

"May as well head for the orchard," he said. "There may be a nymphalid or two at the rotting fruit."

"You mean, like the Beauty?"

191

"Oh, most probably just lots of Red Admirals," he said, "But come on. I want to tell you a story."

"Is it about butterflies?" asked Hyslop.

"What else?" he snapped. "You've been reading your book, Miss Smarty Boots, so tell me what you know about the Large Blue."

"The Large Blue," said Hyslop. "Mmm. Can't recall its Latin name, but I know that there are two in your grandfather's collection, and that the species went extinct in Britain in 1979."

"That is correct, yes," said Northy. "A disaster. An absolute disaster. Too many silly idiots ran around collecting them even when there were hardly any left."

"I suppose your grandfather must have been hunting them too," said Hyslop.

"Yes, that was in Victorian times," said the old man, pausing to glare at her crossly. "It was for a valuable scientific collection, labelled and studied. He gave lectures to eminent lepidopterists of his day. He didn't endanger species! Not like modern day cretins who want to make pretty pictures with butterflies in their suburban living rooms! Anyway, the problem was more to do with us messing with nature as usual."

Spittle was flying everywhere. He tried, unsuccessfully, to stifle some shouting and cursing and head-slapping, and Hyslop let it all run its course.

"Well," she said after a while. "I read that they re-introduced them to a secret location in the south west of England. All very cloak and dagger at the time but now there are colonies on various sites down there."

"Yes," said Sir Northcote, calming down again. "Yes, they did. The chap who wrote the book I gave you, chap called Thomas, spent years studying them at close hand and they discovered it was all to do with rabbits and ants!"

"Rabbits?" frowned Hyslop. "I think I read that the Large Blue caterpillars are adopted by ants and protected and fed, a bit like a cuckoo in their nest. But where do rabbits come into it?"

"It needs huge numbers of rabbits to graze and keep the grass down to a certain height so that the ground temperature is exactly right for the special type of ant that will adopt the Large Blue caterpillar. Rabbits and sheep." Sir Northcote stopped head slapping and cursing and was able to talk fluently as he only did when he was talking about butterflies. "Man of course messed up as usual, and introduced a vile disease called myxomatosis to keep the rabbit population down. Hideous thing, terribly cruel way to kill the rabbits. So there was not enough grazing, d'you see, to keep the grass down. We changed the livestock grazing so there weren't enough sheep, and killed too many rabbits. So no ants of that special sort, and therefore no Large Blues. It was all part of a cycle, and we interfered with it."

"Well, I suppose even if we humans do interfere with nature," said Hyslop, "we do sometimes try to get it right later. We managed to re-introduce some from Sweden, didn't we? So isn't it sort of a happy ending?"

"There's not always a later, not always a happy ending," growled Sir Northcote. "That is the point. You can't rely on 'later.' Usually it's too late."

"It's weird how ants can think that a caterpillar is one of their own grubs," said Hyslop. "It's just the most extraordinary thing."

"Yes, not just any old grub," said Northy. "But a queen ant grub. They tend it and keep it safe all winter until it pupates. Defend it with their lives, and it repays the poor things by eating all their own grubs, and more or less destroying their colony."

"Nature is cruel at times," said Hyslop.

"Not as cruel as humans."

"I think I read that the caterpillar produces a scent to fool the ants and also it has a funny little song that it sings to them. A song that is similar to that of a red ant queen. How amazingly clever is that!"

"Well, it's not a song that would be audible to human ears, but yes, you're right. It's a song that makes the worker ants treat it like a queen."

"Clever little thing getting itself looked after, I think. Shame it has to destroy its host sometimes. Why are you asking me all about the Large Blue anyway?" asked Hyslop as they reached the fruit trees. "There aren't any round here, are there?"

Sir Northcote pointed with his stick at a pair of Red Admirals on the rotting plums, then slapped his head.

"No," he said. "None round these parts. It's August, so we're too late this year anyway. Oh look, there's a Peacock now."

They watched the butterflies around the rotting fruits in silence for a while, a silence broken only by head-slapping.

"I have a plan for next year," said Sir Northcote. "Next June, if I'm still here, if I haven't popped my clogs and if Hugo hasn't carted me off to the loony bin." He snorted loudly. "Or the Nursing Home! Well, next year, next June I mean, we could do a trip, Hyslop, down to Somerset to a National Trust place where we can see the Large Blues flying. I won't involve Judd." He shook his head dismissively. "We could get Sandy and Penny to share the driving, find a nice hotel, go and see the butterflies and make a bit of a long weekend of it, just the four of us. That's my plan!"

An image of how it would be leapt immediately into Hyslop's mind. It would be a holiday, a holiday that she would actually enjoy, with people that she cared for, and who cared for her. It would be different from holidays with her mother and all her mother's rich friends: there would be no sarcasm or cruelty from hostile adults, no drunk horrid Uncles, no punishments, no feeling alone and hungry. Sandy and Penny would be joking and laughing together, fussing round Hyslop; all of them would be teasing Northy and he would be happy, hardly swearing or shouting at all; there would be picnics full of Penny's wonderful sandwiches and cakes and ginger biscuits and chocolate tiffin; there would be Sandy's home-made lemonade; the two dogs, Sasha and Skye would be there too, of course, running ahead and chasing rabbits; above all, there would be a hillside bathed in sunlight with Large Blue butterflies flying around, all newly emerged and in perfect condition. It was an image so beautiful it brought sharp tears to a prickly place behind her eyes.

The reality was, of course, that there were many obstacles to such an outing. In the first place, Hyslop had no idea where she would be in a year's time. Would her mother have made Hugo an Uncle? If so, would Penny and Sandy and Sir Northcote hate her and her mother forever? Would Hugo and her mother force Northy into a home and turn the butterfly wilderness into a shooting estate? Would she be forced to go back to Italy with her mother just when she had found happiness and good people for the first time in her life since she had lost Nonna? She even found cause for regret in thinking of how sad Zak would be if she left. Everything beautiful that she had found would be destroyed. It was like eating a juicy ripe peach which suddenly turned rotten and maggoty in her mouth. She fought back tears.

"What's wrong, don't you like the idea?" asked Sir Northcote.

"I like the idea very much," said Hyslop. "Oh, yes, Northy, don't worry about that. It would be just perfect. It's just that… well, I don't know what plans my mother has for me. I don't know what will have happened in another year. It's so far ahead."

"Just like with the Large Blues," sighed the old man, "sometimes you have to give nature a bit of a helping hand."

CHAPTER THIRTY THREE

Watchers in the Night

"I have a guest due to arrive any minute," said Vanessa, emerging from her bedroom, with her high heeled shoes dangling from her right hand. "You can stay and make polite conversation for ten minutes, then you can scoot off upstairs."

"If it's Hugo coming, I'd rather go upstairs now," said Hyslop.

"I don't recall giving you the choice of what you'd *rather* do." Vanessa stooped to put the shoes on, admiring first one elegant slim ankle, then the other. "I said that you could stay and be civil for ten minutes first. I think it's time for you to be civil to him."

"And I'm saying that I don't *want* to be civil to Hugo," Hyslop had been careful to hide her precious butterfly book in case her mother became destructive again, so there was no danger of it being snatched from her and hurled across the room.

Vanessa looked at Hyslop first of all in a slightly incredulous way, then anger flashed across her eyes and it seemed for a moment as if she was going to fly at her daughter. She made no move to strike, however, and Hyslop decided it was because she did not want to be caught out in a temper if Hugo arrived at the door.

"I should like you," said Vanessa coldly, "to stay for a minute or two and pay your respects. Hugo may well become an important part of our lives."

"Well, he's not an important part of *my* life and he never will be." Hyslop felt a strange surge of power as she realised that her mother was not going to shout at her or slap her with Hugo likely to arrive at any moment. Unlike the Uncles in France and Italy, Hugo was not living with them, and he had so far posed no physical threat. Besides, she had her own allies now: she had adults who cared for her.

"That's what *you* think, Hyslop. You'll find that he's quite an important person whether you like it or not." Vanessa's anger turned to a sneering laugh. "Go on then, off you go upstairs to your silly books and your insects. Enjoy it all while you can!"

They stared at each other and for once Hyslop did not lower her eyes. Two pairs of dark eyes flashed at each other, and Vanessa lowered her gaze first.

"I hold all the cards round here, Hyslop," she said, wandering over to look out of the window.

Hyslop said nothing but took a handful of peanuts from a small bowl and went upstairs.

It was not until she reached the safety of her room that she felt her legs shaking. She had stood up to her mother and it felt good. It felt like she had just run a race, and burst over the finishing line first at sports day and her heart was beating loudly in her chest. Normally she could not hear her own heart beating, but now she did. She was aware of her own breathing too. She felt alive and vibrant and strong.

Downstairs she heard the doorknocker and the exchanged "Darling!" and "God, I've missed you, Vanessa!"

She went to the top of the stairs to listen. For once she would not shut it all out, but would find out what was happening. There was a silence and she imagined them kissing. Then Hugo was asking her mother what was wrong as she seemed upset, not herself at all. Hyslop wondered if Hugo would like it if he knew what Vanessa was like if she *was* being herself. For a while Vanessa fobbed him off, saying it was nothing in a little-girl-being-brave voice, and that she really would rather not tell him. Hyslop listened intently; not much in life upset Vanessa and she wondered what it could be. How unlike her mother's normal tone this silly voice was; anyone with a brain could surely tell that it was false, and also that Vanessa had every intention of telling Hugo what was troubling her. It was the whole point of the exercise. Men were so stupid.

"Tell me, darling," Hugo sounded so tender and loving that Hyslop wanted to be sick. She forced herself to listen and heard her own name mentioned.

"It's Hyslop," she heard her mother say with a stifled sob.

"What has happened?" There was another silence and Hyslop imagined Hugo putting his arms round her mother in a consoling sort of way. "Here, let me pour you a drink, darling. What has Hyslop done to upset you?"

"I don't like to be disloyal to my own daughter," Vanessa said. Hyslop almost laughed aloud at this. "Hugo, please don't tell anyone what I'm going through. I know I can trust you, and I just don't know where else to turn."

There followed protestations of love and sympathy from Hugo that were both tedious and nauseating. Hyslop kept thinking of poor Penny and Sir Northcote.

Finally Vanessa said: "I just don't think I'm a good mother to Hyslop."

Hyslop nodded her head. For once her mother had said something truthful, though unfortunately Hugo did not agree.

"Darling, no one could do more than you do. You're a wonderful mother!"

"Tonight," Vanessa actually appeared to be crying. "Tonight Hyslop shouted at me and defied me openly. I can do nothing with her, Hugo. Nothing. I mean, I don't expect her to understand how tough things have been for me. She's too young to appreciate that." There was a particularly realistic sob here. "I just can't go on like this, a single mother, struggling to keep things afloat, with no money, no home of my own, nothing. And now not even the respect of my daughter!"

"Of course you can't," there was another long silence and Hyslop tried to block out thoughts of the cuddling and kissing.

After what seemed a long time, she heard Hugo murmuring things to Vanessa that she could not make out. There were snatches of sentences, like: "… I'll do what I can, darling… " "… it won't be easy, but I'll do anything so we can be together… " and "… it's an enormous risk for me professionally but that doesn't matter if it makes things all right for you at last… "

There was a clinking of glasses and then they moved into the kitchen. What they hoped to get there was a mystery as there was only another bowl of salted peanuts, some jam and a packet of Italian coffee. It was frustrating for Hyslop as she was unsure what her mother's intentions were, and what Hugo meant by "an enormous risk." They were plotting something and it sounded serious. For the first time in her life she was fearful not just for herself, but for the others she had grown to care for.

She did not need an imaginary Nonna hug, however, and she did not feel that she had to hide under her bed-clothes humming to herself.

She was going to get her butterfly book out in a minute and read more about Large Blues, but in the meantime she went to her window and stared out into the night. Darkness was falling, though it always looked darker when you were looking out from a room with the light on. Probably it would be quite easy to see if you were outside and your eyes were accustomed to the twilight. Her bedroom light was on, and the curtains wide open. She stood right by the window, aware of how visible she would be, a dark figure in the square of bright light. It was not long before two moths appeared, beating their heads against the glass, trying to get in.

Hyslop put her fingers out to them as if to touch them through the glass. She wondered if Northy was outside somewhere setting his moth traps, and if Zak was still up and about. He would surely be able to see her, silhouetted against the light.

Hyslop ran her fingers through her long dark hair, then stretched her arms above her head. She was not going to stay in the shadows any more. She had had enough of blending in with the background, hiding in corners, trying to be invisible. If she was being watched she didn't care. She had always had Nonna and Papa in heaven to watch over her, though up until now they had not been able to help her a great deal. She gazed at the moths on the other side of the glass, and thought of Sir Northcote and Sandy and Penny and Malcolm and Zak. She now had more substantial guardian angels to watch over her.

CHAPTER THIRTY FOUR

Storm Flies gather

As was her custom now, Hyslop hurried out of the cottage early, long before her mother would be awake, and headed for Sandy's barn. She was never sure these days whether her mother was in the cottage or in London with Hugo.

She and Sandy had gone beyond the polite "Would you like something to eat?" stage where Hyslop had to look faintly surprised and reluctant before accepting a brioche or a biscuit. Even the dogs greeted her less with the excited barking they reserved for strangers, and more with familiar high pitched yelps. They looked expectantly at her as if they suspected that she would be the one giving them breakfast. While she went for their bowls amidst whines and nudges, Sandy called out from the kitchen: "I fancy a fry up this morning, Hyslop. I was just waiting for you. Do you want your eggs fried or scrambled?"

Hyslop made Sasha and Skye sit and stay before she let them have their breakfast, as Sandy had taught her to do, then she wandered into the kitchen. Bacon was sizzling and the smell made her realise how ravenous she was.

"Can I have two fried eggs, please," she said.

"Sweetie, I assumed you'd want two eggs, so don't worry. I've come to realise that there's hungry and then there's hungry-caterpillar-Hyslop-hungry! I've got some really thick butcher's bacon," said Sandy, "and some big mushrooms. Get the cutlery out, could you?"

Hyslop had eaten expensive meals with her mother's friends in restaurants throughout France and Italy. She had eaten breakfasts on villa patios and on board yachts with the Mediterranean sparkling in the background. Servants had waited on her and called her "Madam" or "Signorina" or "Mademoiselle", and, as long as her mother had staff to deal with the cooking, she had eaten tasty and delicious food. Nothing could compare with this bacon, egg and toast, however. She recalled her mother saying when someone handed her a glass of champagne: "Oh darling, this just hits the spot!" She had never really understood what "the spot" was before, but she suspected that whatever it was, Sandy's fried eggs had just hit it.

"This is an amazing breakfast!" she announced, breaking open her second fried egg and dipping her buttery toast in it. "It has hit my spot."

"Well, I'm glad it's done that, but it's hardly a gourmet feast. I'm not renowned for my cookery skills. I think it's a case of the old saying 'Hunger is the best sauce' and you do always seem to be a hungry little thing."

Hyslop looked up at Sandy and put her knife and fork down.

"I wish I could live here always," she said. "With Sasha and Skye and you."

"Glad you've got us in the right order," Sandy tried to laugh, but Hyslop continued staring at her fiercely, and instead of finishing with a joke about the dogs coming first as she had intended, Sandy merely said: "Oh, sweetie," in a choked voice.

"I've never really liked adults before," said Hyslop. "Apart from Nonna of course."

There was a silence where Hyslop could, or should, have mentioned her mother.

"You've been unhappy for a long time," Sandy said at last. It wasn't a question, just a statement, and Hyslop knew she did not need to reply.

After another silence, Sandy said: "Nothing would make me happier, Hyslop, than to have you live here with me. You say you've never liked adults before, and, to be perfectly frank, I've never had much to do with children before I met you!"

Hyslop continued to stare with her huge dark eyes.

"I don't like you because you're a child, or my Goddaughter, or whatever. I like you because I like you. And that's that. As for living here, I don't see how it's possible, much as I'd like it too," said Sandy. "Vanessa wouldn't give you up. I'm sure she loves you in her own way, Hyslop. She's just not a person who lives by the normal rules of life, and that probably includes being a mother. She never was one to abide by rules even when she was at school. I can see that things are tough for you. In the meantime, my humble café is always open for breakfast, lunch and dinner. And of course, if you need to stay here there's always a bed made up." Sandy put a hand out and placed it on top of Hyslop's hand, and Hyslop gazed down at the stubby fingernails, so different from her mother's manicured talons.

"Have you hated all the travelling around Europe?" Sandy asked.

Hyslop found herself plunging into her familiar tunnel of misery, but this time coming out the other end in a blaze of light. She felt something on fire inside her, churning around, swirling, changing: she thought of her life with Vanessa over the years, and she knew she didn't want things to go on as they had before. She knew she had done with all the travelling around, moving from Uncle to Uncle. She had changed into a different person, and she was no longer going to stand for it.

"I was happy with my Nonna until I was five," she said. "I was safe."

"Safe?" queried Sandy, puzzled. "In what way safe?"

"Yes, safe like I am with you," said Hyslop. The word was good in English: it was a short comforting sound, which began with a gentle hiss and then ended at the front of her mouth, like breathing out. "I like being safe."

"Were you… were you in danger when you lived in Italy then?" Sandy was looking worried and concerned and Hyslop wondered if she had gone too far. She was way beyond her mother's rules already.

Sandy had assumed that the opposite of being safe was being in danger and Hyslop considered this. Vanessa had always made sure that she tagged along in her wake; she had been violent, sneering, angry and neglectful; she had let the Uncles be vile and horrid, but she had never actually abandoned Hyslop to them. Thoughts of the past buzzed around in Hyslop's head: there were so many emotions to deal with, sometimes she felt her head would burst with the pressure of them all.

The knowledge that her mother was not going to leave her behind had been a strange sort of security. Even with French Oncle Xavier whom Hyslop remembered only with a shudder, and with the two bad-tempered Italian Uncles, Paolo and Massimo, she had known that her mother would take her with her when she left them. And she always did leave them in the end.

Had she felt in danger all those times locked in dark cupboards as a punishment for talking back, or for not doing as she was told immediately? Insects had been her dear companions, her comfort. With Uncle Massimo, in particular, who always wanted to come into her room to give her a goodnight cuddle, stinking of cigarettes and red wine, insects had been her allies. He had a terror of being stung and she had gathered dead bees and wasps and spread them around her bed so that he wouldn't come near. Hyslop gave a half smile as she recalled him jumping back with a shout when he first encountered all the dead insects. She knew he wouldn't complain about it, though, and she also knew that he wouldn't be back.

People might have let her down, but insects never had.

"It's getting dark all of a sudden," she said.

"Gosh, yes, it looks as if a storm is brewing," said Sandy.

Hyslop got up and went over to the window.

The sky, which had been gloriously blue and cloud free when she got up, was darkening. The trees shook their leafy coats like dogs coming out of the water, and strange little black whirlwinds swirled around the garden in front of her. Hyslop narrowed her eyes and gazed at them.

"What on earth are those?" Sandy said, appearing beside her. "They look like mini tornadoes."

"They're thunder-flies," said Hyslop. "Storm flies."

"Storm flies! I've never seen them do that before. How very odd!"

A swirling swarm of flies broke off from their tornado formation and flew at the window, as if someone had thrown handfuls of soil at the windowpane. Sandy leaped back. Hyslop put her hands onto the glass as if to touch the tiny black flies crawling up the outside of the pane.

Behind her Sasha and Skye began to bark.

"Oh my goodness, I've never seen so many flies," said Sandy. "They look as if they're trying to come in."

"It's all right," said Hyslop. "They are just announcing the storm."

CHAPTER THIRTY FIVE

Zak Hears some Scary News

Zak tried gazing intensely at the courgette plants in Mrs Braithwaite's vegetable garden, but it was no use. They could flaunt their pretty yellow flowers, and display their fruits, both green and golden, of all shapes and sizes, but they could no longer hold his interest. They were like friends from a distant past when he was young and shallow and did not understand the world. They were friends that had served their purpose and could be snubbed without a backward glance. They were merely vegetables.

As he kicked stones and wandered along the path towards the dahlia beds, he recalled a dog which his father had owned when Zak was very young. It was a working dog, a spaniel called Rex, which lived outside in a half broken kennel, and Zak had endeavoured to make it his special friend. He had asked to feed the dog and spent time grooming it and brushing its coat, but whatever he did to please it, the spaniel was indifferent to him. However much affection he lavished on it, the dog loved only his father. Despite the fact, or perhaps because of the fact, that his father spoke roughly to the dog and never showed it any affection, the spaniel lived in a state of quivering excitement, always half listening for its master's voice. It would push Zak out of the way in an instant if it heard his father's whistle, and if he tried to hold it back, the dog would scratch and whine and struggle until he let it go.

Despite his father's rough ways, the dog was happy. If Mrs Braithwaite stooped to stroke it and say "Good boy" in her gentlest tone, Rex was not interested. The faithful creature would wag its tail but kept its eyes, shining and alert, on its master at all times. It would not have swapped the cold kennel and meagre scraps for a room in the big house with chicken and steak and constant petting from the posh folk.

Zak felt that he understood Rex now. His own dogged devotion to the girl Hyslop was all that mattered to him. He thought of all the things that mattered to other kids: a place on the football team, being invited to birthday parties, coming top of the class, winning at sports day, getting new computer games or smart new clothes, and it all seemed so unimportant. No one had used the word "love" to Zak, though he had heard it often enough on television. Soppy parents in American films were always telling their kids: "I love you, honey," and children at his school would say things to their parents at the school gate like; "Bye, Mummy! Love you!" Zak sometimes paused to consider what it would be like if his mother were alive. Perhaps she would be the one to say: "Bye, Zak! I love you!" at the school gate. Somehow he could not imagine it, though. It was such a silly word. If you felt that way about someone, then surely you didn't need to go around saying it in public all the time. His mother and he would have an understanding between them, he decided, and she wouldn't need to go around saying soppy things. If old Rex had been able to speak, Zak was quite sure the dog wouldn't have said: "I love you" to his father. True attachment did not need to be always flaunting itself with words. Silly words like "love." Zak scowled at the thought.

He felt that the girl Hyslop understood his feelings towards her, his solid devotion, without anything needing to be said between them. They had a connection. She was not one of those silly girls in the class, always giggling and whispering to each other. Those girls laughed at him behind his back, but they knew nothing about him. Oh no, Hyslop was different from them. She had a stillness at her centre, a wisdom born of suffering. She *knew* him, the real him that no one else knew: she understood him. The others were like plump domestic fowl, clucking around the henhouse. Hyslop was savage and free, a beautiful wild creature. She knew that he watched her and followed her around, and sometimes she was cold or cruel to him, but sometimes she spoke up for him to the old man, and seemed to want him to tag along. Sometimes, most thrillingly of all, she smiled at him. It was enough.

Today some sixth sense guided him, not to the woods near the old man's house, but to the meadow beside the main garden. The day before had been marred by a sudden storm, but today the sun was hot and the meadow was bound to be full of butterflies. He strode impatiently along the paths and jumped over the style into the field. It did not take him long to spot Hyslop hunkered down, watching something in the grass. He did not feel the need to hide or even to approach timidly now. She always seemed to know if he was there so hiding was pointless. If she didn't want him to stay she would tell him.

She flicked a sidelong glance at him as he walked up to her, and tossed her shimmering hair. He was careful not to let his shadow fall on the butterfly she was watching. He knew that would annoy her. He knew that he should keep a respectful distance and wait until she spoke to him first.

"Just looking at this Marbled White," she said after a while. Zak said nothing in reply. He was happy that she had accepted his presence. "Not many of them left now."

When the butterfly flew off the girl Hyslop turned to face him, looking directly at him with her fierce dark eyes.

"So what did you do, Zak, before I arrived?" she asked. "Before you started following me around?"

Her voice had a note of mockery in it. Although he did not like her tone it was still better than being ignored. He said nothing, but looked down at his feet. A silence ensued but neither of them minded long silences.

"I like it round here," Hyslop said after a while, knocking some grass seeds off a tall stalk of grass and flicking them at Zak. "This is the best place I have ever stayed since my Nonna died."

Zak wasn't sure who or what her Nonna was but he didn't ask.

"I feel I could really make a home here," she continued. Zak felt all fluttery with happiness when she said this. He opened his mouth to speak, but didn't know what to say, so closed it again and returned to examining his feet.

"There are good people here," Hyslop said. "And you don't get good people everywhere, I can tell you."

Zak knew that only too well. In fact he could have told Hyslop that some of the people round here weren't really that good either. It was best not to say this, however, so he simply made a vague "Hmmm" sort of noise and cleared his throat a few times.

Hyslop paused to study another of those chequered black and white butterflies that were flying around the meadow. It had landed on a grass stalk right beside her, and she peered at it closely. When she was looking at butterflies, the rest of the world did not seem to exist for her. The good thing about that was that while she was looking at the insect, he could raise his eyes to look at her. Her hair was catching the sunlight again and he began counting the colours in it.

"Everything I need is right here," said Hyslop after the butterfly had flown off. "Everything." She gave a sigh, and looked right at him again: "I shall be sorry to leave it all behind."

"What d'you mean?" He felt cold with fear.

"I mean that my mother and I never stay long in one place, Zak."

"But surely if you're happy here, like, and you've got everything you need," he began, then stopped, not sure how to continue.

"My happiness has never been part of the equation," said Hyslop. Zak frowned, not quite understanding. He always felt lost when she used teachers' words.

As if realising this, Hyslop explained: "My happiness is not important to my mother. We always move on when she's ready to go. It's nothing to do with me."

Zak felt so many strange emotions buzzing around inside him that he did not know what to say or do.

"Do your family take your happiness into account, Zak, when they make decisions?"

The mere notion was so ridiculous that Zak made a face and shook his head. She certainly had a point there.

"But your mother… " he began, then stopped.

"My mother?" Hyslop pounced on him. "What about her?"

"Well, she seems happy enough round here, doesn't she?" he said. "With all her… you know… her friends."

"Really, Zak," Hyslop's voice was smooth and low. "Why would you think that? Have you been watching her too? Mmm? Following *her* around?"

"No!" he cried. "I haven't. But I've seen her with… with… Mr… "

He paused, not knowing whether to continue or not.

"What were you going to say, Zak?" said Hyslop. "Tell me."

"Well, I've seen her with Mr… Mr Braithwaite." Zak hung his head and waited for her reaction. He did not care what it was as long as she did not send him away.

For a long time there was no reaction, and he dared raise his eyes to look at Hyslop.

"Sorry," he said. "I shouldn't have said that."

"I once asked you to tell me the truth, Zak," she said. "And you just did. There's nothing wrong with that."

It was impossible for him to tell if she was angry with him or pleased that he had told the truth.

"My mother is not like other people," said Hyslop, her voice distant and cold, as if it were coming from a faraway place. "You mustn't think she's like other people."

Zak wanted to say that he didn't care a bit about Hyslop's mother, only about her, but he didn't know how to express himself. Words could get you into trouble, so it was best to use them sparingly.

"I know she's planning something," said Hyslop. "I always know when she's planning something. And when she plans something," the dark eyes bored right inside him, "it means that we move on. You won't want that, will you, Zak?"

He hung his head in sorrow.

"You won't want my mother to take us away from here, will you?" she asked again.

This time, as she seemed to want an answer, he raised his head and said : "No. No, I don't want that to happen."

"Sometimes, Zak, when we don't want things to happen, we have to do something about it."

CHAPTER THIRTY SIX

Mother and Daughter Have a Conversation

"I bought some brioches for tea, Hyslop," said Vanessa, opening a paper bag that looked as if it had come from the baker's shop in the village. She placed a little butter-dish on the table and a pot of jam beside it. "There's butter and jam too. Raspberry I think. No, maybe it's damson."

Hyslop raised her head from her butterfly book and narrowed her eyes. She wondered if she had misheard her mother.

"Sandy said you were fond of these," Vanessa had brought out a china dish and put the brioches on it in the middle of the table. "She said you could eat three or four at one sitting. Now, would you like some orange or apple juice?"

Vanessa was addressing Hyslop in a strange formal tone, and Hyslop found herself looking around the room to see if anyone else had slipped in without her noticing.

"For me?" she said, suspiciously. There had to be a catch. There had to be someone about to arrive any minute for Vanessa to be putting on this loving-mother act. She hoped it wasn't Hugo, and scowled at the thought.

"Well, you could look pleased, Hyslop," snapped Vanessa. This was more like her normal tone, but still, her behaviour was inexplicable.

"I'd like apple juice please," said Hyslop, going over to the table to examine the brioches. She half wondered if the trick was that they would be made of plastic and when she tried to bite into one, her mother would laugh at her.

They smelt delicious, however, and despite herself she took one and bit into it.

"You could wait until you are sitting down with a plate," said Vanessa, coming back from the kitchen with a glass of apple juice, a plate and a knife. "It's what we tend to do in civilised society. It's called good manners."

Certainly the sarcasm was more what she was used to, but Hyslop did not know what to make of the mummy-serving-tea act that seemed to be put on with no audience around to witness it.

"Thank you," she said, as she sat down at the table.

Her mother made no move to leave the room, but stood watching Hyslop. This was so bizarre that Hyslop was almost put off eating her brioches. She felt a deep sense of unease. Something was odd, not quite right.

"Don't you have any conversation, Hyslop?" asked Vanessa after a while. "How are the insects today? Tell me all about them!"

Hyslop almost choked on a particularly large chunk of brioche. She found herself looking around the room again for some invisible visitor who may have sneaked in whilst she was not looking.

"The insects?" she asked incredulously.

"Yes, Hyslop, creepy crawlies, bugs, insects," said Vanessa, still watching her daughter strangely. "You know, those six legged beasties that you like so much. Butterflies for instance. Have you seen any good ones recently?"

"Oh," said Hyslop. She was still not sure what to say. She spread the second brioche with butter and reached for the jam.

There was an expectant silence from her mother. It seemed as if she actually wanted an answer.

"Well, yes, there are butterflies around at the moment," said Hyslop. She paused. Her mother was still looking intensely at her, and her expression was impossible to fathom. "A new generation of Painted Ladies."

Her mother nodded her head as if she had been awaiting just such a report; as if she knew exactly what Painted Ladies were and was pleased to hear about this new generation. As if she cared.

Hyslop, still puzzled, spread the thick damson jam onto the

brioche and began munching. The combination was delicious. Vanessa wandered over to the window.

"I don't see your little guardian angel," she said, scorn beginning to creep back into her tone. "The village idiot boy. But no doubt he's somewhere around outside waiting for you."

Hyslop felt cross at hearing Zak described in such a way, but she was also amazed that her mother had been perceptive enough to notice him.

"You're happy here, Hyslop, aren't you?" Vanessa turned back to stare at her daughter in that strange way again.

Hyslop stopped chewing, and nodded her head. This was not something she could ever recall her mother asking her before.

"Yes, you've found some admirers I must say." Hyslop listened keenly for scorn and resentment in her mother's voice but was unable to detect any.

"Quite a little fan base, in fact," continued Vanessa. Her tone was expressionless, without any obvious nasty undertone.

"Yes, I am happy here," said Hyslop, preparing her third brioche. "I like the people round here more than I've liked anyone in all the places we've stayed before."

"Well, that's good then," said Vanessa in a peculiar tone that Hyslop could not categorise.

There was another long silence between them, and Hyslop, suddenly self-conscious, tried to chew as quietly as she could.

"I've done a bit of food shopping," said Vanessa after a while. "There's lots of cereal and milk and bread for you, Hyslop. There's a pizza to heat up. Some fruit. And a few other bits and pieces. I'm going away for a few days."

Hyslop looked up. "Where are you going?" she asked sharply.

"None of your business!" snapped her mother. They were getting back to normal now. "Well, if you must know," her tone softened slightly, "I'm going to London. I have some business to sort out there with Hugo."

Hyslop no longer felt like eating the last brioche. She felt vaguely sick. Her mother was planning something and Hugo was involved. This could not be good news.

"You'll be all right here on your own," said Vanessa. "You can always go to Sandy's for meals, can't you?" She twisted her mouth into a strange expression. "She's happy to have you. Or you could try the dour Scotsman? He's quite smitten too. Or the shouty old man? Mmmmm? Or you could give orders to the village idiot boy, couldn't you?"

Hyslop said nothing. Her mother disappeared into her bedroom and came out with her cream high heeled shoes on, pulling a small suitcase on wheels. She was on her mobile telephone, telling Hugo she was ready to be picked up.

The thought of being alone in the cottage did not worry Hyslop. After long sessions in dark cupboards, the dear little cottage held no fears for her. She was more afraid of what her mother was planning in London with Hugo.

"Bye then, Hyslop," said Vanessa at the door.

"Bye," said Hyslop. She waited for the door to slam behind her mother, but this did not happen immediately.

For a long time Vanessa stood there, poised to leave with the door open, staring back at her daughter.

"Well, I'll be off then," she said, picking up her case. "And I'm glad about the... um... new generation of Painted Ladies, Hyslop."

The door closed gently behind her and Hyslop sat at the table for a long time. She gazed down at the fourth brioche but found she had no appetite for it.

CHAPTER THIRTY SEVEN

Hyslop Stays with Sandy

Hyslop sat for a long time at the table, staring at the last brioche on the plate.

She wanted to go round to Sandy's house but was afraid that Penny might be there. How could she face either of them, knowing that her mother was off in London for a few days and would be staying with Hugo. She was, after all, her mother's daughter and Penny would be bound to resent her too. They must all feel, with justification indeed, that their warmth and hospitality had been ill repaid. They must surely feel that the guests they had nurtured so kindly, had been imposters, cruel destroyers.

"We've spoilt everything here," she addressed the brioche. She had no desire to eat it now.

After a while she wandered over to the window and looked out. There was no sign of Zak but she knew he must be nearby, hiding somewhere in the bushes. Her mother's words echoed in her mind, and she decided that she could indeed give him an order to carry out.

She opened the window as wide as it would go and leaned out. "ZA-AK!" she called. "Zak Judd! Where are you!"

At first she could see nothing, but out of the corner of her eye she saw a tiny movement in the brambles behind the wooden fence. If he was there he must surely be uncomfortable amongst the thorns.

"Zak!" she called again. "Could you come here please!"

Zak emerged from the brambles and nettles, shaking himself down, brushing off thorns and twigs from his dirty old T-shirt. He looked rather sheepish, but was obviously pleased that she had called him.

"I have something I want you to do for me," she said. Zak said nothing but looked eagerly at her, like a dog waiting for a stick to be thrown.

"I want you to go to Sandy's house and see if she's on her own," said Hyslop. "Look in the windows, do whatever it is that you do when you spy on people. Then come back and tell me."

He stood, uncertain.

"Can you do it now, please," said Hyslop. "Then come straight back and tell me if there is anyone with her. I specially want to know if Mrs Braithwaite is there."

Without a word Zak turned and ran off in the direction of Sandy's house. Whilst he was gone Hyslop went upstairs to her chest of drawers and found some clean clothes. She brought them downstairs together with her toothbrush, and popped them in a plastic bag. She stood by the window waiting for Zak.

He had barely been gone ten minutes when he returned, out of breath from running.

"I looked," he said. "I looked in her house, in all the windows, and in at the window of her pottery place. She never seen me, like."

"Yes?" Hyslop waited whilst he got his breath back.

"I looked and saw Mrs... Sandy," Zak looked slightly uncomfortable calling Sandy by her first name, but probably did not know her surname and had never had cause to use it before. "There was no one in the house. I saw her... Mrs Sandy... in the pottery place, and she was alone in there. All by herself like. No one else there. Just her."

Hyslop nodded.

"Good," she said. "Well, thanks for that, Zak. You can go now. I don't want you following me any more today."

The boy looked crestfallen but turned away obediently.

"Actually, wait a minute," Hyslop called him back. She held out the plate with the brioche on it and Zak returned, and looked down at it.

"You can have this as a reward," said Hyslop. "It's a brioche."

Zak put out a tentative hand and took the brioche. He examined it as if he had never seen such a thing before.

"Bye then, Zak," said Hyslop and she closed the window. Zak was dismissed.

She watched him walk off, gazing down at the brioche. He held it in his hands as if it were a wild bird he had captured, and he was trying to stop it from flying away, yet without wanting to hurt it. He looked back once at Hyslop, then continued slowly on his way.

Hyslop waited until he was out of sight before setting off for Sandy's pottery. She did not bother to knock, but opened the door and stood there, with her bag of clothes, toothbrush and butterfly book.

"I've come to stay for a few days," she announced.

"Hyslop!" cried Sandy, looking up from her work. "Well, how lovely!"

"I've brought a few things with me."

"Sweetie, don't stand there cluttering up the doorway," said Sandy. "Leave your stuff there and come and see what I've been making."

Hyslop walked over.

"Well, I'm thrilled to have you," said Sandy, peering at Hyslop over her glasses. "Is it OK with your mother?"

"She's away," said Hyslop, aware that her words were dropping into Sandy's consciousness like stones chucked into a pond. She could almost see the ripples. "Away. In London. For a few days."

"London!" exclaimed Sandy. "Oh, I see."

She did not explain what it was that she saw or didn't see about London, but began to show Hyslop a newly glazed teapot that she had made.

"I like this dark green glaze," said Hyslop. "Green's my favourite colour." She took the lid off and replaced it carefully. "And the lid's a perfect fit. That's really clever."

Sandy beamed at her.

"Would you like to make something else?" she asked.

"Mmmmm, yes," said Hyslop. "I should like to make a mug for drinking hot chocolate. I should like it to be green, maybe a different green from this though. I should like a mug the colour of a Green Hairstreak."

"Well, I presume that is a butterfly," said Sandy. "I think I said that I would make you a butterfly mug."

Hyslop nodded: "I can show you a picture if you like of the Green Hairstreak."

"First things first, Hyslop," said Sandy. "Making a mug means a lesson in throwing. Are you ready for a shot on the wheel?"

"Yes," said Hyslop. "Yes, I think I am."

CHAPTER THIRTY EIGHT

Zak Feels Thunder in the Air

August continued to be hot, oppressively hot. No one had ever endured such a stifling August. His grandmother, who seemed to have lived forever, said it was the hottest summer she could remember, and she grumbled about how "close" it was. Zak did not understand what she meant by this, but knew to keep out of her way as much as possible as the heat made her specially grumpy. She sometimes had to go and lie down after lunch, which was not something he had witnessed before. "My bones are getting old," she said, and that was certainly true. Her bones were growing old like the rest of her. "There's thunder in the air," was another of her phrases, and this one he did understand. He could feel it too. The air felt heavy, as if it was struggling to hold back a storm. Maybe the air had to become thick and heavy to hold those heavy rain-filled storm-clouds up in the air. Otherwise they would burst through with lightning and thunder and all the animals would have to run for shelter. It seemed to Zak that the air was holding back more than a thunderstorm, though. There was something else it was holding back, something big that was trying to break through. Everyone seemed to be in a cross mood. Little storm flies were everywhere: they stuck to the butter, died in their hundreds on window ledges, and even got into the milk somehow. Great swirling swarms of them appeared from nowhere, and made his father swipe at them and curse.

"Horrible flies, I'm sick of them," Mr Braithwaite snapped at Zak and his father as they were weeding the borders. "Could do with some rain, Judd," he added accusingly, almost as if it were Zak's father's fault that the garden was dry and parched. "Keep on top of the watering, will you? I'm going to be away in London for a few days."

His father made a respectful, if inarticulate, monosyllable of assent.

"And strim the nettles near Keeper's Cottage," continued Mr Braithwaite. "Seems to be a breeding ground for flies and moths there. I want it all cut back. Be as savage as you like with it."

This time Zak thought first of all about the girl Hyslop rather than about the old man. She wouldn't be happy to have all the nettles cut down. They were probably full of caterpillars and butterfly eggs and insect life. He hoped she wouldn't blame him.

"I promise you, Judd, the day is coming soon when I'll turn this whole place into a civilised place to live," Mr Braithwaite swatted at a swarm of flies that were circling his head. "I'm going to wage war on weeds and insects and vermin and tidy the place up once and for all. Get rid of all the brambles and nettles near the houses. Yes, one of these days we'll put some pheasants down and manage it all properly."

Zak's father made another vague noise of assent.

"In the meantime, I could do with a lift to the station," Mr Braithwaite was looking at his watch. "Get the Jaguar out, could you, and I'll be ready in about five minutes."

With that he walked off, followed by a halo of black flies.

"You get on with the weeding," his father said to Zak, and headed for the garage area behind the big house. His father liked driving Mr Braithwaite's Jaguar better than the old man's ancient Mercedes. It would put him in a good mood for a few hours. Zak knew that after he had dropped Mr Braithwaite off at the station in it, he would drive around for a bit on the dual carriageway, going as fast as he could, enjoying the power of the engine. He would be gone for some time, which was always a good thing for Zak.

Zak hated being stuck in one place as it meant he couldn't follow the girl Hyslop around. He knew that she had stayed with the woman Sandy overnight, and when she was there she spent more time indoors than she did when she was at Keeper's Cottage. She sometimes walked the dogs and he could only follow at a distance, or else the dogs soon sniffed him out. Sometimes she did pottery work with the woman Sandy and made coloured pots out of clay. It was strange, Zak mused. He had lived here all his life but none of the adults had invited *him* to do stuff. Hyslop did pottery with the Sandy woman, she looked at butterflies with the old man, and she even wandered into the Scottish man's furniture workshop. He didn't think she made furniture, but it was impossible to tell what she did as she sometimes stayed there for quite a long time. It wouldn't have surprised him if she suddenly appeared with a chair she had made: she seemed capable of anything and everything.

Zak picked an enormous weed that almost filled his plastic bucket, then covered it up with some chickweed. It was a trick he had learned. It looked as if he had done quite a bit of weeding already. He decided that he might have a wander around whilst his father was safely occupied with driving Mr Braithwaite to the station. He set off towards the big house, careful to keep behind the fence out of sight. His father would have gone to get the car out of the garage so there was no chance of being spotted by him. Suddenly Mr Braithwaite came out of a side door of the big house and Zak ducked behind the wall just in time. This was unusual. He normally came out the front door, with Mrs Braithwaite giving him a kiss on the cheek, saying: "Goodbye, darling."

He was pulling a large suitcase with one hand and holding his mobile with the other. There was a lot of "darling" on the telephone but it was a different sort of "darling", nothing like the voice he used with Mrs Braithwaite. Zak knew he was talking to the girl Hyslop's mother. He was arranging to meet her and stay with her somewhere. Probably London. Everyone seemed to go to London. It was such a huge place that Zak wondered that they didn't all get lost there. How would you ever find someone in such a vast area of pavements and roads and houses and shops and buildings? You could be stuck there forever.

"So glad you love the flat, darling," Mr Braithwaite was saying. "Mmm, yes it was the view that sold it to me." He gave a silly laugh. Zak didn't like Mr Braithwaite or his silly laugh. "I shall be with you in just over an hour. Then we can have three whole days together. God, I can't wait… "

Zak stared miserably at the wall in front of him. Mr Braithwaite was going in to London to meet Hyslop's mother. It was sad news for poor Mrs Braithwaite, who was a kind, good person and whose husband had found another "darling." It was sad news for Hyslop, as surely she wouldn't want to go and live in London with her mother and Mr Braithwaite where there were no butterflies. Most of all, it was sad news for Zak. He would never be able to find the girl Hyslop if she went to London with her mother and Mr Braithwaite.

Zak realised that it was not just a storm that the air was holding back: it was change. Everything was going to change. Somehow he had to stop them from taking Hyslop away from the butterflies and the beautiful garden. He had to stop Mr Braithwaite from destroying all the insects in order to shoot poor pheasants. He had to stop Hyslop from leaving him forever, as the thought of life without her was unbearable to contemplate.

He had stop things from changing, but he had no idea how to go about doing it.

CHAPTER THIRTY NINE

Painted Ladies Emerge

"Look, the first one is emerging!" cried Sir Northcote. "Come quickly!"

Penny, Sandy and Hyslop left the ceramic pieces they were working on and all hurried over to the table by the windowsill in Sandy's pottery.

"I must admit, it's something that even I find exciting," said Sandy, bending down to survey the pale brown chrysalises. "It takes me back to my childhood when we came to visit, and Uncle Northy, you always seemed to have some chrysalises ready to turn into butterflies. We seemed always to be releasing Painted Ladies when I think back to my visits here! Such happy memories!"

"Yes, I like them too," said Penny. She looked fondly at her father. "And I've seen quite a few in my time, haven't I, Daddy?"

"None of you were *properly* interested," snorted the old man, with a vigorous head slap. "I have much higher hopes of young Hyslop."

"Oh, well," said Sandy. "We won't even try to compete. She is streets ahead of us on that score. A proper lepidopterist in the making, I'd say."

Sir Northcote had purchased five Painted Lady caterpillars in a small clear plastic container, and had placed it in Sandy's pottery so that Hyslop could visit it every day. She had been watching them double in size, as they munched and munched without ceasing. They were very hungry little caterpillars. The stage where they all decided to become chrysalises had been incredible. Somehow, after three weeks of constant eating, the soft wiggly caterpillars had shed their skins and even their heads and transformed into hard pale brown chrysalises before her eyes. It was strange to contemplate that one's head was a sheddable part of one's body. Hyslop had never seen anything so extraordinary in her life, and now the next miracle was about to take place, an even more spectacular and beautiful miracle: the chrysalises were rocking and shaking, and unmistakeable butterfly wings were pushing out.

"I've set up this lens so that you can look closely at what's going on," said the old man, fiddling with an ancient looking brass lens which he angled towards the first chrysalis. "Here, look through this. It belonged to my grandfather," his voice rose to a shout, "so be careful with it!"

Hyslop hardly dared breathe as she watched the first butterfly emerge in glorious detail through the magnifying lens. The wings were crumpled and feeble looking.

"It won't be able to fly for some time," said Sir Northcote, with only a tiny head slap. "It has to pump fluid into the wings to harden them. You'll have plenty of time to watch it before it's ready to take off. A few hours probably."

"The butterflies must be very vulnerable to predators at this stage," said Hyslop. "It looks so helpless."

"Oh yes," said Sir Northcote. "Very vulnerable indeed. But if they're females they will already be exuding a pheromone, a scent to attract male butterflies. Life is short and there's no time to waste."

"Well, there are no predators in here," said Sandy. "My pottery is a safe place!"

"It's thirsty work all this pottery and butterfly watching," said Penny. "I'm going to put the kettle on. Daddy, do you want some tea?"

"No, I'm fine," Sir Northcote shooed his daughter away with a wild gesture that ended in a head slap. "You two have your tea. Hyslop and I shall be fine here on our own. We're busy."

"We'd better not disturb such important work," said Sandy. "I'll join you, Pen. I'm in dire need of a cup of Earl Grey. "

Hyslop watched the newly emerged Painted Lady through the microscope. It was a moment almost as close to perfection as the finding of the Purple Emperor in the forest. Here was a new life, a beautiful new butterfly about to spread its wings and discover the world. Painted Ladies travelled for miles across seas and hills and valleys and forests, and there was no telling where this fragile little one would end up. At least these five were getting a good start in life: no predators could get at them whilst they were hardening off their wings. She smiled as she thought of how wonderful it would be to see them flutter into the air and discover the joys of flight. Sir Northcote shuffled and head-slapped and muttered "Dunderheids!" a few times beside her, and Sandy and Penny chatted quietly over their tea-making.

Just as the third butterfly was beginning to emerge, and Sandy and Penny were finishing their second mugs of Earl Grey, the door of the pottery opened.

"Hi, everyone!" said Vanessa brightly, stepping into the room. The peace and tranquillity in the room felt threatened, as if the sky had just grown dark.

"I thought I'd find Hyslop here with you, Sandy." Vanessa gave her familiar throaty laugh, but no one responded. She was greeted by silence. "I told you, Ilga, didn't I?"

Ilga walked in behind her.

"Quite a beehive of industry here, darlinks," she said. "I have been neglecting my pottery recently."

"I had noticed that, Ilga," said Sandy.

"SO kind of you to keep an eye on Hyslop," gushed Vanessa. "I had to go away for a few days, Sandy, darling. I knew she'd be in good hands."

Hyslop returned to staring down the lens. The pottery suddenly did not seem such a safe place any more. Sir Northcote began slapping his head so violently he left red weals on his forehead.

"I must be going, Sands," said Penny. "I didn't realise what time it was."

She took off her apron and made for the door, pointedly ignoring both Vanessa and Ilga.

"Hey, Penny!" said Ilga. "I thought we could all have a nice cup of Earl Grey together!"

"No," Penny was trying to force a smile, but failing. "No, Ilga, I really must be off. Lots to do."

"You've just missed tea-break," said Sandy. "I'm afraid I must get back to work. I'm right in the middle of something here."

This was so unlike Sandy's normal kind hospitality that Ilga looked startled.

"Sandy!" she exclaimed. "I've not offended you, have I? Darlink, I've never been turned down for a cup of your funny old Earl Grey before."

"Not turning you down at all, Ilga," said Sandy, returning to her work. "Help yourself. I must just get down to some work, though."

"I'm *so* sorry we disturbed you, Sandy," said Vanessa gently, her voice full of concern. "And you've been so kind with Hyslop too. Well, we'll leave you in peace and let you get on. Come on, Ilga, it's either second-rate coffee at my place or proper coffee from that wonderful espresso machine at yours."

Vanessa looked over at Hyslop.

"Hyslop!" she said sharply. "Can you come too, please. Sandy has work to get on with. You've outstayed your welcome here."

"No!" said Sandy sharply. "No," she said again, this time in a more controlled voice. "There's no need for Hyslop to go. Of course she hasn't outstayed her welcome."

Hyslop looked up and waited.

"Well, in any case, she must come back home," said Vanessa. "I want to hear all about what she's been up to in my absence."

This was so unlikely that there was a long silence as each person present mentally chewed over the statement, found it indigestible and spat it out.

"We're watching Painted Ladies emerging," said Sir Northcote suddenly, his eyes glaring and angry. "Hyslop is needed here."

Hyslop returned to peering down the lens and did not even look at her mother.

"Oh, I see," said Vanessa in an unnaturally high cheerful voice. "Butterflies, is it? Well, I shan't compete with them."

She waited a moment more as if for something to happen, and then turned to Ilga and said: "It's just you and I then, Ilga. Let's have some espresso at your place. I'm gagging for some caffeine."

She added something in German and Ilga laughed.

As they went out of the door, chattering in German, Sir Northcote stopped slapping his head, and stared after them.

"Dunderheids!" he called out loudly.

No one else said a word.

CHAPTER FORTY

Tomatoes and Pistachio Macaroons

Vanessa had ignored Hyslop since her return from London, and had been permanently on her mobile telephone. There was a lot of laughter and chatting in English littered with "darlings" to Hugo; there was sharp business talk in Italian to what sounded like bank managers; occasionally there were conversations in German to Ilga; and several times, rather unusually, she seemed to be laughing and flirting in Spanish which was much too quick for Hyslop to understand, and "Buenos Aires" was mentioned several times, a city that Hyslop knew to be the capital of Argentina. Something was being planned. Hyslop could feel it in the air, but she knew there was no point in asking any questions. She was being punished with especially cold treatment for not coming with her mother and leaving Sandy's pottery when asked. She had not rushed to obey, and had made her mother look foolish in public. Sir Northcote, Penny and Sandy had supported her against Vanessa, and it would never be forgotten or forgiven. There may not be a suitable dark cupboard in Keeper's Cottage, but her mother was definitely plotting something and Hyslop knew the punishment would be a bad one. There was an urgency about Vanessa's phone calls that was new, and there were ominous cold glances in Hyslop's direction.

The morning was particularly hot and heavy. The thunder in the air that everyone kept talking about was so heavy that surely it had to break through soon. It felt hotter than Italy. The little storm flies were still around and appeared randomly and irritatingly in the oddest of places. Vanessa had found several, unaccountably, in her morning espresso and Hyslop had sneaked out of the house, to the sound of her mother spitting out coffee and cursing in a singularly nasty manner.

She went into the greenhouse to find some tomatoes for breakfast and found Zak there before her. He wiped his mouth and looked sheepish at being caught.

"Are you eating the Braithwaites' tomatoes, Zak?" she asked.

"Well, I did just taste the one," he said. He paused. Hyslop watched him struggle with the desire to lie that came naturally to him as a survival technique, and the desire to please her by telling her the truth. She could read his facial expressions as easily as an infant's reading book, and, as she had predicted, his desire to please her was strongest. "Well, I think I tasted a couple," he added. "Actually, four. I ate four."

Hyslop looked along the rows that were becoming more depleted of tomatoes every day. She wondered if Penny knew that she and Zak were eating them at quite such a rate.

"I might just try one myself," she said casually. She picked one and ate it. Its ripe-to-bursting sweetness exploded in her mouth. "They're quite good," she said, taking another one, and popping it in her mouth. She nodded her head in an interested manner, as if savouring one for the first time. "Although," she took a third tomato, "not as good as in Italy of course."

"I helped Mrs Braithwaite plant the seeds," said Zak. "And then we planted them on in the special tomato compost. From the grow-bags, like."

"I see," said Hyslop. She eyed up a fourth tomato that looked exquisitely ripe.

"Have another one," said Zak. "Mrs Braithwaite don't use them all. She never misses them."

Hyslop raised her head in a haughty manner at the implication that Zak was giving *her* permission to take one, and she decided to leave it. Silence descended, and neither of them moved or spoke for a while, though the greenhouse, even this early in the morning, was stiflingly hot.

"There's never much breakfast in my house," Zak blurted out finally. "Don't s'pose that mother of yours cooks much either, does she?"

Hyslop said nothing to this but her dark eyes flashed at Zak and he looked down and kicked an empty fertilizer bottle. She didn't seem to like it when he mentioned her mother.

"I am going to visit Malcolm," she said abruptly. "I don't need you around me today, Zak."

Zak continued to stare at the ground, and she could feel the hurt emanating from him.

"Didn't mean nothing 'gainst your mother," he muttered.

"It's nothing to do with that," said Hyslop. "I have things to do this morning and I don't need you following me around." She paused, watching how crushed he looked. "But I do want you to go all around the estate for me."

Zak looked up, pleased at being given a task.

"You haven't forgotten about the Camberwell Beauty I hope, Zak."

"No!" he cried vehemently. "No! I look for that Beauty every day. I go round and round the fields and the woods. Everywhere."

"Well, you need to keep looking," said Hyslop. "I read on the internet that one was sighted twelve miles away, and we have a very attractive garden here." It felt strangely right for Hyslop to say "we" when describing the estate garden, "so it's not impossible that one might turn up."

"I'll keep looking," he said. "But what if I see one?" Hyslop was amused to see a look of cunning flash across his face. "I'll need to know where you are so I can come and tell you."

"I shall be at Malcolm's," she said. She smiled at Zak and saw how her smile affected him. "For an hour or so anyway."

"The furniture man?"

"Yes, Malcolm is a friend of mine, and he lets me go upstairs to his study and use his computer," Hyslop turned and left the greenhouse, with Zak following eagerly. "I shall check on the internet which butterflies have been sighted in our area."

"Does that internet tell you where to find a Beauty?" asked Zak.

"There was a possible sighting not that far away from here," said Hyslop. "But nothing definite. It's not a butterfly that you can just go out and find. It may come and find you. That's all you can hope for."

Zak was right behind her and Hyslop turned round abruptly and frowned.

"You don't need to follow me," she said. "I don't have time to make conversation with you. You have work to do, Zak. Buzz off."

Zak ran off at once and Hyslop made her way to Malcolm's workshop.

"Hullo, wee one," was Malcolm's greeting. "Just sorting out some veneers."

He had long strips of veneer all around him and seemed to be pondering over them. Hyslop knew how valuable they were so she did not approach too closely for fear of stepping on one.

"Come to look for butterflies on the computer, have you?" he asked. "Or have you time for a quick tea break with me."

When Hyslop said nothing, he added, by way of incentive: "Got some pistachio macaroons that Ilga made last night. Have you ever tasted those?"

"No," said Hyslop, stepping forward.

"I tell you, it's a close run thing between my late mother's shortbread and Ilga's macaroons," said Malcolm. "Now, I know you don't like tea, so I've got some apple juice for you in the fridge."

He bustled about, making himself a mug of tea and brought out a glass of juice and a little plate of greenish looking biscuits.

"That's one of Sandy's mugs you're drinking out of," remarked Hyslop.

"Oh yes," said Malcolm. "And see here," he pointed at the blue ceramic coil pot full of pencils, "I'm using your pencil pot too. I never lose my pencils these days. Very handy."

Hyslop took the green macaroon and examined it. She had eaten pistachio ice cream in Italy, but had never seen a biscuit like this, sandwiched with some greenish icing together with another biscuit.

"What d'you think then?" said Malcolm, wiping crumbs from his mouth. "Good, eh?"

Hyslop had her eyes closed. She did not particularly like Ilga, but she had to admit that these biscuits were delicious.

"More than good," she said, her mouth full. "What is the icing stuff?"

"Lime curd," said Malcolm. "Go on, you have to have another. Next time you can try an almond one filled with peanut butter. They're pretty special too."

Hyslop did not need to be asked again.

"Do you know what I like round here?" she said, between mouthfuls.

"What, apart from what wonderful people we all are?"

"I like," pronounced Hyslop, "how everyone creates stuff."

"Stuff?"

"You know, like making furniture and pottery," said Hyslop. "And you grow your own vegetables and eat food you make from scratch. It's not all bought from shops. And everyone's always doing interesting things."

"I think you're right. We do pretty well round here." Malcolm nodded in agreement. "But most interesting of all for you I think are the old man and his butterflies. Go on then, up you go. The computer's switched on and Miss Hilda's up there. Miss McKenzie is out hunting I think."

Hyslop ran up the little staircase, taking the stairs two at a time.

CHAPTER FORTY ONE

Paradise under Threat

Although Hyslop preferred her precious butterfly book with its exquisite illustrations to photographs on the internet, she found that an hour could slip by quite easily just looking at local websites, which listed all recent lepidopteral sightings.

There were some good stories: someone had seen fourteen Red Admirals feasting on rotting fruit in their garden; a butterfly enthusiast had been so intent in chasing what he thought was a Clouded Yellow that he had ended up falling into a stream; a young boy had photographed the grey-blue Valezina form of Silver-washed Fritillary which he happened to see whilst out riding his bike; someone else had photographed a very fuzzy, indistinct Fritillary of some sort and was asking for identification. Most exciting of all, there were rumours of an unidentified dark butterfly which two people claimed might be a Camberwell Beauty.

Hyslop felt akin to these people. The world contained those who appreciated butterflies, and those who didn't. Most people would of course profess an interest: butterflies are, after all, attractive and summery. People wore them as motifs on dresses and hairslides and jewellery in much the same way as hearts or flowers. Her own passion went far beyond this. She scorned those who thought butterflies should be pink and glittery and who never bothered to learn their names. Those people probably wouldn't notice real butterflies if they were flying all around them. They preferred fake versions. For Hyslop, butterflies were embedded deep within her, and she knew she was obsessed, pinned to her passion as surely as those specimens in Sir Northcote's collection. Every waking moment was filled with them, and sometimes even her dreams too. Butterflies flocked in their thousands and filled all the vast spaces inside her which had been empty for such a long time. They chased away all the ugly dark dreams of the past. It had been a rough journey, but she had found her habitat, her home: a garden of Eden which she never wanted to leave.

She looked on-line at various sites all over Britain where she and Northy could view different species. There could be a glorious Somerset trip with Sandy and Penny to see the Large Blues. There could be a trip to Norfolk to see its unique Swallowtails; perhaps a crossing to the Isle of Wight to see Glanville Fritillaries, and of course trips to Scotland and the Lake District to see Chequered Skippers, Scotch Argus and Mountain Ringlets. Hyslop shivered with delight as she anticipated her future, discovering all the British butterflies with Northy and Sandy. She stroked a delighted Miss Hilda who was purring on her lap.

"Hugo! Didn't expect to see you around at this time of day!" she heard Malcolm exclaim suddenly from downstairs. "Oy! Mind my veneers, would you. Don't stand on them!"

Hyslop froze, one hand poised over the keyboard, and the other over Miss Hilda's head.

"Sorry, Malc. How are you, old chap?" Hugo didn't sound at all sorry, Hyslop decided. He had come for some reason of his own, and although he was asking Malcolm how he was, she knew he wasn't really interested at all. She pushed Miss Hilda off her lap gently and crept to the top of the stairs to see what was happening. The cat shook itself indignantly and stretched.

"Don't pace around like that," said Malcolm. "Look, sit down and I'll make you a cup of tea. I'm going to carry on working, mind you. I'm just trying to… "

"What? Oh sorry, yes I'll sit down here, shall I?"

"Tea? Coffee?"

"Um, tea please, Malc, thanks."

There was a silence broken only by Hugo clearing his throat several times. Hyslop lay at the top of the stairs, silent and alert.

"Thanks, old chap." She presumed he had been given a mug of tea.

"You… um… seem busy. What are you working on?"

If one asks a question like this it is polite to wait for an answer, but Hugo was like her mother's rich friends in Italy. He was not interested in other people's answers. He had come to talk about himself.

Malcolm began to say something: "I'm making a cabinet at the moment, English oak with… "

"I had to come, Malc." This was Hugo's interruption.

Again there was a silence. Both Malcolm and Hyslop waited for Hugo to get to the point of his visit.

"I'm in pretty deep," was what she thought she heard Hugo say in a low voice.

"Pretty deep in what way?"

"You know, Malc. It must be obvious. With Vanessa."

Malcolm said nothing.

"I know you won't approve," said Hugo. "I know you will think I'm a swine." Hyslop nodded to herself at this point. "It's not some casual affair, though. God, no. Casual is the *last* word for it, believe me. Malc, I've found the right person for me. The right person in every way." There was another long silence, whilst Hugo perhaps waited for some comment from Malcolm. When none was forthcoming, he carried on. "My marriage to Penny has been a sham for years. A complete farce. You must have seen that. I have a chance of real happiness now with Vanessa. She is just the most incredible woman I have ever met. If I don't take the chance now, I will lose her. I couldn't bear that, Malc." It almost sounded as if the man was on the point of bursting into tears. Hyslop narrowed her eyes and waited for more.

Again, there was a pause but Malcolm said nothing.

"The thing is," Hugo said, and then for a long time he did not say what the thing was. After a while he repeated: "The thing is," but still did not elucidate.

."The thing is?" said Malcolm.

"Yes, the thing is, Malc, I may have got myself in a bit of trouble."

"In what way?" Malcolm's voice was sharp.

"Professionally."

"Professionally!" repeated Malcolm. "What has your profession got to do with that woman?"

"Don't call her 'that woman' Malc," pleaded Hugo. "Please try and get to know her. For my sake. If you give her a chance, I know you will come to see what a wonderful person she is. Sandy has known her since school-days. Ilga has got to know her too and likes her a lot, and you know she's an astute judge of character. Give her a chance for Ilga's sake, if not just for mine."

"What about for Penny's sake?"

"Malc, you're my friend," said Hugo. "Please try and understand. I will see that Penny is all right. You know I would never just leave her without the means to fend for herself. She will be left well off, unlike poor Vanessa all these years."

"Poor Vanessa seems to do all right if you ask me."

"Malc, her Italian husband died and left every penny of his estate to his mother, then in trust for Hyslop when she comes of age. This man was seriously wealthy, I mean *loaded*, but he left *nothing* for Vanessa. Nothing at all to help her bring up their daughter. Somehow that was allowed in Italian law. Can you imagine the selfishness?" Hyslop dug her fingernails into the palms of her hands as she heard this. She wished her nails were longer and sharper: she wanted to draw blood. "Every penny is in trust, Malc. Vanessa can't touch it. She's had to bring the kid up on her own, in a foreign country with absolutely no income. Not easy for her I can tell you."

"My heart bleeds."

"Be sarcastic if you want, but just try and imagine how hard it would be," said Hugo. "Penny's never wanted for anything materially in her life, but Vanessa has had it tough. Really tough."

"And what did she get you to do professionally?" asked Malcolm.

There was a lengthy silence. Miss Hilda McKenzie rubbed her head against Hyslop, demanding attention.

"You mustn't tell anyone, Malc." Hugo sounded anguished. "I know I can trust you."

Malcolm said nothing, but Hugo continued: "Vanessa needed help. Legal help to overturn the terms of the Italian will. I have assisted her in getting the trust fund into her own name."

"I see."

"It's only right, Malc. It's the way it should have been left in the first place but for some vindictive old cow of a mother-in-law."

If Hyslop had been a cat she would have arched her back and hissed at this point, as she realised that Hugo was referring to her Nonna. She felt her lips curling back in a snarl. Miss Hilda sprang back from her in alarm.

"Well, if as you say it's only right, then there shouldn't be a problem professionally," said Malcolm. "I assume everything was done legally and above board?"

This time Hugo was silent.

"What the devil have you done, Hugo!" Malcolm sounded harsh, angrier than Hyslop had ever heard him. "Have you compromised yourself professionally for this woman?"

"Malcolm, you have to understand… "

"Well, I don't, Hugo, I don't understand at all."

Upstairs, lying trembling in a shaft of sunlight, Hyslop understood only too well.

CHAPTER FORTY TWO

Flight

Hyslop had no idea how long she lay there, or how the conversation between the two men continued.

Hugo's words had pierced deep within her immediately like arrows into armour. How fragile and thin had her armour been all this time. Who would have guessed? She had thought she was hardened. Now, she lay as if wounded and tried to extricate them one by one from her flesh. She tried to make sense of what she had heard, to regain control. All she could hear was her own panicky breathing, a rush of air in her ears, her heart beating: thump, thump, thump.

Her father, who had died shortly after she was born, had not been the villain that her mother had described. He was the wonderful Papa that her Nonna had told her about. He had left money, a great deal of money by the sound of it, for Hyslop.

Beat. Beat. Beat. Blood seemed to be pumping violently all around her body.

Her mother, who had mysteriously appeared after Nonna died, had only come on the scene because of the money.

Beat. Beat. Beat. Beat.

Only because of the money.

Boom-boom-boom-boom. Her heart was pounding so loudly it was almost deafening her.

Hyslop's one consolation over the years was that somehow she had known that however awful the Uncles were, however unhappy she was, her mother was not going to abandon her. Her mother had come for her when Nonna died. Her mother always took Hyslop with her wherever she went.

Boom-boom. Boom-boom. Boom-boom. Hyslop found it hard to think over the noise of her beating heart.

The truth was that her mother had only dragged Hyslop around because of the money, the trust fund that she was waiting to get her hands on. Hyslop felt exposed and wounded. The greatest wound of all was the final truth: her mother had *never* loved her.

Boomboomboomboomboom… Hyslop could not breathe properly.

She stood up. Dimly she was aware of Miss Hilda retreating to a corner of the room.

She needed fresh air, she felt constrained in the room. She had to get out, yet going downstairs past Hugo and Malcolm was out of the question.

Gasping for breath, she opened the skylight window and looked out. She simply had to get out of the stuffy attic room. Nothing could hold her there. As if in a dream, she pulled a chair over to the wall beneath the window and stood on it. With her heart still pounding, she climbed up and out onto Malcolm's roof.

There, stretched before her, was the estate garden in all its late summer beauty. The trees looked fresher and greener than she had ever seen them, the air was full of the buzz and hum of a thousand different insects, the sky was a strange shade of dark blue. It was a stormy blue, menacing yet beautiful, but not as oppressive as the storm gathering inside her head. She had to be out there. She had to be free.

There was a tall tree some distance from Malcolm's workshop and Hyslop slid down to the edge of the roof and surveyed it. She stood up and stretched out her arms.

Somewhere, in a tiny part of her consciousness, she was aware of an inarticulate cry from Zak. He was watching her of course.

Hyslop jumped.

She flew through the air. It was a marvellous sensation. Nothing else mattered in the world. And somehow, there in front of her, was the foliage of the tree. Although some of the outer twigs were too feeble to hold her, she managed to grasp at the stronger branches beyond them and haul herself into the tree. In later years, when she contemplated what she had done, it was a mystery how she had made such a leap. Zak Judd would describe it to her as the most amazing thing he had ever seen.

She was scratched and both her arms were bleeding, but she did not care. She clung to the trunk of the tree, and remained there, in its green centre for some time. She waited until she could no longer hear her heart beating, the air rushing in her ears, then decided to get away. She did not want to be found by Malcolm, or – she shuddered at the thought – by Hugo.

As she shimmied down, Zak was there waiting for her. A single gesture fobbed him off and she began to run.

Hyslop ran and ran. She raced through the garden, weaving through flower beds and shrubs, hurtling over lawns. Her feet hardly seemed to touch the ground. It was as if she were still flying.

She reached the woods and continued on through the trees, barely pausing in her flight. The woods were dark and welcoming, but she still had to be free, out in the open.

It was only when she reached the meadow that Hyslop slowed down. The field was full of tall grasses and thistles and wild flowers. As Hyslop plunged into it, she put up a myriad of butterflies. The grasses parted before her and it seemed like a million Painted Ladies flew up in the air to join her.

It was only there, breathing in the hot earthy smell of the summer meadow, amidst the flapping and fluttering of the wings all around her that Hyslop stopped. She stretched out her arms and immediately butterflies landed on her. She gazed down at them and breathed calmly.

As one landed gently on her hair she threw her head back and exhaled.

CHAPTER FORTY THREE

Zak is filled with Wonder

Although Hyslop had commanded Zak to wander round the estate to look for The Beauty, he had given up circling the woods and fields after a short time. He did not feel at ease until he had returned to wait outside the furniture maker's workshop. He knew at every point of his wanderings that Hyslop was there at the centre, magnetically drawing him back.

He wanted to be on hand when she came out. He would pretend that he had searched everywhere with great thoroughness. It did not seem to Zak that Hyslop herself held out much hope of finding this butterfly. If he saw one, would anyone believe him? And even if he did see one, how could he catch it and hold it? The chances were remote: it was an impossible dream. Every part of him longed to be near the girl Hyslop. He could not help it. It was like breathing. If someone asked you to stop breathing for a while, even if they ordered you or begged you to, it wasn't something you would be able to do. He hunkered down to wait. Waiting was what he was best at.

So it was that he was hiding behind a low hedge when he caught sight of Hyslop climbing out of the skylight window onto the roof of the furniture maker's workshop. Whatever was she doing? Despite his intention to remain hidden, Zak stood up. There was something about her face, her expression – her whole demeanour – that frightened him. There was something strange and terrible about her. Something was not right.

As she clambered right out of the window and made her way down to the edge of the roof, Zak opened his mouth in horror. The roof was dangerously high. She would fall if she was not careful. Then, as he watched her stand up at the very edge of the roof, Zak realised that Hyslop was not going to be careful. Her eyes blazed like black stars, and there was nothing careful behind them. She *didn't* care. He saw that she was going to jump and he let out a cry.

The world went into slow motion for Zak like it does sometimes in films. Hyslop bent her knees slightly then leaned forward. There was no way back now. Her arms were outstretched, and she flew through the air. Zak found himself gasping for air. She soared towards the tree. It had seemed an impossible distance away, but somehow she landed in it. She crashed through its branches and then all was quiet.

For a moment or two he stood there, unable to move. He began to breathe more normally again. She was not going to fall. Somehow, incredibly, she was inside the tree.

Just as he was about to step forward to look up into the tree for her, she scrambled down. Her arms were gashed and bleeding, and her eyes were still blazing fire.

She did not actually look at him, but he knew that she was aware of him. She put her hand out in a gesture which unmistakeably told him to keep away. Zak shrank back from her.

When she began running he hesitated for a moment, before the invisible cord that attached him to her began to pull him after her. Zak could run fast but there was no way he could keep up with Hyslop. She ran as if a wild beast were chasing her, she ran as if she had wings, and Zak, running as fast as he could, was left behind.

When she reached the woods she did not pick her way between the trees but seemed to dive and dodge through them, scarcely slowing her pace. Zak was seriously out of breath by the time he saw her reach the meadow and slow down at last.

There it was that Zak witnessed the strangest sight of all, even more memorable than her fantastic leap. Brightly coloured butterflies in their hundreds flew up from the long grass and flowers as Hyslop ran through the field. They weren't Beauties or Admirals as far as Zak could see, but they were all of one sort. The air around Hyslop was filled with them. She slowly came to a stop and let them circle around her head. Her arms were still stretched out, and several butterflies landed on them. A single butterfly landed on her hair, and the girl Hyslop threw back her head, and seemed happy at last.

"The females of most species take enormous care during egg-laying, placing their offspring in situations where they are best adapted to survive…"

(from The Butterflies of Britain and Ireland by Jeremy Thomas and Richard Lewington)

CHAPTER FORTY FOUR

The Beauty at Last

Zak had been unable to sleep. It was nothing to do with the heat, which always made his grandmother grumble.

"Didn't sleep a wink," she would say every morning as she thrust a cup of tea at his father. "Not a wink."

Well, a wink of sleep wasn't much. But surely winking was closing one eye briefly whilst the other eye was open. If his grandmother had been winking all night long, it was hardly surprising she hadn't been able to sleep. Neither Zak nor his father ever commented, however. They would sit in silence while she ranted on about how hot it was.

"How is someone of my age meant to sleep in this heat?" she would demand, clattering dishes around in the sink. "How, in God's name, I ask you?"

She would ask, but they weren't meant to answer. Adults often asked questions like this: questions that weren't really questions.

It was questions in his head that had kept Zak awake, however. Questions like : What was Hyslop doing? Why had she jumped from the roof, and risked breaking her neck? Were her arms still bleeding? Why had she run into the field of butterflies, and why did they land on her? How soon could he see her?

He crept out of his room once it was light. He knew it was very early in the morning, and he paused on the landing to listen to the sounds of the house. He could hear snores coming from both his grandmother's room and his father's. No doubt the old woman would claim the heat had kept her awake, but it sounded like more snoring than winking was going on.

There was nothing worth grabbing on the way out. There was no bread left, and the fridge contained only milk which smelt sour and some raw meat, dripping blood onto the shelf. Zak decided that Mrs Braithwaite's tomatoes were more appetising for breakfast, and he made his way out of the house, along the path through the woods to the estate. It was too early for butterflies but he glanced around him just in case.

He had always loved the garden in the early mornings before anyone else was around. The birds were singing loudly all around him, and the greenhouse was already hot and steamy. He pulled a couple of radishes from the soil, wiped them roughly, and ate them with his greenhouse tomatoes. Now that Hyslop had come into his life he loved the mornings even more. Each morning held the promise of seeing her, being with her, maybe speaking to her. He didn't ever want to go back to the prospect of a day without a chance of seeing her. One or two days might be bearable, but there had to be something to hope and wish for. If that mother of hers took her away, Zak knew he would not be able to bear it.

As always, he was not good at judging how much time passed as he sat by the vegetable patch, but it felt like a "whole hour." His father was due to take Mr Braithwaite's car in to town to be serviced, so there was no fear of him bursting in on the scene and barking out orders. Zak felt unusually restless, and he got up and wandered towards Keeper's Cottage.

There, just coming out of the cottage door, walking purposefully towards him, was the girl Hyslop.

"Hello, Zak," she said. Her voice was flat and neutral, and the terrifying flashing was gone from her eyes.

Zak found himself looking at her arms. One was scratched and scarred. She saw him looking and held it out in front of her.

"It's not too bad," she said, examining it closely herself. "Could have been worse. A lot worse."

Zak didn't know what to say. He had questions in his head, buzzing around, but didn't know how to ask them.

"I'm going to see Northy," said Hyslop. "You can walk with me as far as his house if you like."

She set off and Zak fell into step behind her. It was such a short distance. He wished it could have been ten times as far. He wished it could have been ten miles. He wished he could think of something to say to her. Her hair was shining in the morning sun, and he wished he could reach out and touch it.

"You… you jumped into the tree," he said awkwardly, as they approached the old man's house.

Hyslop did not turn round.

"From that roof," added Zak, desperate to get her attention. "That roof that was high up."

"Yes," she said, half turning this time, "it was quite a jump, wasn't it?"

That was clearly all she was going to say on the matter. She let herself into the overgrown garden by the little gate.

"Bye then, Zak," she said. "See you later."

Zak made an inarticulate noise of farewell and watched as she rang the doorbell and was let into the house. Why did she prefer the company of the old man with his yellow teeth and his odd head slapping and swearing, to being with him? He kicked a stone and wandered around crossly. A period of time that felt like half an hour went past. It may have been longer. A butterfly landed on the path just ahead of him. It was one of those he had seen in the field with Hyslop. It flew up and then landed again, a little way ahead. Zak took a step towards it and it flew up again.

For a long time it just sat on the path. Zak watched it. Butterflies were fine, but he didn't know why the girl Hyslop had to spend hours watching them and then reading about them in books. He knew that the other girls in his class at school weren't interested in butterflies. But then, Hyslop wasn't like those other girls. Zak sighed. She wasn't like anyone else at all. Anywhere.

He wondered what it was that she was doing in the old man's house. His grandmother had said it was a weird house. They were probably looking at books about insects together. Or maybe at jars of poison, or stuffed owls, or animal bones. She was interested in the strangest things and he wished that she were more interested in him. He sighed again.

A butterfly rose up and did a little dance in the air just ahead of him, then it flew towards a nearby tree. Zak wandered after it. It wasn't one that Hyslop would want to know about. After all, she had seen hundreds of these in the field yesterday. They were quite common at the moment. He kicked at some gravel.

The butterfly was joined by another. It wasn't the same sort. Zak screwed up his face. This was different from any that he'd seen before, and he scratched his head as he tried to remember if he'd seen a picture of it before. It fluttered around the original butterfly, and the sun caught its browny-blackish-red-purple wing colouring. It reminded him of all the colours in Hyslop's hair. As it stopped and displayed its wings, Zak stood still, his mouth wide open: it was a dark butterfly with cream borders. He gasped.

"The Beauty!" he whispered. "It's The Beauty!"

He walked backwards away from it. What was he to do? If he turned and ran to the old man's house he might lose sight of it. If he ran up to it he might frighten it away.

"Hyslop!" he called, as he kept walking backwards towards the old man's gate. He did not dare turn round. He continued walking backwards, never taking his eyes from The Beauty.

Then he began shouting as loudly as could : "HYSLOP!"

Over and over and over again he called her name.

CHAPTER FORTY FIVE

The Mourning Cloak

"Can I see the empty drawer again?" Hyslop asked Sir Northcote. "You know, the one where the Camberwell Beauty is meant to go."

The old man slapped his head and muttered to himself. He seemed even more agitated than normal this morning. He was not himself at all.

"What did you say?"

"You know, Northy, the bottom drawer."

"Well, there's nothing to see," he said shortly, "just an old label."

He was definitely in an odd mood, but Hyslop was feeling rather strange herself.

"Yes, well, I'd like to see that label."

Sir Northcote shuffled over to his butterfly drawers and laid the empty drawer on Hyslop's lap.

"Not the most interesting drawer," he said, his hand hovering near his head, as if about to slap, but trying not to. "I thought you wanted to look at the Blues today."

"Mmmm, yes," said Hyslop. "I do, but I just wanted to see this label again. It's hard to read it's so faded."

"Yes, well, it's over seventy years since it was written," said Sir Northcote. "And it's copperplate script which no one can write nowadays. No one takes the time to write elegantly." Hyslop looked up, waiting for the inevitable: "Dunderheids!" which Sir Northcote obligingly spat out with some venom in the Scottish accent of his long-dead Nanny.

"Everything nowadays is printed off computers, Northy," she

said. "OK, I was mistaken. The label just says Nymphalis Antiopa, and I knew that name. It's just that I thought there was another name. You know, one of the names you said last time"

"It has been called many things," said Sir Northcote. "The Camberwell Beauty. The Grand Surprise. The Mourning Cloak."

"The Mourning Cloak!" cried Hyslop. "That's it! Yes, I like that name. Did people wear actual mourning cloaks in the olden days when someone died? "

"In Victorian times people were always mourning one thing or another," said Sir Northcote. "There was a whole cult of mourning. Queen Victoria wore black for forty years after Albert, her husband, died. Quite tedious of her."

"It does seem rather extreme," said Hyslop. "Ah well, let's start with the Common Blue, Northy."

She put her head to one side. Through the open window she could hear her own name being called.

"Hi – i – slop!" and then louder and more insistently: "HYSLOP! HYSLOP!"

Sir Northcote scowled. He could hear it too. Her name was repeated over and over again.

"For goodness sake, it's that boy," he said crossly. "The Judd boy."

"HYSLOP!"

"I shall tell Judd to stop him from pestering us," snapped the old man. "I'm sick of him hanging around all the time."

There was something about the way Zak was shouting that made Hyslop put the drawer down and rush towards the door.

"Come with me, Northy," she said. "Come quickly."

They went outside into the bright sunlight together. There, a short way up the path towards the main house, was Zak, standing with his back to them, calling Hyslop's name at the top of his voice.

"What is it?" cried Hyslop. Zak still did not turn round to face them.

"The Beauty!" he shouted, pointing straight ahead of him.

Hyslop broke into a run. Sir Northcote slapped his head and followed.

"For Goodness sake, that's a Painted Lady, Zak," said Hyslop crossly.

"No," said Zak. "Not that one." He took a few steps forward and pointed again. "The one beside it. That one there, see."

As he did so, a dark-coloured butterfly flew up into the air.

"Good God!" cried Sir Northcote, staring open-mouthed at the butterfly, then he said it again: "Good God!"

"It's The Beauty," said Zak. "Oh no, it's flying away!"

The butterfly flew high up into the tree and all three of them groaned in unison.

"It's coming down," cried Hyslop. "Look, over there. Quickly!"

She set off along the path and the other two followed, the old man a little way behind.

"Don't lose sight of it," he called. "Don't wait for me. You young ones must run! Follow it! Oh heavens, I don't have my jar. I need my jar!"

The beautiful dark butterfly was flying now in a reasonably straight line, and it led them across the lawn in front of the main house. Hyslop hoped it might stop and nectar on the buddleia, where several brightly coloured butterflies were already congregating. The Beauty did not pause, however, but flew, in an even more direct line towards the dahlia patch.

"It's going for the vegetables!" called Zak.

"Keep up, Hyslop!" cried Sir Northcote. "Don't lose it! I need my net! And my killing jar!"

"I can still see it!" Hyslop and Zak were running together.

"Oh, it's too late!" The old man shouted. He was some distance behind them now and out of breath from trying to keep up.

The butterfly soared over the dahlias to the vegetable garden, where it hovered above the runner bean wigwam. It looked as if Zak was right, and the vegetables were going to attract it.

Down it fluttered, down onto a yellow courgette flower. Hyslop put her hand out to stop Zak.

"Not too close!" she said in a low voice, as if the butterfly could somehow hear her. "We don't want to scare it."

At that moment they heard a scream. It was a sound that smashed into the heat haze of the morning sunshine and made the whole scene shatter like a broken mirror. It was a hideous sound, more animal than human in its horror, a sound that entwined itself into the memories of all three of them forever afterwards. The Beauty itself seemed to hear it and shudder in the air, then it was off, heading for Keeper's Cottage.

Like an airborne pied piper it led its three followers towards the source of the scream. They zig-zagged past the vegetables and the greenhouse, round past the nettle patches to the patio behind Keeper's Cottage, in pursuit of the beautiful creature they had longed to see for so long. There was another scream, and the name "Vanessa!"

Despite the terrible scene that awaited them, for two of them at least, the memory, the hideous memory, would always be glorified by the sight of the morning sun shining on those aubergine black wings, edged with gold.

Sometimes it is hard for the mind to make sense of what the eyes take in immediately. The screamer was Sandy, bent over Vanessa. Vanessa, in her black dressing gown, was lying face down on the patio. Her arms were stretched out and her skin seemed to have taken on a strange purplish hue. Thankfully they could not see her once beautiful face. The York stone all around her was stained dark red, and glittered with jagged broken glass. As the breeze lifted the folds of the flimsy dressing gown and made them flutter like wings above her body, it was obvious at once to all of them that Vanessa was dead.

Still magnificent in its flight, the Mourning Cloak circled once round the tragic scene then soared up over the hedge. By now no one had any inclination to follow.

CHAPTER FORTY SIX

The Butterfly Mother

"We don't need to do this now, Hyslop," said Sandy. "Not if you'd rather wait. There's no hurry."

Hyslop said nothing but gazed around Keeper's Cottage.

"No one will be needing this cottage for a very long time," said Sandy, watching Hyslop and following her gaze. "What do you think?"

Hyslop walked over to the little sofa and sat down.

"It seems so empty," she said at last.

"Yes." Sandy came and perched on the arm of the sofa. Her large blue eyes were full of sorrow and sympathy. "Yes, it does. Penny and I cleared most of your mother's things. Everything's in boxes and some time, much later, when you're ready, you can look through it all."

Hyslop was silent.

"As I said, there is no rush for any of it, you know. We can come back another time?" Sandy let the question hang in the air.

"I want to get my stuff, Sandy," said Hyslop. "I'll get everything from my bedroom now."

Hyslop walked over to the foot of the tiny staircase, then turned back to Sandy.

"The patio," she said. "Has it… "

"The patio's been cleared, of course, Hyslop. All the broken glass has been taken away. Everything. Long gone."

It had not been the broken glass that Hyslop was thinking of. She recalled the terrible sight of her mother's body lying there. She recalled the blood, darkly soaking the paving stones.

"I don't want to go out there."

"Well, of course you don't. There's no need for us to go out that way."

"What… what's going to happen to Northy?"

Sandy looked down at the floor for a while.

"I don't know, Hyslop," she said softly. "I really don't know. It's been suggested that he stays in a… well… a sort of special nursing home."

"They're blaming him, aren't they?" Hyslop's eyes blazed fire at Sandy, who could not meet her gaze. "They're blaming him for my mother's death. The police, I mean. Why do they keep questioning him?"

"Well, after a sudden… or… a suspicious death," said Sandy, "they always want to ask questions. I don't think anyone is accusing Uncle Northy of anything, but they just don't know why his cyanide killing jar was broken into pieces all over the patio."

"It's not Northy's fault!"

"No, sweetie, of course not. No one's saying it is. But, it's just something the police have to clear up. There was an extraordinary amount of cyanide encrusted on all those shards of glass, quite lethal amounts, and when Vanessa went out with bare feet and… "

"Northy only wanted to kill The Camberwell Beauty," said Hyslop. "He needed it for his collection."

"Well, I'm sure he'll have explained all that to the police."

"It's Hugo, isn't it?"

"What do you mean, Hyslop?"

"It's Hugo who's accusing him, who wants him to be put away in a nursing home! It's what he's always wanted."

"Hugo isn't saying much to anyone at all at the moment."

"Oh," said Hyslop. She put her foot on the bottom stair.

"I'll go up and get my things now," she said.

"You sure you don't want me to come up with you?"

"No. No, I'd rather just do it on my own. There's not much, so I shouldn't be long."

"Well, I'm here if you need me."

It was comforting for Hyslop to know that Sandy was downstairs, sitting on the sofa waiting for her, but she wanted to go into her room alone.

In truth, the little room held no memories of her mother, as she could not recall Vanessa visiting it much.

So much had changed since she had last been here, yet everything was just as she had left it. The top drawer was still half open in her little chest of drawers and Hyslop pulled it open and began laying out her clothes on the bed. She pulled out her suitcase from under the bed and opened it. There were her three childhood books, the old familiar books that she and Vanessa always took with them everywhere. Since her arrival in England and her new butterfly book, she had hardly looked at the old books.

This was indeed a memory of her mother. Hyslop picked up The Lion, The Witch and The Wardrobe and opened it to look at the familiar prize label at the front. She gasped as she did so.

An envelope fell out of the book. It was in her mother's handwriting.

Hyslop laid the book down and picked up the envelope. Her hands were trembling so violently she could hardly hold it still. There was a single word on the outside of the envelope and that word was her name.

She stared at her own name, in her mother's hand, for quite a while, then she opened the letter.

"Dear Hyslop," she read. The letter was dated a few weeks earlier, the day before her mother had died. Hyslop's hand trembled all the more. She had never received a letter from Vanessa before. What could it mean?

"By the time you read this I shall be far away, somewhere in South America, with friends that you have never met. I am sure I don't need to urge you not to come looking for me. You shall never find me."

Hyslop went back to the beginning of the letter and re-read this part. It made no sense. Why did her mother think she would be in South America?

"To be frank, you probably won't want to find me. I have taken the money from your trust fund, Hyslop, but then it was never really yours anyway. I earned that money by marrying your father, and it was always meant to be mine. Believe me when I say that my marriage was harder work than you will ever know. Hugo helped me with the legal side of things and imagined that we had a future together, but I have left him to make things up with his little wife.

I have provided well for you, daughter. I chose Sandy and her community carefully. They are all crying out for someone to nurture, someone to look after, and they all adore you. I don't need to tell you this – I've seen how you can wind them round your little finger. It's as it should be – just as my powers seem to be waning, yours are waxing. I can leave you there in the certain knowledge that you will be happier with Sandy and the others that you ever were, or ever could be, with me."

Hyslop paused here. A single tear petered down her cheek, but she wiped it away and continued reading.

"If you are clever – and you are, after all, my daughter – you should find yourself set up for life. That is more than I was at your age. I had to keep moving, had to keep one step ahead of the game, and it has been tiring all these years. At last I have my independence, the financial independence I should have had years ago, and I have left you in a place where you can achieve anything you want to. Just learn to smile more and charm people.

It's amazing what you can achieve if you smile.

Goodbye, daughter. I won't insult your intelligence by pretending to send love. It's not an emotion I have ever felt, but I have never admitted that to anyone else before.

That's quite a big deal I think, Hyslop.

Your mother,

Vanessa."

Hyslop had no idea how long she stood there in the little bedroom, staring at her mother's letter. Her hands were no longer trembling. She was acutely aware of her surroundings: the clothes laid out on the bed in neat piles, the books, the suitcase, the coil pots she had made with Sandy on top of the little mantelpiece, the dark green tiles, the dead woodlouse still curled up in the fireplace, and finally, the sound of Sandy's footsteps on the stairs.

"Is everything OK, Hyslop? I can help if you want me to. What's that you've found? A letter?"

"Oh, it's nothing at all. Just a bookmark that I have had for years." Hyslop put the letter back into the Narnia book.

"I'm nearly finished here, Sandy," she said.

And smiled.

Acknowledgements

My heartfelt thanks must first of all go to Lesley Paton, whose support, friendship and nurturing made this book possible from the start. She provided the perfect blend of encouragement and constructive criticism all the way through the writing process and without her it would not have been written. I am also deeply indebted to David Dennis, current Chair of Butterfly Conservation, who introduced me to the world of butterflies in the first place. He not only advised on Lepidopteran details for this book, but was inspirational in his enthusiasm for butterflies and for the characters in my book at all times. He and Lesley were incredibly generous with their time and made me believe the book was worth publishing. They even sat up late proof-reading my manuscript!

Next, I should like to thank my friend (and fellow author), Lynette Kerridge, who provided valuable literary critique, specially at times when I was struggling with the writing process.

A major source of inspiration for me was (and remains) that masterpiece "The Butterflies of Britain and Ireland" by Jeremy Thomas and Richard Lewington. Every household in the UK should own one of these amazing books. Read all about the life histories of our native butterflies and marvel at the fantastic illustrations. You will appreciate summer walks as never before, and a butterfly will never be "just a butterfly"again.

I must also thank the following people who took time to read extracts and offer constructive advice: Ben Batten, Ian Bowie, Aileen Jones, Jacqui Kean, Janet King, Dinah Latham, Eleanor McDonald-Pratt, Moira McKenzie, Elisa Sibille, Candida, Freya and Zanna Spencer and Katherine Vincent.

Last, and certainly not least, I must thank Marc, David and Roy for their love and support throughout the writing of the book.

We hope you enjoyed this book. If you would like to comment/leave a review, please contact the author at:

www.kathleennelson.co.uk

Join Butterfly Conservation Today!

Butterflies and moths are among the most threatened groups of wildlife in the UK. By becoming a member of Butterfly Conservation today you can do something important not just for Britain's butterflies and moths but for the planet as a whole.

To celebrate this wonderful book Butterfly Conservation is delighted to offer readers the opportunity to become a member for half price*.

Join online at **www.butterfly-conservation.org/join** using promotional code **CLOAK** and we will send you a welcome pack bursting with essential information about butterflies and moths. You can look forward to receiving our exclusive magazine *Butterfly* three times a year - packed full of fascinating features, conservation news and stunning photography. You will also have plenty of opportunities to get involved with events and activities in your local area if you wish.

Please don't forget to use promotional code **CLOAK** and the direct debit payment method to ensure you get your first year's membership for half price.

*Offer available for new members only paying by direct debit.